By Victoria Lee

A Shot in the Dark

Books for Young Adults

A Lesson in Vengeance
The Electric Heir
The Fever King

A SHOT IN THE DARK

A SHOT IN THE DARK

A NOVEL

VICTORIA LEE

DELL
NEW YORK

A Shot in the Dark is a work of fiction. Names, characters, places, and incidents are the products of the author's imagination or are used fictitiously. Any resemblance to actual events, locales, or persons, living or dead, is entirely coincidental.

A Dell Trade Paperback Original

Published in the United States by Dell, an imprint of Random House, a division of Penguin Random House LLC, New York.

Library of Congress Cataloging-in-Publication Data
Names: Lee, Victoria, author.
Title: A shot in the dark: a novel / Victoria Lee.
Description: New York: Dell [2023]
Identifiers: LCCN 2023012578 (print) | LCCN 2023012579 (ebook) |
ISBN 9780593500514 (trade paperback) | ISBN 9780593500521 (ebook)
Subjects: LCGFT: Romance fiction. | Novels.
Classification: LCC PS3612.E34877 S56 2023 (print) |
LCC PS3612.E34877 (ebook) | DDC 813/.6—dc23/eng/20230407
LC record available at https://lccn.loc.gov/2023012578
LC ebook record available at https://lccn.loc.gov/2023012579

Printed in the United States of America on acid-free paper

randomhousebooks.com

9 8 7 6 5 4 3 2 1

Book design by Sara Bereta

For A.

I loved you before I was born.

In loving memory

Christine (d. 2022)

ברוך דיין האמת

AUTHOR'S NOTE

This book contains vivid scenes of substance abuse.

A SHOT IN THE DARK

1

ELY

My problem, generally speaking, is that I care too much.

I'm an artist, so maybe I'm supposed to. That's the stereotype, right? The prodigy obsessed with perfection, shivering in a frigid garret, huddled over their masterpiece, bourbon drenched and brilliant. If I didn't care so much, maybe I wouldn't be able to see the true shape of things, how lines and shapes smudge together perfectly in the light. I wouldn't be willing to spend hours in the darkroom with my lungs full of chemicals or waiting in the park with my tripod for hours until that split second right before the sun goes down when the world is cast in shades of rose and red, shadows stretched out long and skinny like bones.

I should have listened the first time someone told me it was a problem, that time Chaya Levy and I had our big fight when we were fifteen and she told me that I was a threat to her Yiddishkeit and we needed a friendship break. *You're just a little too intense,* she said, and the accusation flung me into the kind of immediate, reactive rage that pretty much proved her point.

I can't stop myself from caring, though, no matter how many times it gets me in trouble. Which is why it's incredibly stupid of me to be here at all, standing at the baggage claim in LaGuardia with my backpack digging into my shoulder, watching the carousel grind by. I've been waiting over half an hour already, long enough that I'm starting to worry my luggage didn't make it, because the baggage guys at LGA are nothing if not efficient and it's just me and this one family left waiting. Their five-year-old keeps trying to climb onto the moving belt, and judging from the pained look on the mother's face, she's thinking about giving up and just letting him cycle through.

I never thought I'd be back here. When I left New York for LA nearly a decade ago, I had every intention of never stepping foot in this place again. I was gonna be all tan lines and margaritas. No more subway. No more bodega cats. And most important, no more bad memories. It's amazing how easily I was seduced by a big, fat art scholarship.

The screen still says *LAX—Arrived,* so I figure my bags have gotta be coming sometime soon. Or not. Because this is what I get for arriving at the airport just forty minutes before my scheduled departure time. Parker is the most prestigious arts program in the country, and I still had to gamble with my flight, like, *Well, if I miss the plane, maybe it was never meant to be.* I'm not sure how to fit lost luggage into that calculus. If I make my flight but arrive without my portfolio, or my lenses, or any of my clothes, am I only half-destined for greatness?

Maybe my problem isn't caring too much after all. Maybe it's that I take every possible opportunity to gamble away the things I care about on high stakes for stupid prizes.

Or as my sponsor would put it: "Ely, you sure do like to fuck around and find out."

A normal person would probably choose this moment to go up to the booth and ask after their luggage. Maybe provide the little sticker receipt they so intelligently kept, make arrangements for their belongings to be shipped to them on the next flight out.

That's what the family does. I, however, stand there while the area fills up again with the passengers from a flight from Berlin, chattering in German as their practical drab-colored luggage begins to rotate around the carousel—as if I'll find my mint-green suitcase with the Ripped Bodice sticker among them.

"Sorry" is the first thing I say when I finally, reluctantly drag myself to the luggage counter. "I think . . . I think maybe my bags got lost on the flight over?"

"Tag."

I might have been born and raised in New York, but the past eight years in LA have made me weak. I flinch. "Sorry?"

"Your luggage tag," the woman says, holding out an expectant hand.

"Sorry," I say—and holy fuck, if I say "sorry" *one more time,* I will personally eviscerate myself—"but I think I threw it away."

The woman fixes me with a flat, unimpressed look, even though I'm pretty sure most people throw their luggage receipts away the first second they get. "Did you throw away your boarding pass too?"

We manage to muddle our way through the process, although most of the muddling happens on my end. I leave the airport sweatier than before, skin chafing where my backpack straps rest, and trudge toward the taxi queue. I look longingly after the bright, perky young things heading toward the Uber and Lyft pickup zone; I demolished my rating on both apps within six months of moving to LA. I'm pretty sure if I logged on to Uber, it would present me with an individualized pop-up message reading *Don't even bother*.

I wonder what it's like to exist in the world as someone who didn't ruin their life when they were eighteen.

I get into an anonymous yellow cab, like a tourist.

"No bags?" the driver asks, meeting my gaze in the rearview mirror.

I shake my head. "Just me."

I tried to memorize my new address on the flight over, but I don't trust myself to get it right after the whole luggage debacle, so I read it off my phone just to be safe.

"Astoria," the driver says as we peel away from the curb. "Why?"

"What do you mean?"

"Tourists usually stay in Manhattan. Maybe Brooklyn."

Good to know my disguise is impenetrable. "I'm not really the Brooklyn type," I say, which is very much underselling it.

"I like Astoria," the man says with a solid nod. "Greek food."

The rest of the ride proceeds in silence, which is one thing I will always appreciate about New York. In LA everyone wants something: a connection, a hustle, a hookup. You can't go half a mile in a cab without hearing about somebody's real estate ventures or upcoming EP. And to be fair, I was part of that—always switched on and looking for a chance to get my art in front of the right pair of eyes. In New York, everyone just wants to get where they're going.

I'm staying in an apartment I found on Reddit, two strangers seeking a roommate for their three bedroom. Risky move, but I couldn't bring myself to fly back here to see places in person. I figure if it's a bust, well, I only paid the first month's rent up front; that cost less than an extra flight out here plus a hotel would have. The building is unassuming from the outside, four stories high with a flat brick façade. I loiter on the stoop, backpack resting against the wall—no one tells you how fucking heavy a Nikon and some film are when you're just getting started—and text Ophelia that I'm here.

She responds almost immediately: **Be right down.**

I arch my back against the railing behind me, as if that could work out the kinks in my spine. It does nothing, of course, except make me feel a little ridiculous when someone walks by.

It's only two or three minutes, though, before the front door of the building swings open and Ophelia appears. She's short—no taller than my shoulder—and plus-size, dressed in a trendy crop top and jeans, her hair done up in a cascade of lilac braids that contrast perfectly with her dark skin.

She'd look incredible on film, I think—because apparently I can't help viewing everyone through a mental camera lens.

"Hi!" she says. "Are you Elisheva?"

"Hey," I say, pushing off the railing and stepping toward her, holding out one hand to shake hers. "Yeah, I'm Ely. Ophelia Desmond, right?"

"That's me! Where's your stuff?"

"Lost." I grimace. "They said they can get it to me by tomorrow, but I guess we'll see."

She makes a face. "Yeah, good luck with that. It'll be at least three days." She pauses. "Come on. I'll show you the apartment."

We climb three flights of stairs to get there. We lived in a fourth-floor walk-up when I was growing up in Crown Heights, but that was a long time ago; it's May, it's hot, and I've been living in an elevator building for almost a decade. I hate it, and my thighs hurt by the time we step out onto the final landing. On the upside, by the end of summer, I'll have an incredible ass—just in time to cover it up with heavy winter coats.

That's another character flaw of mine: I'm perennially pessimistic.

I should probably try to get over that.

The apartment has a green-painted door, and the welcome mat outside reads *OH, HI MARK*—a reference to the cult-classic best/worst movie ever made, *The Room.*

Somehow I gravitate to a very specific kind of person, even if that person is a Reddit stranger living on the opposite coast. It's a talent.

"I like the mat," I say as Ophelia lets us into the apartment.

She arches a brow at me. "You're my favorite customer."

"Anyway, how's your sex life?" I quote back, and my timing, as ever, is impeccable, because the shirtless guy draped over the living room sofa moans, "*Nonexistent,*" and covers his face with a throw pillow.

"Aaand now you've met Diego," says Ophelia. "He still thinks it's 2006 and emo is cool."

"Emo *is* cool," Diego mumbles from behind the pillow.

I smile despite myself; whatever Reddit Ely was thinking, she made good choices. I can already tell we'll all get along just fine.

"Diego, make yourself useful and put some tea on," Ophelia commands, then moves deeper into the apartment, gesturing for me to follow. "Ely, your room is back here. It's a little small, which is why we were advertising it for lower rent, but our ex-roommate didn't complain *too* too much, so I presume it's livable."

"I'm sure it's just fine," I say, although when she shows me the room in question, it turns out she's right. The place is about the size of my bathroom back in LA, barely large enough to fit a twin bed and a tiny desk shoved against the window. There's no space for a dresser and no closet; I'll have to use a portable wardrobe, one of those metal contraptions on wheels with a bar and hooks.

But it's kind of cozy too. I can imagine it in candlelight, warm and flickering, the bed draped in a pile of blankets, and pillows littering the floor. It'll be even nicer if—god willing—I do well enough at Parker that they ask me to stay here past summer and into the fall, into winter.

"You know what?" I say to Ophelia. "I fucking love it."

"You better," she says, but when I look at her, she's grinning; she has a gap between her two front teeth, I notice, and it serves to make her even prettier than she looked before.

When we emerge back into the living room, Diego has

acquired a shirt and is standing in the kitchen, assembling a cheese and charcuterie plate.

"I know you're moving in here," he says, "but this seems hospitable."

"I love cheese," I admit, and he stabs a cube of Gouda with a toothpick and holds it out to me.

For a moment I feel the reflexive twinge in my gut, from some old and buried part of my mind. I stare at the plate for a moment, at the cheese cubes nestled right up against the soppressata. But as I decided after two years in LA, what's a little treif when you're already so far off the derech as to be swimming in the metaphorical ditch?

Of course the guilt's back, now that I'm in New York. That makes sense. But it still makes me feel fucking weak.

I eat the cheese.

"You should try this properly," Diego tells me, and begins layering a cracker with a fruit spread and prosciutto and Brie. I eat that too.

It's been a long time since I kept kosher. Almost as long as it's been since I felt bad about breaking kosher—which says a lot, I think, about how nervous it makes me to be back in New York. But it'll be worth it, of course. It's got to be. I'll have the chance to work with Wyatt Cole, who is only my single most favorite photographer of all time.

And it's easy, here with Ophelia and Diego, to forget everything else I'm afraid of. I used to dream about living in a place like this, with people like this. I sat through classes with my books open but my mind among the stars, fantasizing about eating cold pizza on the floor and watching bad sitcoms with friends who didn't care what religion the protagonists were or what gender they preferred to kiss. But even in my most florid fantasies I didn't imagine Diego's hot-pink stiletto nails or Ophelia's taste for ambient music that sounds like a slowly evolving minimalist tone but turns out to be the Windows start-up chime played in slow motion.

"This is the sound they play when you die," Diego says.

"You're fucking weird," says Ophelia.

They're both fucking weird, but it turns out I like that. "Fucking weird" is what I thought I'd be when I moved out to LA—as if living on the West Coast would somehow transform me into a svelte and sun-glazed bohemian with too much style and too little money. Instead I just turned into one of the emaciated Venice Beach junkies who used to beg me for cash when I first moved there.

It took me four years to crawl my way back out of that hole. But ever since getting clean, I've existed in this liminal space where I'm afraid to have a personality, like if I think too hard or feel too deeply I'll find myself spiraling down, down, and this time I won't come back up again.

"It's the sound that Quicksilver hears when he starts up his computer," I suggest, and Ophelia smacks both hands down hard on the island, the sound loud enough that I jump.

"*Oh my god,*" she says, her voice rising in pitch. "Finally. *Finally.*"

"Um . . . ?"

"Ophelia's been pining for an X-Men nerd to come into her life for like three years," Diego informs me.

Ophelia nods effusively. "Yes. Diego literally couldn't tell you the difference between Magneto and the Juggernaut. I've been dying here."

I lift a brow, and—in the end—I just can't help myself. "One's a tormented antihero fighting for social justice," I say. "And the other is *the Juggernaut, bitch.*"

This earns me another screech from Ophelia and a hearty eye roll from Diego, who covers his face with both hands like he's in physical pain.

"Sorry, Diego, normies wouldn't get it," Ophelia declares. "So exactly how many arguments did you get into on Tumblr about whether or not Erik could have controlled the direction of the bullet that paralyzed Charles in *First Class*?"

"At least three," I say. "I also wrote a forty-chapter *Phantom of the Opera* crossover fan fiction starring Magneto as the shadowy opera ghost."

"*Wait,* I've read that one," Ophelia says, jabbing a finger toward me. "That was you? No shit!"

I make a face. "To my great shame."

"No, shut up. I commented on like *every* update. You aren't allowed to be embarrassed."

Diego groans loudly. "Please stop talking about bad comic book movies. I literally cannot stand another second of this."

"We're actually talking about a fan fiction crossover of *great* comic book movies and Broadway musicals—" Ophelia starts, but she's interrupted by a piece of prosciutto flung in her face.

Dinner ends up being a mishmash of Diego's cheese-and-pork towers plus some leftover lo mein and a rather impressively green salad that Ophelia concocts out of lettuce, scallions, cucumber, and a slightly overripe avocado. I've never been happier to consume what I imagine "college food" would have looked like if I'd ever actually attended college and explored its culinary idiosyncrasies.

"We have to go out," Diego declares once dinner is finished and the dishes are cleaned and it's getting close to the time that I would normally start making excuses to turn in, especially with tomorrow being my first day at Parker. "It's Ely's first night here; she needs to go to Revel."

"Right," Ophelia says, "it's Ely's *first night here.* She does *not* need to go to Revel."

"What's Revel?" I ask from my spot on the sofa, where I have beached myself for the past half hour, still waiting for my overstuffed stomach to deflate.

Diego fixes me with his laser gaze, which is extra piercing thanks to his lime-green mascara. "You're gay, right?" he asks.

"I . . ."

Ophelia grimaces and says, "You don't have to suffer the Inquisition if you don't want to, Ely. Say the word and we can punt Diego safely back into his bedroom where he can't bother anyone."

"Do you like guys? Girls? Hot nonbinary people with lots of piercings? All of the above? *None* of the above?"

Diego says it so matter-of-factly, so *easily*. I wish I could do that. It's not like I haven't been honest with myself. It's not like I haven't had relationships. But I've never felt the need to label myself before now—that felt like it would have been claiming something that didn't belong to me. Even though that doesn't make sense, because identity is something you belong *to,* not the other way around.

But apparently I'm giving off major gay vibes, at least per Diego's radar, so.

"I guess . . . Well, I've dated both girls and guys," I venture at last, which seems like the safest answer. "But gender doesn't really matter much to me. It's more about the person."

Don't overthink it, I order myself, but of course it's too late; I'm overthinking it. What I said is true, but I worry it comes across as pandering. That maybe Diego and Ophelia can tell how badly I want them to like me—and if they can tell that, they might think I'm making this up to seem tolerant or whatever.

Only I shouldn't have worried, because as it turns out, most people don't have my habit of being bitterly suspicious of everyone they meet. Ophelia and Diego simply exchange looks, some silent conversation passing between them that my anxiety desperately wants to hyperanalyze, and Diego rubs his hands together like a Disney villain. "I *knew* it. You're coming to Revel with us, pansexual icon."

2

Revel, as it turns out, is a gay club.

A *queer* club, to be more accurate, as the crowd mingling out on the sidewalk is a mishmash of genders, not the standard flock of cis gay dudes I associated with places like this in LA. No, these are New York queers—painfully, effortlessly cool queers—and . . . I can't relate. I tried the baggy jeans trend once, and it made me look like Gumby. The only style I typically muster is best described as "grunge meets cottagecore." Not that my day-old airport clothes even rise to that level.

Diego's brought a flask, which he surreptitiously offers to me as we stand in line. I shake my head and one of his eyebrows flicks up. "Don't like tequila?" he asks.

"Not my favorite," I say, because *I don't drink, period* is always a bombshell to drop on people. As soon as you admit you're sober, they start asking questions. Worse, they start insisting that you should loosen up. Have a drink. Or three. Or six. What, are you watching your figure?

Half the time they don't let up until I lose my temper and snap that I'm clean, I'm *in recovery,* my brain literally wants to kill me and I cannot be trusted with the weapons of my own destruction.

Which tends to put a damper on things, and I want these people to like me. So, personal-disclosure hours can wait.

But to Diego's credit, he just shrugs and passes the flask to Ophelia instead, and by the time we're at the front of the line, they're both slightly tipsy. I'm better than I used to be; I can be around drunk people now. Good thing, considering the nature of the photography social circuit out in LA, a booze-drenched, drug-fueled fuck fest where the quantity and lethality of the drugs you consumed while creating a given work were treated almost like accolades. *I heard she went into rehab right after the gallery opening,* someone would whisper. *Heroin.* And they'd all hum discerningly and make comments about artists and their vices.

We make it through the line faster than I expected. The bouncer up front barely even glances at our IDs before letting us in.

Stepping into Revel is like stepping into the past. Forty years into the past, specifically; the décor is firmly eighties chic, all neon lights patterned like the zigzag slashes on vintage dad jackets, everyone dressed in polyester and denim. Some guy with bleached-blond hair has taken over one of the poles and is doing an impromptu show up there, and he's wearing overalls for some reason. The DJ plays a mash-up of Madonna and Hayley Kiyoko, and honestly, it kind of slaps.

Being here wakes me up, as if I've been underwater for years and have finally surfaced into the sun. It's the feeling I used to chase with whiskey and drugs and the bodies of strangers. I take a breath and my lungs expand. My head clears.

And for the first time since I got off the plane, I think maybe being here—maybe New York itself—will be okay.

"Come on," Ophelia says, and she grabs my hand, pulling me deeper into the club.

She and Diego get shots at the bar. I make an excuse to go to the bathroom, and when I come back, they're already dancing. It's easy to slip into the crowd alongside them, to let our bodies become fluid and anonymous. I end up with Ophelia, my hands on her plush waist and her hips grinding against mine. It's not even sexual, not really; it's the kind of hyperphysical flirtation queer girls get into sometimes, where movement becomes its own language. It's special. It's something I worried I wouldn't find when I left LA and its queer-lit bookshops, as if people like us only exist in the spaces I'm familiar with. I knew I was wrong, of course, that this was just me being self-absorbed and navel-gazey about my own experience, but still.

I thought I wouldn't be able to make friends anywhere else. That if I left the people who'd been putting up with me for the past eight years, I'd find I was in fact an intolerable person to be around.

We dance until the heat gets to be too much and I have to excuse myself to catch my breath and find something cold to drink. I end up at the bar, leaning in past the crowd of brightly colored gays, trying to get the bartender's attention. Which is kind of difficult when you're the only one present who isn't plastered in glitter and glow stick goo. I'm starting to get low-key irritated about it, which probably shows on my face, because when I accidentally make eye contact with the guy standing next to me, he laughs and says, "Yeah, around here you need to be wearing about seventy percent less clothing to get service. Sorry."

I feel my cheeks flush. The comment would have landed a lot differently if it had come from a different sort of guy—or at a straight club, where douches outnumber reasonable people four to one. But this man isn't looking at me like I'm a piece of disappointingly overdressed meat. He's smiling, has the kind of face that aggressively reads *himbo* despite his scruffy jawline and strong features. The thick Carolina accent certainly helps. He's wearing a plain white T-shirt, James Dean style, and I can't avoid noticing the way his black jeans cling to his muscular thighs a little *too* well.

Statistically speaking, I remind myself, he is almost definitely gay, so there's no point in fantasizing.

But holy *shit*. He looks like he could crush my head between those thighs, and to be honest, I would probably let him.

"I suppose I could always take my shirt off," I say, and his grin widens slightly, revealing—fuck me—dimples.

"You could," he says. "Or you could let me give it a go. I'm kind of a regular around these parts." He rises up on the balls of his feet, which is necessary considering he's around my height or maybe even a little shorter, and extends a heavily tattooed arm over the bar. "Greg!"

The bartender, presumably Greg, who has somehow heard hot guy's voice over the throbbing bass line, glances over his shoulder at us and shoots my new friend a thumbs-up.

"There you go," says my friend, dropping back onto his heels again. "All sorted out. Maybe I could buy your drink for you?" He pairs that question with an arch of a brow. I wish my arched brow looked that sexy.

My blush deepens, which is humiliating because I've never been an attractive blusher. My whole face tends to turn red, not just my cheeks, making me look more like I'm doing a lobster cosplay than flirting with a sexy stranger.

"Sure," I say. "I mean . . . yeah. Okay. If you want. But you don't have to actually. . . . That is, it won't cost much. I'm just ordering seltzer with lemon."

Something shifts in the guy's expression. The way he looks at me isn't teasing anymore; it's more . . . *considering*. "You're sober?"

I nod. I'm not sure where he's headed with this. Some people—men, mostly—are really turned off by the realization that they can't simply ply me with liquor and have me fall drunkenly into their beds. But this guy isn't like other guys, apparently, because if anything, my answer makes him lean in closer, bracing one elbow against the bar and facing me more fully, as if I just became the most interesting person in this place. I have to keep reminding myself that this is a gay club, meaning *he's* probably gay, meaning I shouldn't get too far ahead of myself.

He's hot, but he needs to be hot in the way that fictional characters are hot. He's unattainable.

"Me too," he says. "A little over ten years now."

"Four," I say, a little shyly, which surprises me. But then again, I don't get many opportunities to talk about my sobriety with people who actually give a shit. "A little more."

"Four's great," the guy says. "Four's awesome. Congratulations."

A couple comes up to the bar, trying to get the bartender's attention; they sidle their way in behind my new friend, who has to shift closer to me to make room. I'm near enough to him now that I can smell the smoky, salty scent of his deodorant—or whatever that smell is, because I'm pretty sure this guy isn't the type to wear cologne.

The bartender chooses this moment to finally show up, and the guy—whose name I still don't know, but he looks kind of like Jamie Dornan, so I'll call him Jamie—orders us both seltzers in martini glasses with lemon garnish.

"Cheers," he says, and clinks our glasses together.

We each take a sip, and I can't stop watching him over the rim of my glass—which he notices, apparently, because his grin when he lowers his drink is a little sharper than before.

"Here's the thing, though," I say. "These places always use well seltzer. When really, Sanpellegrino is the only sparkling water option worth considering."

He rolls his eyes, slapping one hand down against the bar. "Oh, come on. I can't believe you would shit on my boy LaCroix like this."

"LaCroix? Are you a thirty-five-year-old mommy blogger?"

"Don't knock Pamplemousse."

"I will knock Pamplemousse. You know the 'natural flavoring' all these brands crow about comes from like . . . beaver anal gland expression or whatever." Which is actually true. I didn't think it was when Chaya told me, but then I looked it up—much to my regret.

His smirk tugs a little tighter, a crooked smile I want to kiss right off his face. "I personally consider myself a connoisseur of beaver butt juice. A delicacy in some parts of Brooklyn."

"Sorry, my Sanpellegrino-trained palate must not be discerning enough."

"Cultural differences," he says with a sage nod. "They must not have a wide enough variety of anal flavorings where you come from. Where is this fabled land of milk and overpriced seltzer, by the way?"

He assumes I'm not from New York. Which I guess is fair; maybe I've fully assimilated into LA culture at this point by necessity, if not by intention. Not that I ever felt like I really fit in.

"Crown Heights," I say.

"No way. I thought for sure you were gonna say some Chicago suburb I've never heard of."

I make a face at him. "Please. With that accent, it's not like you grew up on the hard streets of the Upper West Side."

"North Carolina," he admits, "but I've been here for thirteen years. Plenty of time to drink every flavor of LaCroix from every bodega in the tristate area."

He's standing closer to me now, somehow, even though I don't remember either of us moving. I bend my knee slightly, and it brushes his leg; our hips are near enough I'm hyperaware of it, our proximity like a heat that only intensifies in the space between us.

"I'll keep spending half my paycheck on overpriced seltzer. Better than spending my whole paycheck on bourbon."

"Valid," he says. "Do you want to dance?"

I can tell I'm blushing from the way my cheeks suddenly feel sunburnt. It's dark enough in this place, though, that he probably doesn't notice. "Yes," I say. "But . . ."

One of his brows goes up. "*But?* I'm bracing myself."

I'm not entirely sure how to put this.

"But . . . aren't you gay?" I say at last, and punctuate it with a sip of my lemon seltzer. It's a fair question. I mean, he's in here. A gay club. "I mean, not that I won't dance with you if you are. I just want to make sure we're on the same page here."

Jamie Look-alike laughs and shakes his head. "No. I'm not gay."

"Bi, then?"

"Nope."

I feel like there's some obvious puzzle piece here I'm supposed to see that I'm somehow missing. I frown. "All right . . . cool, I guess. But why are you here if you're straight? Please tell me you aren't one of those het guys who thinks they can convert lesbians."

"*Are* you lesbian?"

"Well . . . no, but that's beside the point."

He's laughing again, and I'm still trying to decide if that's irritating or not when he says, "I'm trans. That's why I'm here. I'm a heterosexual trans man."

"*Oh.*" Now I feel like an asshole. "That makes sense. Sorry."

"Don't worry about it. Seriously."

My whole face is burning; I try to hide it with a quick gulp of water. I feel like some kind of weird gatekeeper now, interrogating him for being here, trying to figure out if he's straight or not, like there aren't options under LGBTQ besides gay and bi.

But Jamie Look-alike just offers me his hand, brows lifting. "You look like you want to disappear right now. Maybe instead of a vanishing act, you give me that dance?"

"Yes. Please."

He takes my water with surprising gentleness and sets it aside on the bar. And then he's leading me into the crowd, into the humid, sweat-scented, bass-thumping surge of human bodies. On the floor, the lights glitter silver and pink; they warm Jamie's pale-gold skin and gleam along his sharp cheekbones, melding like watercolors among the tattoos on his forearms, his chest. I have no idea what happened to Ophelia and Diego, but the moment I would have spared to worry was subsumed by the man's hands finding my waist, drawing me in close.

We fit together a little too perfectly: his firm body against mine, my hands on his broad shoulders, and his face close enough to mine that, even in this light, I can make out the faintest smattering of peppery freckles scattered across his nose. Something in my stomach coils just a little bit tighter—and we begin to dance.

Two hours ago I would have said I was a shitty dancer without liquor. Self-conscious, awkward, too aware of all the places my feet are and aren't supposed to go. Maybe it's that I know my partner is sober too, that we're both inebriated by nothing but the music and each other, but it's easier now. The beat finds its way into my bones, and I shift a little closer to his heat. His hands slide down to my hips, and I reach for his wrists and redirect them so his palms are cupping my ass instead.

He smirks, the cut of his lips knife-sharp in the flickering strobe lights—a blade I'd all-too-willingly impale myself on.

"What's your name?" I ask.

"What?" he mouths back.

It's loud, the bass line a steady thrum that all but vibrates in my core. I repeat myself, shouting a little to make sure he can hear:

"What's your name?"

The guy says something back, but it's impossible to hear over the music.

I scrunch my brows together and say, "What?"

He says it again, and at this point it would be embarrassing to ask him to say it a *third* time, so I just grin and nod as if I understood him. Doesn't matter anyway; I seriously doubt I'll see him again after tonight, as he doesn't strike me as the long-term-relationship-with-a-dog-and-a-rotating-chore-list kind of dude. I shout back my own name when he asks (or, well, I assume that's what he was asking), and he grins at me too. Whether he heard me is anyone's bet.

Normally, I start making my excuses to find a new partner around the third song. But I keep dancing with Jamie—or whomever—into the fourth song, the fifth, sixth. When his touch skims my bare skin, I feel electrified, the soft gust of his breath against the curve of my ear sends a thrill spinning down my spine. And then I'm kissing him, my hands slipping into his messy brown hair and his sliding down my ribs, pulling me in closer. He tastes like lemon and something sweet. Something sugary.

When the kiss breaks, he stays there, near enough that our lips graze, the tip of his nose warm when it brushes mine. And this time I can actually hear him when he says, "Do you want to go somewhere that isn't here?"

"Yes. Absolutely."

I shoot off a quick text to Ophelia as we wind our way through the crowd toward the doors—texting one-handed because my new friend has laced the fingers of my left hand together with his, guiding us between strange bodies without losing that link between us. He picks up a backpack at coat check, and I shake my head when he asks if I left anything there.

The night air is cool when we step out onto the sidewalk, refreshing on the nape of my neck after so long in the overheated club. The guy is still holding my hand, his palm soft and his grasp firm, steadying, around mine.

"I live in Bushwick," he tells me. "Are you any closer?"

I make a face. "No. Queens."

And there's something unbearably awkward about the prospect of an hour-long subway ride with a stranger I met at a random club. I don't want the magic to dissipate under the fluorescent train lights, to see the sweaty lines and crevices of another human instead of . . . this, his eyes reflecting the amber streetlamps, his body still tilting in close to mine. Jamie like the perfect photo of a perfect man, or something out of an oil painting.

But I'm also fucking broke, so I'm about to open my mouth and suggest we split cab fare when he says, "We could get a hotel." And before I can start calculating the impact of that on my grocery budget, he adds, "My treat."

Well, I'm not arguing with that.

3

The hotel he chooses is in Hell's Kitchen, the kind of place that exists to serve the throngs of upper-middle-class businessmen and Javits convention attendees, with stylized modern interior décor and a rooftop bar that is probably great for selfies and terrible for your wallet. Not that we go to the bar. Instead we take the elevator up to the tenth floor, and I follow Jamie down the hall to the room he's just now reserved. These floor-to-ceiling windows are definitely out of my price range, so I can only assume that whatever Jamie does when he isn't picking up girls at queer clubs is extremely lucrative.

"Sorry," he says, frowning at the slick all-white king bed. And the thing I find bizarre after meeting the confident guy at the bar is that he really *does* seem sorry. "I didn't realize it would be this bougie."

"It's okay. I really like the . . . art." I gesture vaguely at the mass-produced contemporary art framed on the walls, and Jamie gives me a long, flat look before I finally break—and suddenly we're both laughing, me with one hand clapped over my mouth.

"Come here," he says, and he reaches out both hands to

gesture me closer. I go, helplessly obedient when he's looking at me like *that,* his deep brown eyes gone a little darker, shaded by the lowered fans of his lashes.

When he kisses me this time, it feels different than it did in the club. There, we were in public—and even if making out on the dance floor isn't exactly an uncommon occurrence, it still felt visible. Here, there is no one to see us. It's private. It's intimate. His teeth catch my lower lip, and I make a soft sound that's muffled against his mouth.

His fingers slide beneath the hem of my black T-shirt. "May I?" he murmurs, our lips still moving together. His voice has the low, husky quality that comes with desire.

I nod. His palms glide up over my ribs, and I lift my arms to make it easier as he strips the shirt off over my head. Then his gaze falls to my exposed body, its weird moles, the sharp edges that never quite softened, even years after I got off drugs. But he touches me like I'm delicate, fingertips skimming over flesh with the same care as I would use to touch the edges of my photographs as I dip them into developer—like he half expects me to tell him to stop.

I catch one of his hands with mine and move it to my breast. He quirks one corner of his mouth and gives in, tipping forward to scatter kisses along my neck, my shoulder, as his free hand does the work of unclasping my bra. Always love a man who can figure out bra hooks without help.

I'm not sure what I did to deserve to be here with him, in this fabulously expensive hotel room that probably cost $400 for the night and seems like it should be reserved for women in evening gowns whose diamonds are worth the GDP of a small country. But I'm not going to question it. I'm going to take his shirt off instead, exposing his firm, tattooed torso, the pale scars that curve like faint smiles beneath his pecs.

I can't get enough of him, touching skin as it's exposed and feeling his strength shifting beneath my hands. I kiss one of his tattoos, a rose illustrated in blackwork, its petals blooming over his heart. His fingers twine in my hair, twisting the loose dark waves around his knuckles.

I manage to get off my shoes and jeans without toppling over, which is an achievement for me. Then Jamie Look-alike—it is *way* too late to ask his name again—hitches me up off the ground, my legs automatically circling round his waist as he carries me over to the bed and tosses me down onto the plush mattress. I push up onto my elbows and watch as he undoes his belt buckle, the *fwip* sound the leather makes as he tugs it free of his jeans sending a frisson of want through my gut. The jeans come off and he crawls onto the bed after me, laying a trail of kisses from the inside of my ankle up to my thigh to the hollow below my hipbone. I shiver as his breath tickles my skin, palpable through the thin mesh of my underwear.

He hooks his thumbs under the waistband of those panties. "Tell me if anything's too far," he says, which is charming enough that I actually want him to give educational presentations to other guys I've dated, the ones who acted like getting consent is a socially uncomfortable transaction to be dealt with as perfunctorily as possible. "We can always slow down or take a break."

"You're fine," I assure him, and lift my hips to help him peel my panties off. And this, I realize, is probably my cue to return the favor.

I've slept with trans women before but never a trans man. Everyone's different, obviously, and everyone has different boundaries, but I'm still trying to find the right words to ask what his are when he reaches down from the edge of the bed and retrieves his backpack. He unzips it to reveal a strap-on harness and a very realistic flesh-colored dildo, the kind that has a bulb at one end that can go inside the wearer to stimulate them as well as the person being fucked. A girl I dated briefly last year used one, and though I never tried wearing it myself, she certainly seemed to enjoy it.

Jamie holds it up with an arched, questioning brow. "Yeah?"

I grin. "You came prepared," I say, and he's still blushing, the color visible in his cheeks despite the half-dimmed light as I push myself upright to help him put it on.

For a guy who's been to Revel enough times that he knows the bartender by name, he sure seems self-conscious about being called out on that fact.

Which reminds me all over again that I really have no idea what to expect from this guy. I don't know his lines, and I need to figure those out before we go much further.

I pause with my hands on his hips, glancing up to meet his gaze. "I don't know if you . . . Some people aren't comfortable with . . ."

"I'd rather you didn't," he says firmly, rescuing me from having to fumble my way toward completing that sentence without humiliating myself somehow. "There's a vibrator in the strap, and that's good enough for me."

"Okay," I say, "sounds good."

"It's nothing personal," he assures me. "But I don't really know you, and it's a whole thing."

"No, I know." I tip toward him and press a kiss to his sternum, my hands sliding up to his muscular waist as he pushes off his underwear. Once the cock is in place, he lets me take over buckling the harness onto his hips, my hands lingering long enough to enjoy the feeling of his firm ass held in both palms. "Why are you so freaking ripped?" I mumble against his clavicle, tongue tracing the shape of the tattoo there, which lies like a slash of ink along the bone. It's very hot. Tattooed guys are universally hot.

He laughs and one hand dips between our bodies, his fingers teasing along the seam of my cunt. And then I forget to make stupid comments at all, because he touches me like he's playing an instrument, tugging a sharp gasp from my lips.

I muffle the sound with another kiss, this one sloppier, needier. His tongue slips into my mouth and I twist my fingers up in his messy hair, keeping him near. Heat pools low in my stomach as his lips shift to my jaw, my throat. I wrap my hand around his cock too, stroking it in the same slow rhythm with which he's touching me. The movement must be grinding the vibrator attachment against him because that earns me a soft moan and the sharp bite of teeth. The pain lights something warm inside me, and it's been a long time since I've felt like this, where I could touch pain and not immediately want to blot it out, drown it in a cascade of alcohol or drugs. Instead, I . . . I like it.

Maybe too much.

"We could pause and check the minifridge if you want," he mumbles against my lips. "They probably have Sanpellegrino."

"Shut the fuck up," I tell him, and punctuate the demand with a rake of my nails down his spine.

A sly smile cuts across that beautiful mouth. "Yes, ma'am."

This is supposed to be a one-night stand. I'm not supposed to be imagining lazy mornings, teasing him over his terrible seltzer taste, finding out the meaning of the tattoos that slide beneath my fingers as I touch him. Those are the kinds of little mysteries that will exist forever. I'll never unravel him. He'll just be a story I tell one day, a shadowy figure from my past.

Jamie shifts down the length of my body, leaving kisses in his wake. I push up onto my elbows, and our eyes meet as he grasps one of my thighs, easing it up and out of the way. He's still looking at me as he dips his head and traces his tongue along me. I shudder—I can't help myself—and reach down, lacing my fingers together with his and holding on tight as he swirls the tip of his tongue around my clit, teasing.

My want is a living, throbbing thing inside me, unignorable. I squirm beneath him as he does it again; fucking *torturous,* it really is, and when he finally breaks eye contact, it's to slide two fingers inside me and stroke me from the inside too. He touches me like he actually cares if I get off, like he actually cares *more* about my getting off, even, than his own. And maybe that shouldn't be a rare quality, but it kind of is.

Or maybe I have a habit of giving myself to people who want me for very different reasons. I've never asked for more. Never thought there was more to demand.

"Fuck," I whisper, and he curls those fingers, earning a sudden jump and a gasp on my part.

I expect him to spend just a minute or so down there, to give up the second his jaw starts to hurt and move on to what most guys perceive to be the main event. But he *stays.* He keeps going, driving me closer and closer to the edge—until my body is liquid heat, until I'm coming, clenching down around his fingers again and again as he works me through the finish.

I'm breathless, my chest rising and falling erratically as he makes his way back up the bed. I taste myself on his lips when he kisses me, and I'm too strung out in the afterglow to care. I can't even feel self-conscious about my nakedness, spread out before him; he looks at me and touches me like I'm beautiful, and so I believe it.

"Come here," I say eventually, reaching for his cock and guiding it to my entrance.

The dildo attachment is pretty big, but it's not *too* big—enough that it hurts a little as he slides in, but then my body adjusts, accommodating him. He hovers above me, braced on one elbow, our noses nearly brushing.

"Good?" he asks. And judging from the rough, husky quality of his voice, he's as affected by this as I am.

I nod and curl one leg around his waist, using it to urge him in deeper.

He fucks me slowly at first, rolling his hips against mine in steady waves. I can't stop touching him; I can't get enough. My hands grip his thighs, his ass, dragging up his long spine to tangle in his hair.

"Is this okay for you?" I ask him, because in this half-light it's hard to see his face, hard to tell—but he blows out a heavy breath, half a laugh, and says, "Yeah. Yeah, it's fantastic."

He reaches down to touch me again as he fucks me—and if I'm sensitive at first, that's quickly overwhelmed by a new and building pleasure. His body is over-hot against mine, our skin slick with a faint sheen of perspiration as we move together. I can't take my eyes off his face, memorizing the way it shifts from parted lips to furrowed brow, his teeth gritting as he gets close, and always—always—his gaze hot and dark and fixed on mine.

I come again before he does, not even bothering to try to be quiet this time. My head tips back, and he drags his mouth along my exposed and vulnerable throat, his hips stuttering against mine as his climax hits a second later. His moans are muffled against my shoulder, breath hot on my skin, my nails digging into his back, dragging down, leaving my mark.

He stays inside me after, during the several long seconds that we remain intertwined, his weight heavy atop my chest and my arms hanging lax and loose about his body. The Midtown city light slants in from the windows, bluish, casting deep shadows between us and making this moment feel out of time—otherworldly.

At last he pulls out and rolls off of me, hands making quick work of the harness buckles and casting the thing onto the floor. I shift onto my side and slide my palm over his flat, damp stomach, kissing the place where his collarbone meets his neck. Some men find this to be an erogenous zone. Jamie, it seems, is no different. I relish the shiver that rolls through him at my touch.

"Was that okay?" he asks me at last, perennially, it seems, the gentleman.

I kind of want to smack him and tell him to stop being so nice, that someone in this city is gonna take advantage of that eventually. Instead I coil in closer and say, quite honestly, "That was some of the best sex I've ever had."

We drift off together like that, tangled up and listening to the arrhythmic music of horns and ambulance sirens that careens through the city below—until he turns toward me around midnight and asks if I want to go again, and I, helplessly, agree.

4

I wake up with drool on my face and my phone alarm blaring pop-punk music. I fling my hand over to mute the alarm and accidentally knock my phone onto the floor; it takes several seconds of sightless fumbling before my fingers finally touch cold glass and I seize blessed silence.

I squint open heavy eyelids and glance at the other side of the bed. The guy from last night is already gone, the sheets mussed but cool. A slip of paper with the hotel watermark rests on his pillow. It reads: *So sorry to walk out on you like this, but I'm late for work and didn't want to wake you. Sleep well. If you want to get dinner sometime, text me.* And then he's written out his phone number.

Great. At this rate, if I want to find out his name, I'm going to have to actually admit to not knowing it.

I push myself upright and reach for my phone again, glancing down at my lock screen. *Shit.* It's past eight. It's past eight, my first class at Parker starts at ten—my *best* class, really, because it's my mixed-media photography course with *the* Wyatt Cole—and *I'm so fucked.*

I launch out of bed, tripping over the overlong duvet in my haste to grab my clothes off the floor and get dressed. My phone keeps buzzing. Probably Ophelia or Diego, or maybe my sponsor saw the photos from the club last night and wants to know if I threw my sobriety away. I'm dying of thirst, but the water bottles in the minifridge cost fourteen dollars, so I end up sticking my head under the sink faucet instead.

Do I have time to go by the apartment and change? Shower? Debatable. But my camera and portfolio are both there, so I'm gonna have to.

I double- and triple-check the room before leaving, making sure I didn't leave anything important behind—like my wallet or Jamie Look-alike's phone number. Google Maps says it's a forty-five-minute trip back to the apartment from here, but an Uber would be fifty bucks in rush-hour traffic, and I'm more broke than I am late.

Fuck you fuck you fuck you, my brain whispers at itself as I power walk down the overheated Hell's Kitchen sidewalk, because this hotel *had* to be in Hell's Kitchen, because a twenty-minute walk just to get to the subway is totally normal, because catching a train at Times Square station during peak assholes-in-business-suits hour is something that humans ought to do, ever.

Muscle memory takes over as I stab my forefinger against the greasy MetroCard machine, which is good because my actual brain is too busy calculating how fucked I am to worry about whether I should get a seven-day ticket or just go ahead and commit to OMNY so I can pay with my phone. It was only yesterday that I kept thinking how losing my luggage might mean the universe didn't want me to go to Parker at all. And now here I am, late on day one because of my own stupid, reckless choices. I could have made Jamie come home with me and dealt with the awkwardness of being on the subway together. I could have gone home after instead of sleeping in the hotel. I could have changed my alarm to go off an hour earlier.

Instead I'm sweaty by the time I dash up the stairs to the apartment, hands fumbling the keys twice before I manage to let myself in. Ophelia and Diego are both nowhere to be seen, their doors shut; they're probably sleeping last night off. I'd forgotten that I don't actually have a change of clothes, thanks to the luggage issue, but I do manage a quick cat bath in the sink, piling my wild hair atop my head and securing it with a velvet scrunchie before grabbing my camera bag and portfolio and running right back out the door.

I stare at the clock on my phone practically the entire train ride downtown. I text Jamie at Queensboro Plaza while we still have service before the train goes underground: **Next time the Sanpellegrino's on me.** I can't afford to fuck up on my first day of class, so that phone stays in my hand. I keep staring at Google Maps like a goddamn tourist the whole way to the building on Washington Square that houses Parker's photography program. I still don't have my actual photo ID—we're supposed to pick those up this afternoon—but luckily the lady at the reception desk lets me get away with showing her my driver's license and the program acceptance email instead.

My first class, Mixed-Media Photography, is on the sixth floor. I take advantage of the mirrored walls in the elevator to apply a layer of brick-red lipstick and rip open one of those perfume sticker samples and rub it on my wrists. I figure it's not like I'm going for an interview at Goldman Sachs. This is an art program. It's totally acceptable for artists to look like they slept in a coffin instead of a plush luxury hotel bed the night before. I tell myself this because it's better than wallowing in my anxiety over making a shitty first impression on Wyatt Cole, who is basically the whole reason I applied to this program. The first time I saw his work was at an LA gallery, a big classy one that I only got admission to because I was (at the time) fucking the curator's sister. I remember standing in front of a massive black-and-white print of two lovers, hands entwined and legs entangled, the canvas embroidered with jewel-colored thread that twisted into vines and flowers binding them together, and thinking, *The only thing I want in life is to make someone else feel like this.*

There were other artists on display too, but I kept coming back to that one piece. And even after the curator's sister took me to our dinner reservation, all I could talk about was how much I wanted to make art the way Wyatt Cole made art.

It turned out I was the last one aboard the Wyatt Cole hype train, which had been running full steam for over a year by then. Everyone was obsessed with him, and the fact that he was notoriously reclusive and rarely made public appearances only made him more appealing. I imagined him as a hermit locked away in a garret somewhere, a shrouded figure in a darkroom backlit in red.

Then Parker announced Cole would teach in its photography program. I never thought I'd get in. Never.

Until I did. And now all I have to do is not ruin it for myself.

I take a moment in the hall to suck in several deep, steadying breaths before going into the classroom. I can be a couple of extra seconds late; that's better than coming in flush faced, sweaty, and breathless. But when I finally open the door and step inside, I find that all the students are still buzzing in conversation, twisting around in chairs, and perched on desks, the podium at the front of the room still empty.

Thank god. I'm late, but Wyatt Cole is later.

I slide into an empty seat, take my portfolio out of my bag, and open it on my desk to glance through my work—not that I haven't spent hours poring over these photos already, but the anticipation of someone else seeing them puts me on edge. I can't help but see them through Wyatt Cole's hypothetical eyes, criticizing the highlights here and the shadows there, wondering if I should have cropped this piece differently, if that one will evoke the same emotions in him as it does in me.

"Are those yours?" the girl next to me asks. I look over and immediately, reflexively, sit a little straighter in my chair.

She's frum. Which is to say she's Jewish and religious and observant. Maybe to anyone else she looks a little out of place with her three-quarter-length sleeves, her long skirt and high neckline, in late spring. But I know tznius—the set of Orthodox Jewish modesty standards—when I see it. And the purple and silver scarf wrapped around her head isn't just for decoration; it's a tichel, the traditional head covering worn by married women.

The urge to slam my portfolio shut hits me so hard I have to physically sit on my hands to resist it. But then I look at her again, and it's different this time. Her nails are long and spiky, painted black. A gold hoop pierces one of her eyebrows. She's frum, but she's unlike any frum person I grew up with. And her eyes—large, dark brown, framed by gold eyeliner—are kind.

"Yes," I say eventually, and glance back down at my work. My cheeks flush hot with mixed embarrassment and shame.

People used to stare at me too, when I was frum. They used to stare at my father with his long beard and black hat, my brothers with their kippot secured to the crowns of their heads, my mother wearing her wig and stockings. They looked at us like they thought we didn't belong in the same city as everyone else. And the fact that I left the community—was kicked out, rather—doesn't mean I should become part of the same judgmental, derisive, xenophobic culture I despised.

It's just . . .

"Can I see?" says the frum girl, and I have no choice; I push my portfolio over to the edge of my desk as she leans over to take a closer look.

The photos tell a story. They're my life in LA in two parts: before I got sober and after. They show the way the same bridge can look different if I took the photo while I was high and if I took the photo after I was clean—the photo of my feet in the sand next to used syringes, my weight off-kilter, uncertain, juxtaposed with that same angle as water crashes to shore, sea-foam swirling about my ankles and my skirt caught in the wind.

Plenty of people have seen these photos; they were in a gallery in Venice, later in Santa Monica, and they served as part of my application process to Parker. But it's one thing to know that people are looking at my art—seeing past the flimsy film and into my life, my history, *my soul*—when I don't have to personally witness it. I drift through my own gallery shows like a ghost, there but not. I can hit Submit on an application portal and never think twice about what it means. But every time I have to watch someone look, watch them *see* me in this way . . .

It feels like I have opened up my stomach for them and let them reach their hands inside to fumble with my organs, twisting my guts between their fingers.

"These are really good," the girl says, and she gestures, implicitly asking permission to turn the page. I nod and let her. My heart is beating too fast, and I stare at the side of her face rather than look at my own work. She's probably just being polite. Everyone here is good; being *good* isn't impressive anymore.

I need to be spectacular.

"What's your name?" she asks when she's done.

"Elisheva. Ely."

"I'm Michal," she says. "Michal Pereira. Are you the—"

But before she can finish, the door opens, and a hush drops over the classroom as our professor, Wyatt Cole, walks between the rows of desks to the front podium. I'm staring alongside everyone else as he goes, drinking in the sight of him, our first glimpse of the mysterious, notorious artist who rewrote the landscape of mixed-media photography. The man whose work has been on the cover of *Time,* who otherwise avoids the public eye as if it will scald him, who is single-handedly responsible for my application to Parker, who can break my heart with a single photograph.

"I can't believe it's really him," Michal whispers, and I can't either, because the man at the front of the room, our new professor—Wyatt Cole—is the man I had sex with last night.

5

The whole class is like a fever dream.

Wyatt keeps speaking words, probably important ones, but it's like my brain is made of oatmeal; I don't process a single thing he says. He doesn't look at me the whole time. Every time he scans the class, his gaze jumps right over me and onto Michal, as if I occupy a black hole, as if G-d just clipped this random fourth-row seat on the sixth floor of the Parker visual arts building right out of existence.

I kind of wish I actually were invisible. Life in the soul-crushing core of a black hole is probably better than whatever awkward-as-fuck conversation Wyatt and I are gonna have after this class is over.

What is wrong with me? How did I end up in this situation? Normal people don't. I have never in my life met another human being who accidentally had a one-night stand with their professor. This is not a thing that happens to responsible people. This is a thing that happens in sitcoms.

How am I going to survive an entire summer like this? How are either of us? Is he going to be able to take me seriously now that he's seen me naked? Am I even going to be able to learn a single word in this class when I've seen *him* naked?

But then I hear Wyatt's voice say, "Ely," and I glance up, and he's finally looking back, his eyes on my eyes, and he says, "Please stay after class for a few minutes."

Shit.

I haven't felt guilty in front of a teacher like this since I was a teenager and got caught using an unfiltered phone during Midrash class. At least Wyatt is unlikely to call my mother.

Still, Michal arches her pierced brow at me as we pack up our things. She graciously doesn't ask me why Wyatt knows my name; it's not like he took roll or anything. And she doesn't ask what I did wrong.

I wonder what I'd tell her if she did.

The other students filter out the door, some of them casting curious glances at me over their shoulders as they go. I pack my things away slowly, lingering over the clasp on my bag like delaying this interaction will somehow make it better.

"Ely."

When Wyatt says my name, all I can hear is the way he said it last night, low and soft, sweet as honey. I close my eyes for a moment, digging my nails into my palms. Then I make myself look.

He stands at the front of the room, one hand braced on the edge of the table and his weight shifted over onto his left foot—uneasy. Or maybe just embarrassed. He looks the way I feel, like I want to break apart into my component atoms and disappear.

I make my way up to the podium. He seems to be having trouble meeting my gaze; his eyes keep flicking down and to the left, as if to stare at me is to stare directly into the sun. So, obviously, I keep my own attention fixed on his face. One of us will refuse to be embarrassed about fucking the other one.

"Hi," I say. "I feel like I know you from somewhere."

His cheeks flush a dull red. "Did you realize? Before?"

It takes me a solid fifteen seconds to process what he's trying to say. And then once I do, I'm embarrassed all over again. It's not like New York is positively littered with guys named Wyatt, after all.

"I couldn't hear you in the club," I admit. "You kept saying your name, but I couldn't understand it, so I just . . . went with it. I didn't know you were—well—*you*."

Which is the truth, but once the words are out of my mouth, they don't sound all that convincing.

"I see," Wyatt says. "There's nothing to be done about it now, and obviously neither of us—that is, we didn't expect— What happened happened, and the important thing is . . . well. It can't happen again, obviously."

"Obviously," I echo.

He must have taken that as agreement because he clears his throat and nods, even if he still can't quite look me in the eye. "The last thing I want is to make you uncomfortable, so . . ."

"Do I look uncomfortable?" I ask, and so what if it comes out flirtatious? I *do* want to fuck him again. *Gladly.*

Wyatt sighs and—finally—meets my gaze. I can practically *see* him piecing together what he wants to say to me, pulling the guise of *responsible, grown-up, sober professor* over himself like a cheap Halloween costume.

"I can't have power over you after what happened," he says. "It's not right."

"I won't tell anyone if you don't."

He shakes his head, lips pressing into a grim line. "That's not good enough. I'm sure you're a wonderful person—but my career and my reputation mean everything to me."

What a slap in the face. He says it as if he just *assumes* I'd want to continue the relationship. As if I'm some silly girl with notions of forbidden love floating in her head.

"My reputation matters to me too" is the only thing I manage to get out. "This could hurt *my* career, and I haven't even really started it yet."

At least I get some kind of reaction: It's his turn to flinch, something complicated passing through his expression before he schools it back into professionalism.

"I know. I—I don't know what to do here. I don't want to be in a position where I have to decide your grades with last night living in the back of my mind. If anyone ever found out . . ."

He pauses for a second, like he's waiting for me to reply and say I totally understand where he's coming from. Like he's waiting for me to relent.

"It wouldn't be fair. To you or the other students," he adds eventually.

"Fair," I echo. A bitter laugh boils up from my chest. "Nothing about this is fair to me."

I learned a long time ago that there is nothing I hate more than people who are obsessed with their own moral virtue. Particularly when it comes at the expense of, you know, having a fucking life.

"So what are you trying to say?" I press on.

He looks distressed, which is fucking rich because *I'm* the one who ought to be distressed in this situation. He realized he slept with a student—so what? He's the one in power here. He gets to decide what happens moving forward.

"Are you telling me I need to drop out?" I ask.

Years. Years of my life, dedicated to rebuilding a sense of myself as an actual person and not just a collection of impulses and fraying nerves—years learning how to exist outside the scaffolding of the world I was raised in and then relearning that world without drugs. Years, all of them leading here, to this, to my first shot at making it outside LA, and now Wyatt is going to yank it out from under me over a stupid fucking one-night stand?

Wyatt sighs, pressing the heels of both palms to his eyes for a moment. "No. No, of course not. I wouldn't do that to you. But you'll need to drop my class."

Somehow, that's even worse. I only cry when I'm angry, which is embarrassing and probably comes across as manipulative, but unfortunately my tear ducts are not responsive to the threat of social humiliation. I scrub a hand quickly across my cheek and hope the gesture looks brusque, efficient—that Wyatt doesn't think I'm trying to get away with anything by having a breakdown in front of him.

"You're the reason I came here, Wyatt. You're—literally, you are *literally* Wyatt fucking Cole. This was my chance to actually—I need this. I can't just . . ."

Although if he *does* change his mind because I cried, that'd be okay too.

"You know, I didn't go out and sleep with Wyatt Cole specifically, on purpose. I don't think I deserve to get punished for the universe's idea of a dumb joke."

This is literally TV-drama behavior, without the benefits. I'm pretty sure this is the plot of the first episode of *Grey's Anatomy*. Only McDreamy didn't kick Meredith Grey out of her surgical internship afterward—we got multiple seasons of yearning stares and steamy scenes in surgical supply closets.

"I could make sure you get into Ava Zhu's class instead," he says. "She has a waiting list a mile long, but I can pull some strings. That's trading up, really."

Ava Zhu is a legend. A titan of digital photography. One of my friends from back in LA has a coffee-table book of her work. Working with her would be a dream come true, obviously. But that's not the point.

"She isn't mixed media. I came here to study with *you*."

Wyatt is gazing at me with these big brown cow eyes like he's begging me to give him a break and take the damn bone. That look probably works for him most of the time. But I've seen that same look from plenty of addicts desperate for a loan, and it doesn't do a goddamn thing to me.

"Don't you get it?" I say. "No matter what happens in this situation, you're still the one with power. You can keep me in your class, and like you said, maybe one day someone finds out and it ruins my career. Not yours, not really. You'd be embarrassed for a few months, maybe. But you're still Wyatt Cole. You still keep getting the good shows, get good reviews, and get covered in *Vanity Fair* or whatever. But what happens to me?"

I can tell I'm affecting him. He looks like I just punched him in the chest. The part of me that hates confrontation swells up, and I have to swallow the urge to immediately apologize. I swipe a fresh wave of tears with the heel of my hand. Fuck him for looking so torn up over this. Fuck him for having the luxury of wallowing in his own conscience.

"I only ever thought of you as a one-night stand anyway," I make myself say, even though I'm already shaky, with that drowned-fish feeling of my throat closing up. "You're a professional. So you ought to be able to be a *professional* and let this whole thing go. It's not like we're exes who had a bad breakup. I don't know why we can't behave as colleagues."

He swallows, throat bobbing visibly. For a second I almost think I've got him. That he'll relent, acknowledge he's being stupid and arbitrary, and take me back into his class. But then:

"I can't grade you," he says.

"*Wyatt—*"

"I can't," he goes on doggedly, "but I can still teach you. Just not in the regular class. All right? I'll help you with your portfolio, one-on-one. Informally." He makes a face, like he isn't 100 percent certain on whether that is morally acceptable. "And you can do your capstone project with me, if . . . if you're still interested in working with me, that is."

I hate how pitiful he looks right now. How yearning. Like he's the one afraid of *me* saying no.

This entire situation makes me want to tear my (and his) face off.

"All right," I say at last. My throat feels swollen, like I've swallowed something that scraped the inside raw. "Okay. Fine. Sure. I guess I don't really have much of a choice, do I?"

Which only makes the kicked-dog expression on his face worse. "Thanks. . . . I'm sorry."

"I don't know what you're apologizing for." My hands are sweaty as I clench them into fists at my sides, then flex my fingers again. This whole conversation just got way more awkward than I bargained for. "I'm gonna go, then."

He clears his throat and nods. "I'll take care of it with the registrar. And with Ava."

He's still standing so close, as near as he did at the club last night when I could smell the heady mix of sweat and deodorant on his skin. Today he's more pulled together, professional. He's even got a collared shirt on.

Not that I can't very easily imagine him with the shirt *off.*

"And you'll email me about setting a time to look at my portfolio and discuss my capstone," I remind him. If I'm not mistaken, that color is back in his cheeks.

"Right."

"Great. I'll see you, then." I'm halfway to the door, portfolio tucked under my arm, when I pause and look back. He's watching me, still blushing like a teenage boy, as I throw out one last barb: "Last night was amazing, by the way."

The choked sound he makes in response to that is worth all the drama. I leave before he can say anything that would ruin my tiny victory.

■

The rest of my classes feel like they speed by in a haze. Maybe it's sleep deprivation; maybe it's just Wyatt fucking Cole. Either way, my brain isn't exactly present for Brianna Earnshaw's Art Criticism syllabus review or even Héctor Pérez-Wahid's demonstration of platinum printing. Michal is a familiar face in a few of my courses, although I don't see her at lunch—which maybe makes sense if she has to go off campus to find something kosher to eat.

It's still blazing hot out by the time classes are over, right in time for the rush-hour commute. I find myself crammed into a hot box on the N train, some man's elbow in my stomach and my face shoved against a girl's fuzzy pink backpack. Half the people empty out at Queensboro Plaza, but at that point there aren't that many stops left before mine, so it's small consolation.

Ophelia and Diego are both home already when I get there. Diego's fussing around in the kitchen with something that smells like onions, and he catches me before I can even sit down—one arm flung out, finger pointing, declaring, "*Ely Cohen,* you didn't come home last night!"

"Hi yourself," I tell him.

Ophelia is on the sofa drinking out of the most ornate teacup I've ever seen. "The prodigal daughter returns," she says. "So I'm guessing you had a good time."

I kind of love that this is the way the two of them are. We've only known each other for, like, twenty-four hours, but already it feels like we've been best friends for ages. Not that I'd know much about best friends: Ever since Chaya, I've erased all my friendships the second they start to get too close.

But Ophelia and Diego aren't afraid of things like that. They're brash and open and wear their hearts slathered across their sleeves.

I wish I were a little more like that.

Right now, if I can judge from how hot my face feels, my

cheeks have gotta be bright red. "Sorry. Maybe I should have waited for you guys . . . ?"

"We're your roommates, not your prison wardens," Diego says, punctuating his words with a rap of his wooden spoon against his skillet. "Hell no. Tell me who it was, you saucy minx."

Is it too late to pretend I forgot something on campus and leave? Ophelia's watching me over the rim of her teacup with a devious grin curling around her lips as if she already knows what I'm going to say, which of course she can't possibly. Hardly anyone knows what Wyatt Cole looks like and certainly not outside photography circles. Which is precisely how I ended up in his bed last night.

I could always lie, of course. But lying reminds me of addiction, and I won't do that. Not ever again.

"Was it that hot guy I saw you dancing with?" Ophelia asks. "The one who looked like he'd play the rugged but charming Scottish laird in a historical romance?"

"Probably," I say. "Yes. I mean . . . yes. Which was fine. But."

"*But?*" Diego prods, and he's even tilting forward slightly, spoon in hand, like I've left him on tenterhooks.

Please kill me. "But today I went to class, and it turns out the rugged Scottish laird is my professor."

I swear it's like I just told them I found a million dollars lying on the street. Diego crows out loud, and Ophelia puts down the teacup a little too hard before clapping her hands together. I don't know how they can be so delighted about me ruining my life, but they really, definitely are.

"You absolute fuckup!" Diego cries, and I collapse onto the sofa facedown—which is what I should have done as soon as I walked in the door.

"Please stop talking and let me die," I mumble against the cushions.

"Wait, like your actual professor?" Ophelia says. "Not just a professor in your program but, like, the one that is teaching your course?"

"Yep. Well. Sort of." I lift my head and blow a wad of hair away from my mouth, where it had gotten stuck to my lipstick. "He kicked me out of his class."

"He *what*?" Diego sounds scandalized but the kind of scandalized you get while watching *Love Is Blind*. He's enjoying this.

But it's still validating to see someone else as pissed off about Wyatt as I am. "I know. It's bullshit. He says he doesn't want to be in charge of grading me or whatever. Which I guess is fine; that's his decision. It's just that he's the whole reason I came here, so . . ."

Ophelia leans forward, offering me her teacup—which makes sense until I realize it's full not of tea but red wine. I shake my head and offer her a thin, grateful smile so I don't seem too weird.

"That really sucks," she says. "I mean, he's right that he probably shouldn't be in that position. But it's not like you slept with him on purpose."

"Exactly." I exhale heavy. It's the kind of exhale that feels like collapsing into a pile on the floor. "At least he said he would help me with my portfolio separately. So I still get to, like, benefit from his genius. Just not as his actual student."

And now that I'm explaining it to the two of them, I wonder how serious Wyatt is about the offer. It's easy to say he'll help me with my capstone, but I want more than that. I came here for a whole summer of learning from him and hearing his feedback on my work. What's he gonna give me instead—a quick glance through some of my photos and a hearty clap on the back?

"That's still shitty," says Ophelia, and I could hug her; I really could. But I'm pretty sure we aren't there yet friendship-wise.

"Agreed. Like, is this dude *that* certain he can't keep it in his pants? We're all grown here," Diego says.

I finally push myself up to sit properly, toeing off my shoes so I can cross my legs on the couch. "Well, there's nothing I can do about it. I have to take what he's willing to give me."

Even if I hate it.

Even if it feels a little bit like he's punishing me.

I don't get a choice in any of this, after all.

6

WYATT

I've spent the majority of my career practicing calculated invisibility.

Fortunately for me, photography isn't one of those fields where you need much of a public social presence to succeed. When news outlets want to talk about my work, they use a reproduction of one of my artistic photos, not a picture of my face.

But taking the Parker job means interacting with people in an actual flesh-and-blood space—something that seemed a lot easier until I actually had to do it.

"This is obligatory?" I ask Ava Zhu for the third time, standing in the doorway to her office while she packs up her bag at the end of the second day of classes.

"Oh yes," she says. "It's supposed to give the students an opportunity to mingle and get to know all the professors in the program. And each other."

"Surely the students want to see less of us, not more."

"Count yourself lucky there aren't icebreakers. Last year Scott made us all go around in a circle and tell the story behind our favorite scar."

Ava smiles at me as she squeezes past, out into the hall. And I stand there, awkwardly watching her lock up, imagining all the disgusted ways she'd look at me if I told her the main reason I'm not looking forward to tonight.

It feels like the kind of coincidence that shouldn't happen in real life. New York is huge. That's one thing I like about this city: the anonymity. I've lived here long enough to have plenty of stories about missed connections, people I ran into one time on the subway or at the grocery store and never saw again. I have neighbors in my building who I've only met one time in six years. A part of me thinks I should deconstruct my office and search for hidden cameras, because surely this is some kind of joke.

It's not, though, and I know it's not. I just have that kind of luck.

I wonder if I brought it on myself. I mean, I gave Ely my number for a reason. I wanted her to call me. I didn't want it to be only one night—I had all these secret hopes for a second date, a proper one this time, in a sit-down restaurant with zero glitter or glow sticks. I do like dancing in a club like Revel from time to time. But I'm not really in the habit of having one-night stands either, so maybe the universe thought it was trying to make things easy on me. Well. Thanks for the effort, universe, but I was good on the relationships front.

Now I'm not the cool, mysterious, hot guy from the queer club. I'm the creepy perv professor sleeping with his students.

"You'll be fine, Wyatt," Ava says as we start off down the hall toward the elevators. "Promise. The students' bark is worse than their bite. And you already know the rest of us."

Which is true—thanks to Ava herself. Ava was one of my first art friends when I moved to New York. She introduced me to everyone at Parker, which is how I got nepotismed into this position in the first place. I'll have plenty of people to hide behind.

The welcome banquet is held in one of the larger galleries on the ground floor. They call it a *banquet* even though the only food options are catered sandwiches and a few hors d'oeuvre trays of sad-looking stuffed mushroom bites. As soon as we arrive, I scan the room, looking for Ely—I can't help myself—but she's absent. I can't decide if I have mental fingers crossed that she stays that way or if I'm secretly hoping she does show up, if only so I can see her again.

No, definitely the first one. I'm a responsible, ethical human.

"How were the first two days, Wyatt?" asks Carmen Moreno, one of the Parker old guard; she's been faculty here since the program was founded. "Still in one piece?"

"Rumors of my death have been greatly exaggerated," I say. "The students took pity on me."

"It gets easier," Carmen says, and gives me a sympathetic pat on the arm. "First week is always a little awkward. Especially when you're young. I remember being your age—so worried the students wouldn't take me seriously."

I'm not sure precisely how old she thinks I am, but I decide to take it as flattery. After thirty you're supposed to start worrying about fine lines and gray hairs, right? Then again, I found my first gray at eighteen.

But if she's trying to imply that I should be concerned about my ability to assert authority over the students . . . well, I've already failed on that front pretty miserably. Cue the world's most pitiful cheer.

"We should mingle," Ava says, her gaze scanning the slowly swelling crowd of students. Most of them are bunched up in the corner by the refreshments table, like a herd of deer wary of encroaching predators. "I don't want Scott accusing us of cliquishness again."

I try to shoot Ava my best *Et tu, Brute?* look, but she is—possibly very intentionally—not looking at me.

And that's how I find myself clutching a tepid lemon water and a little cup of cheese cubes, cornered by Elisheva Cohen.

"Good day so far?" she says while I'm still struggling to figure out how a normal person is supposed to interact with other human beings, specifically ones they've never seen naked.

"Oh, you know," I say, which doesn't quite live up to the eloquent vision of myself I had in my head.

But Ely doesn't seem to mind. She has a plate of those stuffed mushrooms and keeps fiddling with them—she's as nervous as I am. Only where I choose avoidance, she's clearly decided overt confrontation is the best solution.

"Hope you've been settling in okay," I say, attempting an olive branch. Normally I can't stand small talk, but right now I'm incredibly grateful for whoever invented meaningless, space-filling platitudes. "Getting along with your roommates, and so on."

"Oh yeah. They're great. If they're hiding dead bodies anywhere in the apartment, I haven't found them yet."

"I'm sure there are still plenty of nooks and crannies you haven't investigated."

"Surely the smell would give it away," she says, and the corner of her mouth quirks up. She's wearing red lipstick. The contrast of that shade and her near-black hair with the creamy white dress she's wearing makes her look like a figure in a painting. Not that I'm supposed to be paying attention to students' lipstick choices.

"A dedicated serial killer would find a way to disguise the stench. Maybe some discreet potpourri."

She makes a face. "Oh god. That reminds me of the time my roommate in LA adopted this tiny little kitten. Then she kept going on, quote, *mission trips* and leaving the cat with me. That thing puked in my room and I didn't find the source for like two weeks. I just kept spraying apple cinnamon Febreze and hoping for the best. Trust me, the only thing worse than the smell of rotting biomatter is that plus synthetic fragrance."

"Dead bodies might be an improvement, then."

The comment earns me an arched brow and another one of those crooked smiles. God, those smiles are gonna be what gets me. The first time she looked at me like that, at Revel, it sent a jolt of adrenaline rocketing through my gut, and not much has changed on that front. Ely Cohen still has an impressive talent for turning my veins electric.

I need to get out of here. But of course Ely won't let it be that easy.

"You know, it's kind of weird seeing you in this environment," she says. "You're wearing actual clothes, for one."

My face goes bright red. I can feel it, blood flaring hot beneath my skin. "That does go with the professional territory." *Be professional, be professional, be professional.*

"Don't get me wrong. The clothes look great on you."

I feel like she's pushing me, trying to press every button she can reach just to see what happens. It's the kind of thing I should be immune to, as a thirtysomething grown-up. But being around her clearly turns me into a flushing teenager. It's my first crush all over again, the shiver that uncurls down my spine when she lifts her drink to cheers me. The way I keep looking at her lips, lacquered in burgundy lipstick, and wishing she would leave bloody trails of that lipstick down my throat, my chest.

When I do manage to drag my attention away from her mouth, I discover that she's every bit as distracted as I am. Her gaze has caught on something lower down—my chest, maybe, or my hips. I'm abruptly hyperaware of the fact that this girl—woman—has seen every part of me. She doesn't need to imagine what's under my clothes, because she knows.

She glances up again and I barely, *barely,* manage to look over toward the refreshments table before she realizes I've been staring.

If I harbored any hopes that Ely might change the subject . . . well, she doesn't. "The whole outfit is very redneck chic. The flannel is a nice touch."

"Flannel is cozy."

"Wyatt, it's almost June."

I roll my eyes as dramatically as possible. "You Northerners have no sense of weather. It's May and it's seventy degrees out; I'll wear flannel if I want to."

She looks me up and down once more. Am I imagining the way her gaze lingers on my thighs? *Stop it, Wyatt. Stop it.* Either way, she's smirking by the time she looks at my face again.

"I'd like to see you in a suit, even so," she says. "Maybe next time they make us come to these. Or better yet, do the whole professor thing—elbow patches and a worn gray sweater."

"Why do I feel like you're trying to role-play right now?"

Aaaand now I'm just leaning into the whole thing because I can't shut my mouth to save my life. The question earns me a grin, Ely sticking her tongue out at me like a five-year-old. "So what if I am? What are you gonna do, Wyatt—give me an F?"

"Oh, I'd figure something out."

Which, of course, is just amping up the flirtatiousness. I need to take this down several notches if I don't want to ruin my reputation by dragging Ely off into a janitor's closet somewhere.

"Well." I truly could not sound less awkward if I tried. "If you need help with bodies, you know where to find me." *What the fuck? Stop talking, Cole.*

I press my lips shut to keep from making things worse and settle for a wave instead of a verbal goodbye. Verbal is not working well with my constitution at the moment.

I find Ava as quickly as I can and then stick close to her side for the rest of the welcome reception. It's the safest place for me, because Ava is talkative, and when she's part of a conversation, I essentially don't have to speak at all.

The first thing I do when I get back to my apartment is shut myself in the shower and press my brow against the cold tile wall. I should have done something the second I found out Ely was my student. I should have alerted the administration. That's the right thing to do, isn't it? If I opened up the faculty handbook, it would probably say something about disclosing such things.

I could tell Ava. She was my mentor before she became my friend. I probably need some outside person to check my bullshit before this spirals out of control any further. But as much as I love Ava, she might have her hands tied by university rules. She might have to report this, and I can imagine all too well how that might go. I'm a trans guy; there's a long tradition of assuming perversion of queer and trans people, and the last thing I need is this black mark on my record from day one. Besides, it's not going to happen again, and Ely is no longer in my class. That means the conflict of interest is officially dealt with. Right?

I stick my head under the spray so that the water falls directly onto my face.

The problem is the power imbalance *isn't* dealt with. Ely pointed that out well enough herself.

I keep managing to be an asshole despite my best attempts otherwise. I can basically hear my dad's voice in my head, murmuring, *You'll always be a failure.* It's the same voice I heard in my head the first day of class, I realize now. He lives eternal in my brain, no matter what I do.

My career and my reputation mean everything to me.

My dad cared more about being a good marine than being a good father. Looks like I, too, am more committed to appearances than to being a good person.

I have to make this right with Ely. I'm not sure what that looks like, but I need to figure it out. Problem is, I'm second-guessing just about everything right now, up to and including my offer to help her one-on-one. Clearly I can't restrain myself, even for the purpose of seeming professional at a goddamn school event.

This whole summer stretches out before me, long and full of minefields.

"Mraaaow."

I twist to meet the gaze of my three-legged black cat, Haze, who has parked himself right in front of the misty shower door to stare at me. His little pink tongue flicks out to wet his nose.

"It's past your dinnertime, isn't it?" I ask as Haze continues to give me that reproachful look. "Sorry, buddy. I'll be out in a second."

It took me years to establish myself as an artist—there were lots of part-time jobs at record stores and fast-food joints while I tried to build some kind of portfolio. My first big break came when I was twenty-four and won a local competition that was judged by a big-name dealer. After that, it was another two years until I could afford my own studio apartment and years after that before I could upgrade to a one bedroom. But even the studio was a game changer. My mind feels larger without the encroaching presence of other humans in the same tiny space. With just me and Haze here, I feel as if I stretch wide, filling every corner. I could close my eyes and expand further still, into the streets and alleys, across the bridge over the river, my imagination swimming between the skyscrapers of Manhattan.

My art is better when I'm alone.

I spoon wet food into Haze's bowl, his damp nose nudging at my hand again and again until I finally get out of the way and let him dive in. I scratch my fingers behind his ears, then leave him to it.

My apartment is small even for a one bedroom; I've appropriated half the living room into a mock studio. I don't bring any of my final products back here—I do most of my work at Parker or at a local spot I rent in an artists' workshop—but it's great for rough drafts. I can experiment with paints and glues and textiles without worrying about damaging a final print. Right now, my desk is covered in the detritus from a project I just finished, a meditation on self-image and the masks we wear to construct the image we want other people to see. I've sculpted photos of real people into masks—laughing, angry, afraid, hopeful, sad. The collection has already found a temporary home at a gallery in SoHo. Sometimes I still can't get over the fact that this is my real life—that actual people, actual *buyers,* are going to look at something I created and potentially be moved by it.

Art is a form of telepathy, really. You have an idea, or a feeling, and you try to get someone else—someone totally different from you, with different wants and fears and interests—to share your emotions, even if just for a moment. It doesn't always work. But when it does, it's the best experience in the entire world.

I clear off the old shit and settle in at my desk, now a blank expanse of oak with my pens lined up patiently along the top edge.

Back to the beginning: the worst and best part.

7

ELY

Dr. Zhu's class, as it turns out, is just as good as advertised. Ava Zhu is a powerhouse, having come into photography from a totally different field—graphic design—before she discovered she liked editing her own pictures more than she liked creating logos for someone else. It's not mixed media, but it *is* fascinating. Most of my work has been digital, so a part of me was worried I wouldn't really learn anything new from a class like this. Turns out, hubris is a bitch. I have a lot more to learn than I thought. The point is to be open-minded.

That's why I'm here, right?

(I try to ignore the voice in my head that snarkily replies, *Yeah. Learn from Wyatt Cole.*)

Wyatt Cole, who, it seems, has been content to ignore me ever since the welcome reception. To be fair, he isn't ignoring just me. I've seen students wave at him in the hall and watched him curl into himself, his shoulders ratcheting up to his ears. I'd heard he was a bit of a hermit, but that was extra. Maybe it's not that he hates me in particular so much as that he hates people, period.

Only that's inconsistent with how charming and extroverted

he'd seemed at Revel. He was effervescent, magnetic, as if he could be the center of any world he chose to be in.

The next time I spotted him was between classes, the two of us passing in the corridor, his gaze catching mine—at that moment, it felt like my heart had stopped in my chest from the sudden heat in his gaze. And then there was the color rising in his cheeks, the way he looked away so fast it felt like a slap. It's not that he doesn't see me.

It's that he doesn't want to.

Which doesn't make any fucking sense. He was all smiles and snarky comments on Tuesday—so, what changed? It's like he decides our boundaries based on some mystical kabbalah that is opaque to me.

Or maybe he's just changed his mind.

My problem, obviously, is that I hate to lose. Because surely there's nothing so special about Wyatt Cole that it justifies the way I'm obsessing over this man. He's just . . . some dude, right?

Some dude who is the best photographer alive, who fucked me like a god and congratulated me on being sober for four years and gave me his phone number.

It doesn't help that when I text my friend/sponsor Shannon from LA about the whole fucking-a-teacher situation, the only advice she can muster is a series of increasingly raunchy butt GIFs. As much as I hate to admit it, times like these, I miss Chaya. There was a lot about our friendship that was messed up, but also I know exactly what she'd say if she could see me right now.

Let it go. Move on. Get a life. Et cetera.

She'd ask me which is more important: my sex life or my art.

And to be honest, she'd be right. I only get one shot at making Parker work for me, and I'm not gonna miss it.

My instructors seem equally keen on making the most of every second we spend here. I'm inundated with projects and deadlines by the end of the first week, and by the time I'm packing up my materials after Zhu's class finishes on Friday, my brain feels like I've pounded it into jelly. I'm rubbing at my temples when someone's purple-skirted hip hitches itself onto the edge of my desk; I look up to find Michal smiling down at me, lips painted black matte.

"Hey," she says. "Are you doing anything this weekend?"

"No plans. Just dissolving into stress goo. You?"

She lifts her brows. "It's Shabbat, Ely. I'm doing Shabbat shit. Want to come?"

For a moment I'm frozen. It's the same way I felt that time in LA when I stepped out of the grocery store and there was a guy in a black hat, black suit. *Are you Jewish?* he asked, and I didn't know how to answer.

In the end I just mumbled something that I hoped sounded indistinct and hurried off, head ducked down. If I'd stayed, he would have offered me Shabbos candles. It's a mitzvah—a good deed—for a woman to light them on Friday nights to welcome the Sabbath.

I kept thinking about it for the rest of the week, wondering if he knew people in New York. Wondering if his best friend's cousin had been *my* friend. If his niece was my classmate at Bnos Menachem.

Chabad is big, but it's not that big. He might have heard of me.

I wonder now if *Michal* has heard of me—if tales of my general fuckery have filtered out of Chabad and into . . . whatever type of Orthodox Jewish she's supposed to be.

The type of Orthodox that wears headscarves and black lipstick.

Stop it. I'm not going to waste time making up some fantastical backstory for Michal Pereira. Her life is her life, and as long as she's happy . . . well, good for her. But there's a reason I left.

"Um . . . I'm good. Thanks, though." I feel guilty for saying no, so I guess some things never change.

Her face falls slightly. "Oh. Okay. Just figured I'd ask."

Well, now I feel like a terrible person. "Want to do something after Shabbos instead?" I offer, hoping it doesn't sound too much like a consolation prize. "It's just, I'm not really . . . I'm not shomer Shabbos anymore."

"You don't have to observe the laws of Shabbat to come to a dinner with me," Michal points out. "We'd be happy to have you tonight, even if you spend the whole evening turning light switches on and off."

I can't help but smile a little. Lots of things are not allowed on the Sabbath—anything that might pass as *work,* which includes stuff like turning the lights on or off. Because something something do-not-kindle-a-flame something. It made sense to me once upon a time.

"I know," I say. "But . . . it's a long story, okay? It's just not my scene right now. But that doesn't mean I don't want to hang out."

Shabbos used to be my favorite holiday. Lucky for me, since it happened every week. But for the past— God, has it really been eight years? For the past eight years, it's just been another Saturday.

"I get it," Michal says. "No worries. We have a space for you if you ever change your mind."

She smiles at me as she gets up and heads for the door, but a part of me can't help feeling sad now, like I've disappointed her or something.

Maybe I should have said yes. She isn't Chaya, no matter how much she reminds me of my former best friend. Chaya would have kept prodding until I surrendered. Chaya would have shown up on my doorstep right before sunset with a bottle of vodka and a bag of molly hidden in her school satchel.

I thought I was doing better. I wasn't seeing Chaya around every corner anymore. But maybe that was an artifact of living in

LA, where the sunlight could blot out every shadow. In perpetual summer, Chaya's ghost had nowhere to hide.

The halls are half-empty by the time I finally make it out of the classroom, almost everyone in their next class or out to grab a bite with friends. A few still linger, crouched against the walls poring over their portfolios or gathered in small knots laughing and trading phone numbers.

It takes me a moment to spot him, but I do.

Wyatt leans against a doorframe halfway down the corridor, deep in conversation with another student. I hesitate, but he's between me and the exit. My choices are either to walk past him or to turn around and hide in Zhu's classroom for however long it takes before Wyatt fucks off.

I choose option A because I refuse to stoop to option B's level.

He catches my eye as I go past, and my heart stammers, my skin prickly and hyperaware of the way my shirt fabric rubs against it, like every part of me has just been powered on.

There's this thing your brain does when you're super anxious where it *shuts off* for a little while to protect you. I read about it online. You stop encoding memories for a few minutes, and everything's a sear of white noise, and then—once the moment's passed—it all goes back to normal. The feeling reminds me a little of getting high: that moment right after you take the hit or push down the plunger of a needle. The way your mind fogs up like a cold window. My ears used to pop, even.

Well, that's what it's like for those five seconds as I walk by Wyatt. Once I'm at the other end of the hall, I don't even remember how I got there. My brain simply did not record it.

I glance back at him, which would have been a mistake if he'd done the same thing—although something like that would be perfect in a romantic comedy. He's still talking to the other student. All I can see is the back of his head and the way his starched white shirt strains between his shoulder blades.

I barely know the man. One fabulous night doesn't really count. Nor does obsessing over his body of artistic work for like five years.

Stop. Being. Pathetic. Telling myself that doesn't really make a difference. But at least I'm not indulging this nonsense.

I leave Wyatt and his sexy shoulders in the hall and head to the darkroom.

The darkroom is what I used to imagine the Christian hell looked like, informed by all the horror movies I binged on after leaving New York. Even the slightest amount of natural light will ruin film development, so the darkroom is illuminated in red. The few other students working in here are dark silhouettes moving from the wet side of the room to the dry, lovingly pinning their work on the clothesline that spans the length of the room.

It's quiet, though, which I like. There's no rule against speaking in the darkroom, but despite the hell similarities, something about it feels holy—meditative. People who do need to talk do it in murmurs, heads bent close together, like they're whispering a prayer.

I spent Tuesday developing the negatives I'd shot on Monday for my Printing Techniques class. It's been a while since I've worked with analog film. But I like the ritual of it: Clipping the negatives. The circulation of fluids through the tank—developer, stop bath, fixer. Rinse. Dry—the strips of negatives hanging like ribbons in open air. I left them here and retrieved them this morning to examine on the light table, hunched over a loupe and drowning in shifting color.

That leaves me with five photos that I actually want to print. Sometimes what looks good in negative doesn't hold up in full size, but I can always go back to the negatives if I change my mind.

Working with film is one of my all-time favorite things. It's so . . . *physical,* so profane. I like the way the negatives feel between my fingers, delicate as glass. The smell of chemicals. Maybe it's the ex-Orthodox in me, still addicted to the art of ritual.

I slide the first negative into the carrier and adjust the height of the enlarger, refocusing the image bit by bit until it takes clear and bright shape on the baseboard. The assignment is to work with still life; I took photos of some of Diego's cooking process as he made a truly glorious quiche for us Monday night. The assignment doubled as a symbiotic favor because Diego was in the market for a new food photographer for his hobby recipe blog, and I was in need of both food and subject matter.

Most of the shots I wanted were way more abstract than the kinds of things Diego would want on his blog. I ended up taking process and finished product photos on my DSLR so I could edit them in Lightroom more easily. The film photos were first, when the raw ingredients were still loose on the butcher-block counter, me hunched over Diego's work space snapping pictures as he ran a constant commentary behind me: *Why are you taking a picture of that? Why would anyone be interested in that? It's called tarragon and it tastes like God's backyard grass clippings.*

The first image is zoomed in close: scattered herbs and spices, the swollen yellow belly of a lemon. The blade of Diego's chef's knife is visible at the very edge of the frame, a patient threat. I turn down the brightness until it's slightly too dim and run my test strips. This is the step I'm always tempted to skip—after so many years, I have a pretty good sense of what exposure time will work best for a given picture. But I've been wrong before, and I like to have good habits. So I do it anyway.

Once the test strips for all five negatives are dry, I evaluate them in actual light again, five strips per photo, all in varying degrees of brightness. When I find the exposure I want, I mark it with a Sharpie.

Technically I should have taken these photos in a light box, where I could have controlled every variable down to the color of the background, and I'm pretty sure that's what the professor expected us to do when he gave us this assignment. I might end up having to do just that if he makes me start over. But for now, I prefer this kind of photography. It feels raw. Real. It's a moment of actual time, frozen and preserved. This is why I'm so drawn to narrative photography—I like to be able to tell a story with my images. A *true* story, through a snapshot of someone's life, not a sterile constructed scene.

I'm so absorbed in studying my test strips that I've blocked out the rest of the room, the other students out of focus and blurry, which is why I don't notice someone standing just over my shoulder until they speak.

"I like this one," Wyatt says, and I drop my Sharpie.

"What?" I say as I fumble around on the floor to find my pen. Which puts me on my knees, of course. *Shit.*

Once I'm back on my feet, he steps forward to stand next to me properly and taps below one of my negatives. "Hard to say for sure without a loupe, of course, but from what I can tell, it has great composition. Good balance of tonalities—unique. Is this for Héctor's class?"

My brain is still catching up to the reality that Wyatt Cole is right next to me, his shoulder very nearly brushing mine, and he's *commenting on my art.* My mouth keeps trying to say something in response, but the single neuron in my mind keeps firing at the same fucking frequency over and over: *Holy shit it's him it's him it's him.* Not exactly the paragon of maturity here.

Of course, on the other hand, he still hasn't written me about looking at my portfolio. Maybe I should be less concerned about the famous Wyatt Cole and more concerned about the dude Wyatt Cole, who can't figure out how to send a freaking GCal invite.

My brain, however, can't tolerate that level of bitterness at this precise moment.

"Yes," I manage, maybe a second too late, maybe three—hard to say. Definitely late, though. "Printing Techniques. We're supposed to do a still life."

"Not exactly a classic still life, though, is it?" murmurs Wyatt, who has tilted forward and stolen my loupe already, peering at my negatives like my uncle Chaim the jeweler used to look at diamonds—no doubt searching for a flaw. And I'm sure there are plenty.

"It's just a start," I tell him. "I might reshoot in a light box. Haven't decided yet."

And now that my neural circuits have figured out how to function again, they skip directly from *close proximity to hot man I fucked once* and make a beeline to the safer ground of *asshole who never emailed me like he said he would.*

Wyatt is still looking at the negatives, a small smile lingering around his mouth. Probably laughing at me for thinking I can get away with submitting this bullshit to Pérez-Wahid when I know damn well it isn't the actual assignment.

"You never emailed me," I say.

It comes out forcefully. Maybe too forcefully . . . but you know what? I've waited all week for this guy to make good on his promise. But nope, he clearly planned to ghost me and get away with it. No doubt relying on my insecurity to stop me from ever chasing him down. Which just goes to show how little he knows me, even if he *is* an expert in my seltzer taste. (*And,* a little voice tries to remind me, *other tastes.* But I'm not thinking about that right now.)

Wyatt finally lifts his head. I don't wait for him to look me in the eye before I keep going—no point in giving him a chance to derail the conversation before I've said my piece. "I dropped your class, like you wanted. All nice and ethical. So, what happened to all those promises about looking at my portfolio and teaching me one-on-one? And *don't* say that's what you're doing right now, because it isn't. You can't waltz in here and drop a couple stale comments about my negatives and think that passes for a fair trade."

I have to stop myself from going on. Once I start ranting, it can be hard to hold myself back. (*You're too intense,* Chaya whispers again in the back of my mind.) The last thing I need is to look even more unhinged than I actually am.

In lieu of saying anything else, I cross my arms over my chest and lift a brow in Wyatt's direction. He makes the same expression back at me—although it fails to have the desired impact since it's physically impossible for him to look angry with those big sad cow eyes.

"I'm sorry if it seems I've been ignoring you," Wyatt says after a long moment, long enough that my pulse has started to slow down a little. "To be entirely honest, I've been putting it off. I'm sorry."

He's being too nice, and he can't quite look me straight in the eye. And I don't think I'm imagining the faint flush of color lighting up his cheeks. It's harder than it should be to keep from yielding. "And?" I manage.

"I've been looking at your materials, and I was meaning to email you. . . . Listen. How about Tuesday at five? I can reserve a room for us. And if there's other work you'd like feedback on, send it to me. Let me make it up to you."

Cool. So, I've officially humiliated myself *twice* in front of Wyatt Cole, which has got to be some kind of photography-student record. He freaking owes me . . . but now I feel like I've kicked a puppy. I can't hold his gaze. The big sad cow eyes have become too much.

I pretend to pick a loose thread out of the bottom button on my shirt. "Right. Wow. Okay." *Be the bigger person, Ely Cohen.* "I'm sorry. I shouldn't have jumped down your throat like that."

"It's all right," Wyatt says, showing me the exact kind of quick and easy mercy that I would never have given him. "You're right. I've been avoiding you. It's just . . . I mean, you know. I don't have to tell you what it's like . . . between us. It's hard to keep things . . ."

He trails off and I steal a glance up. Wyatt has one hand braced against the light table, his slim hip jutting out slightly to graze his tattooed thumb. His face, when I dare to look that far north, is tipped away from mine as Wyatt stares fiercely at some point on the far table.

He likes me, he likes me not. And he likes *me!*

Okay. He wants to play professionals? I'll be professional.

This is the problem with being around genuinely good people. They never fail to make me feel about as charming as a nugget of dog poo on Mark Zuckerberg's flip-flops. I feel like a perv for fantasizing about that tattooed thumb digging into my thigh when Wyatt is over here trying to be an adult and shit.

"It's fine," I say at last, stuffing both hands into my jean pockets. "So I guess . . . Tuesday, then."

"Tuesday," Wyatt agrees. He finally looks back at me and smiles, the same smile I remember from the club, with white and slightly crooked teeth. A dumb, golden retriever–type smile.

Well, I think as he finally walks away, my heart still pounding between my ears and my hands clenched into unseen fists. *Well.*

I'm fucked.

8

WYATT

I don't see Ely often during school hours.

It's an intentional choice, obviously. I even double-checked her schedule in the admin office to make sure I knew when to be mysteriously unavailable at my office—which might be overkill at this point, but I don't trust myself. The thing about being an ex-addict is that you aren't under any delusions about being a good person; you know exactly how far you'd go if given the chance. I constantly have to stay one step ahead of my own atrophied conscience. Outsmart myself before I can outsmart myself.

Despite intentionally ignoring her, I come close to texting her one night over the weekend. I have Ely's number programmed into my phone from when she texted me after our night together, before I figured out she was a student. Before I looked at her portfolio again and discovered it was just as brilliant as I'd thought at first glance. She has real talent.

That could be why I haven't been able to bring myself to delete the text I've typed out three separate times: **Still on for Tuesday?** An innocuous question, maybe, but I wouldn't text any other student asking it. Which tells me everything I need to know about my own motivations.

"Fuck it," I mutter at last, erasing the message and tossing my phone onto my desk. It startles Haze, who darts off onto the floor and vanishes into the other room. "Sorry."

I'm not big on Narcotics Anonymous anymore. Not big on twelve-step programs in general. But they do have their place. And right now, I need the sense of stability and grounding that NA is really, really great at providing. I get plenty of support from my SMART Recovery group online. Or I did, anyway; since I started at Parker, the virtual meetings don't fit my schedule anymore. Guess I'm gonna be making more appearances in person.

I toss a couple books in my satchel in case I want to spend time reading at a coffee shop after and head out. The Sunday night meeting is at a church a couple of blocks away. Every time I show up one of the members strongly implies this means I have no excuse not to be there every night—which is honestly part of why I keep my distance.

Most of the group has already gathered by the time I arrive. It's the usual crowd; I spot Marcus, Karabeth, Ji, and Doug clustered together by the sign-in sheet where people on court-ordered meetings get their forms stamped. I occupy myself with the food table. Even when I was the one here on a judge's orders, I had to admit that these grocery store powdered doughnuts hit the spot.

There's no official leader at NA meetings. Everyone's supposed to be on an equal footing here—which means the meeting starts once everyone has found a seat somewhere and one of the attendees volunteers to read the opening text. I have it memorized at this point.

"Hello, everyone." Marcus is the chosen tribute this time. Which is great because Marcus is both my sponsor and my favorite out of everyone who comes to these things. "My name is

Marcus, and I'm an addict. Welcome to Narcotics Anonymous. Let's open this meeting with a moment of silence for the addict who still suffers. . . ."

I might have over ten years under my belt, but being back at these meetings still serves a purpose. Just being here as a sign to people earlier in their recovery that you *can* do this, you *can* get and stay clean long term. But it's good for me too. Sometimes it's easy to forget how bad things used to be if you don't remind yourself.

"Hi, I'm Wyatt, and I'm an addict," I say about half an hour in, when there's been a long enough break without anyone else speaking up.

Everyone murmurs the requisite "Hi, Wyatt," and I plaster on a cursory smile.

"I've been clean for ten years and four months"—this earns a scattering of applause—"and I'm glad to be back with y'all tonight."

I put a lot of effort into *not* looking at Doug, who is probably giving me a judgy look. I honestly have no idea why Doug hates me so much. Instead of looking at him, I focus on Marcus, who offers an encouraging nod and a wink.

"I grew up down in North Carolina, in a military family," I continue. "My dad, both granddads, all my uncles, my brother . . . pretty much every man I knew went into the Marines straight outa high school. It's not that you *couldn't* go to college or get a different job or something, just that nobody did, and so nobody really knew how to do anything else. I had one cousin who got into State, and we all had no clue if we were supposed to congratulate him or not. It was like, *Good for you, I guess, and good luck paying down those loans.* There was always this unspoken implication that my cousin was a coward too afraid to enlist."

I have no idea what happened to Rory, actually. We haven't

kept in touch. Maybe I could have reached out at some point along the line—the two black sheep of the Cole family connecting—but having gone to college doesn't necessarily mean Rory is cool. For all I know, he feels the same way about me as everyone else in our family. Maybe he just learned enough in college to hide transphobia by pretending it was about feminism.

"Anyway, point is, as soon as I got out of high school, I joined the Marines. It was maybe the first time in my life I felt like my parents were proud of me, you know? But that was around the time I started realizing some things about myself. I dunno, maybe a part of me knew all along, but it wasn't until I was out of the house and at basic training that I started piecing the truth together. When I told the base doctor I was trans and asked to get put on testosterone, I knew what would happen. This was back before Don't Ask, Don't Tell got repealed. I knew what was gonna happen, but I did it anyway. And I got kicked out."

I scan the room, just as I always do after telling this part of the story. It's easy to tell who is shocked by the confession, who is okay with it, and whose smile is just a forced attempt to be polite.

"That was pretty much it for my relationship with family. My dad . . . he was always tough on us. Well, I say tough, which is what he woulda called it, but I mean he got violent. After a bad fight, he told me I was no child of his. He kicked me out and wouldn't even let me pack. I spent a couple weeks bumming around Morehead City, sleeping under the bridge at Atlantic Beach, trying to make a little cash selling seashells to tourists. But I ended up spiraling. Got hooked on dope, and then . . . y'all know how it goes. I was miserable, but at least I was numb."

So much of those years exists only as a haze in my memories. All I've got is a collection of disjointed events strung together like beads on wire: the first time I saw someone OD, the sickening jolt back to consciousness after the paramedics shoot you up with naloxone, vomit in my mouth and in my hair, the time I spotted my family on the beach laughing and drinking beers and so fucking happy to have me out of their lives.

"I OD'd more times than I can count. It was only after the third arrest that I got my shit together and actually did the work. I was able to get a spot at a free rehab up here in New York. Even then it took four admissions before I actually stayed clean for good. That's the main thing I wish someone would've told me when I was early in recovery: Sometimes you slip up. In fact, you probably will. But you don't have to give up. You can choose to keep fighting and start over every single day."

My gaze flits over to some of the newer faces, ones I don't recognize. They're watching me, fixated on me. I can only hope some of this is actually sinking in. Recovery isn't magic. You can't show up to a few meetings and get better. You have to want it. That took me way too long to internalize.

But maybe they'll be smarter than I was.

"I've been doing good for a while," I say after a moment, rubbing my doughnut crumbs between my fingers, watching the powdered sugar dust the napkin like a thin coating of snow. "Ten years, like I said. But I recently . . . I met this girl. She's in recovery too. I like her a lot. We hooked up, and I kind of hoped it might turn into something, you know, if I was lucky. Well . . . turns out we have more in common than just being ex-junkies. She's a student in one of the classes I'm teaching this semester. So basically I'm fucked. We had this crazy connection, but is it worth risking my career? My sobriety?" I shrug. "That's all I wanted to say, I suppose. I'll yield to the next person."

There's a moment of silence after I'm done speaking. I suck the powdered sugar off the end of my thumb and stare down at the table, already regretting bringing up the Ely thing. It's not relevant to my recovery, not really. Or maybe it is. Maybe that's what my subconscious is trying to tell me—to tread carefully.

"Don't do it, man," says one of the newer guys. I lift my head;

it's one of the court-ordered attendees. "You got ten years. Don't throw that away. Stay away from her, or you'll both end up right back where you started."

"No cross talk," says Ji, but of course, it's too late. The words have already settled into my brain and put down roots there.

New guy might not know much about recovery yet, but that doesn't make him wrong.

I *do* need to stay away from Ely Cohen.

For both our sakes.

9

ELY

I'm not a patient person. I have friends who are—Shannon is like some kind of superhuman when it comes to waiting. She had a kid last spring and went two weeks past her due date and basically didn't bat an eye. Meanwhile, I struggle to put up with a slightly long Starbucks line. Waiting for my meeting with Wyatt is the worst kind of waiting, because I'm way more invested in this than I am in my iced Americano.

By Monday night, I'm exhausted and annoyed with myself for procrastinating on my very serious deadlines by spending gross amounts of time scrolling through Reddit. I could ask Ophelia if she wants to hang out, but it's crunch time for her on some project, and Diego has flown out to Minnesota to visit family and doesn't get back until next Monday.

I want to text Wyatt and ask if *he* wants to hang out. But that's just asking for Wyatt to shoot me down, and I'm not sure my fragile ego could handle that.

As soon as my last class lets out on Tuesday, I head to the bathroom and spend two minutes trying to wrangle my hair into something resembling order. A useless effort because it hasn't seen a brush in days.

Well, hey. At least this is nothing new. Wyatt saw me in my unfiltered morning state already, all drooly and covered in the previous night's mascara. If anything, this is an improvement.

Plus, I'm not *actively* trying to get in his pants anymore. Obviously. Going after a guy who's made it very clear he doesn't want me going after him would be deeply uncool. This is just about the *art*.

I wrote the room number in my phone's Notes app after Wyatt texted it to me last week, but apparently I have no problem remembering that detail on my own: 36C.

He's already there when I arrive, leaning against a table and examining a set of photos scattered out across its surface. It takes a beat for me to recognize them as prints from my application portfolio.

Wyatt glances up when I close the door behind me. "Hey," he says. "Leave that open, if you don't mind."

Right. I mumble an apology and open the door again, trying to fight the flush rising in my cheeks. *Great—now he thinks I'm trying to come on to him again.*

I clasp my sweaty hands behind my back and approach the table. He gestures for me to come around to stand at his side, and I comply, gazing down at the photos in front of me.

"What do you think of them?" Wyatt says.

I don't know how to respond. I've spent hours—weeks, probably—staring at these images, between choosing them, cropping them, editing them, studying them for flaws long after I'd hit Send on my application to Parker. Looking at them now, trying to see them through Wyatt Cole's eyes, is about as bad as you'd expect. All I can see are the mistakes.

"They're . . . fine," I say, hedging slightly. Nobody likes an overly enthusiastic self-critic. "My work is better now. But it was good enough to get me in here, so . . . they're fine, I suppose. A solid foundation."

"A solid foundation," Wyatt echoes.

I nod. "Everyone starts somewhere."

"Is that what you really believe? That these are only worth the price of admission to Parker? Nothing more?"

I steal a sidelong glance at him, but he isn't watching me; he's still looking at the photographs. I shrug one shoulder and wish I knew what he wanted me to say.

"They're fine," I tell him a second time. "But this one has tonality issues, see? And this one . . . the focus isn't right. I should have cropped it a little smaller, cut out some of this negative space. They have flaws."

"All art is flawed," Wyatt says, sounding surprisingly sage for a guy with neck tats and a penchant for arguing about sparkling water. "You can't chase perfection. You just have to figure out what you wanna say, and then say it."

I keep looking down at my work, the portfolio I labored over for months back in California. Once upon a time, I thought these pictures said everything there was to say about me. Taking them had felt like opening a vein and bleeding out in public. Like everyone could look at these photos and know who I was down to the core, see every muddy, rotten-apple dark spot of my junkie self.

"What do these photos say, Ely?" Wyatt says softly.

I don't know how to answer him.

Eventually he leans over and shifts the photos around slightly, showing some of the images that had been partly concealed under the corners and edges of their fellows. "Do you want me to tell you what I see?"

I nod again, my jaw clenched so hard my cheeks hurt.

"I see someone who was hurting. Someone who did things they weren't proud of but who wanted to be better. Someone who fought as hard as they could to claw their way back to sanity. And maybe it's not perfect yet, maybe they're still ashamed of what they used to be, but it's still something."

I force a shaky, shattered laugh out of my chest. "You're like a bootleg therapist."

He laughs too, although Wyatt's laugh sounds richer, more like it belongs to an actual human. "Nah, I'm just an ex-junkie who likes looking at sad pictures. But I'm really good at looking at sad pictures, so when I tell you these are great, you ought to believe me."

I can't bring myself to look at him. I can imagine the expression on his face—gentle, considerate—and something in me feels like if I were to see that right now, I'd crumble. All the flimsy threads holding me together would snap. I don't know who I'd be then, without those restraints, and I don't want to find out.

"I'll do my best," I say instead, and push a photo from one spot to another on the table as if I'm looking at it more closely. Really it's just to have something to do with my hands.

Wyatt shifts away, moving somewhere behind me. I hear the rustle of fabric, and when I do finally dare to glance back, he's slinging his satchel over one shoulder. "You know what?" he says. "Five P.M. is hitting me kind of hard right now. Do you mind if we go grab a coffee? We can talk more on the way."

Never been so grateful to be invited on a coffee date in my life. "Yes. Please. That sounds perfect right now."

We pack up my portfolio, and Wyatt slips it into his bag. I can't help but fantasize, briefly, about him looking at my photographs again later, alone in his apartment with these pieces of my heart scattered across his desk. But I shove that thought aside and grab my water bottle instead, following Wyatt out.

Manhattan has a Starbucks on every corner, but Wyatt takes us to a smaller indie spot wedged between a record shop and an NYU building. We talk about technique on the way, Wyatt pointing out things he likes about my work mostly and offering a few ideas of things to try for my next project. It would be rude to get out my phone and write it all down in my Notes app, so I do my best to just remember. Which is a tall order for me, but hey, I'd like to think I won't ever forget a single word of photography wisdom that drops from Wyatt Cole's mouth.

Coffees in hand, we end up sitting on a bench in the park instead of heading back to the cramped quarters of Parker's visual arts building. Wyatt stretches his legs out beside mine, and even though he's barely my height, his seem longer. Or maybe that's just the weight of the work boots he's wearing, which look like he's worn them every day for forty years despite being thirty-five, max.

"How old are you?" I ask before I can stop myself.

But Wyatt doesn't scold me for crossing a line, at least not this time. "Thirty-two," he says with a little laugh. "Why?"

"No reason. Sorry. You just seem . . . well, you're younger than I thought you would be, I suppose."

"Yeah, I get that a lot. People seem to assume I'm some crusty relic of Greenwich Village in the seventies. No idea what it is about my work that gives them that impression; it's a little insulting to be honest." He shakes his head and takes a sip of his coffee, watching a pair of kids rocket past us on their skateboards. "Of course, there was great stuff coming out from queer artists at the time, but somehow I don't think that's what they mean."

It takes me a moment to process what he's said, and when I do, I frown. "Are you really worried that people think your work is boring?"

He shrugs one shoulder. "I mean . . . yeah, sometimes. A reviewer once called my show *cold and sterile*. That's the kind of thing you never get out of your brain once it's in there."

Sterile. Wyatt's art is the furthest thing from sterile. I actually want to laugh. "Who the hell would say something like that? That's so . . . You're like the most unconventional photographer out there right now. The last review I saw of your stuff said you might have 'finally gone too far.' "

Wyatt snorts, and when he meets my gaze, there's something smirk-like about the twist of his mouth. "Yeah. But like I said, haven't gotten that criticism out of my head since. It was from Donna Fowler, so, you know." He mimes stabbing himself in the heart. "Used to think about quitting art entirely. Relapsed more than once. But turns out sometimes it's the bad reviews that do the most for your career. I wanted to win out of spite."

I find myself mirroring his grin and resist the urge to cover my mouth with one hand; I've been told I have absolutely gigantic teeth.

I might not know Wyatt very well yet, but all this tracks with my impression of him so far. Too smart not to be gutted by a vicious critic but too stupid to really let it stop him.

"My mentors in LA told me never to read my reviews," I say.

"They're right. You should protect your passion at all costs. Don't be like me." He hides his mouth with a sip of coffee, but he isn't smiling.

I wonder how much of his brain space is still consumed by these thoughts, obsessing over what other people think of him.

Maybe we're more alike than I thought.

"Well, Donna Fowler couldn't take a good picture to save her life, so fuck her anyway," I say. "Normal people think you're great. *I* think you're great, for the record."

Wyatt makes a face and waves his hand in the air as if to dismiss the conversation entirely. "I'm not trying to get you to make me feel better. I know I'm good, or I wouldn't be here. And we're supposed to be talking about your work, not mine."

"Oh, okay, Wyatt 'I know I'm good' Cole, I won't compliment you anymore." I roll my eyes and earn a chuckle in return. At least things seem a little more normal between us now. It no longer feels like we're both holding our breath, waiting for the other person to cross an invisible line.

As worried as he might be about acting professional, I prefer it when he treats me like a normal person. We threw out *professional* back when we told each other about our former drug habits. When he fucked me so hard I came. Twice. That used to be something I thought was impossible. I enjoyed myself during sex, sure, but it always felt like there was a defined end point. I'd never really wanted to go further. I'd never wanted more, and so I'd never *had* more.

Wyatt blew my world right open.

"What are you thinking about doing for your capstone project?" he asks, distracting me from my increasingly florid fantasies about him bending me over this very park bench.

And fuck, of course my face is bright red. He must know exactly what I've been thinking about. He's trying to talk about art, and I'm fantasizing about his cock.

Okay, focus.

"I haven't really thought about it yet," I say. "I've been busy with the course assignments."

"Well, if I can give you yet another piece of advice, it's to start working on it sooner rather than later. People—actual critics—come to the end of program. It's better to half-ass your homework than put off your capstone."

"Critics?" I say, waggling my eyebrows. "Like Donna Fowler?"

"Entirely possible," Wyatt says, "so shape up." But he's still smiling, which means he doesn't think I'm at risk of massively embarrassing myself. That's a plus. "You can text me if you want to talk about it, you know. I'm always around."

Oh, *are* you, now, Professor Cole?

I have to work pretty hard to drag my mind away from careening off into another fantasy and back to thinking of a capstone project idea off the top of my head. You know, how everyone does their best work: off the cuff and under pressure. "I don't know. . . . I guess . . . I was thinking of doing another comparison piece. Like with my application portfolio." I stop myself from adding, *But better, obviously*. "Mixed media, maybe. Not for any particular artistic reason, but just because it's something I want to try."

"A good start," Wyatt says. "Did you have a subject in mind?"

Nope. "Something narrative. I want to tell a story. Or . . . multiple stories, perhaps. I've always liked the kind of art that pulls back the curtain and shows you that your reality isn't the only reality."

"And what is this other reality you want to show people?" Wyatt asks.

It's a good question, but this is about where my creativity ends. That must be clear from my expression, because Wyatt goes on:

"One place to start is to ask what makes you different from other people. You've shared your addiction, but is there something deeper, more innate to explore? What about your story makes you feel the most vulnerable?"

One thing comes immediately to mind. But I'm not sure it's the kind of answer Wyatt's looking for. He probably wants me to say something about my worst fear or whatever it was that made me start using drugs in the first place. But those are harder questions to answer. And maybe it's just that I've been thinking about Chaya, but—

"I grew up Chassidic," I say before I can think better of it. "You know, like . . . black hats."

His expression hasn't changed. He's watching me with placid brown eyes, calm as anything. I don't know what I expected. Shock, maybe. A little rivulet of disgust running through whatever else. People hate us. I know that—have known it since I was three years old. Even as a small child you notice the way people step to the far side of the sidewalk to avoid getting too close to your father. The stares. The whispers under breath and surreptitious photographs snapped by tourists who seem to think your family just waltzed in from the shtetl in *Fiddler on the Roof*. One time, when I was twelve, my father took me to a bookstore near Prospect Park; as we were checking out, the store owner congratulated me on knowing how to read.

As much as I'd like to give folks the benefit of a doubt and assume that *smart* people, people who care about social justice and protecting marginalized religions or whatever, will see through the bullshit—sometimes those people are worse. Like a girl I knew in LA who watched the TV show *Unorthodox* and found it utterly mesmerizing. She went on a rant about how horrible it must be for Orthodox women to be so oppressed and uneducated, ground under the heels of old men and a dying religion. I told her that most Chassidim thought *Unorthodox* did a bad job representing the community, and besides, those people in the show were Satmars, and there are as many kinds of Orthodox Jew as there are stars in the sky. I said if a woman was happy on that path, well, why not let her walk it? Which earned me a disappointed sigh and a pompous statement about how *some women* won't fight for what's in their own best interest.

But Wyatt hasn't taken the bait. There's no monologue forthcoming, or at least not yet. I gulp at my coffee to give him the chance to speak. If he's got Big Opinions, then I may or may not want to keep talking.

Just silence. Patient, completely unreadable silence.

"I left the community when I was eighteen. I haven't talked to anyone in my family since." I work my thumbnail against the lip of my cup, flicking the waxed paper back and forth. "I don't know if that's the kind of answer you were looking for, but if you want to know what I wish people understood about me, that's it."

Wyatt nods at last, slowly. "That's a lot to go through at such a young age," he says. "Losing your family, all at once . . . it's like a death. Like the part of you that used to exist is gone, and you have to become someone new."

My breath catches in my throat. "Yes," I say. "Yes . . . exactly. Exactly."

It's like he knows. The way he describes it is too familiar, as if he reached inside my head and tore out the words. I wonder if he's lost anyone. I'd ask, but . . . after that conversation about his own insecurities about art and how quickly he shut it down, I suspect he'd consider it inappropriate for me to ask about his family.

And fucking me isn't inappropriate?

I shunt that voice aside. It's not like he knew I was a student back then. Or when he told me about being an addict. Or when he slid his hands down over my ass and rolled our hips together as we danced, his breath hot on my neck and the taste of his sweat on my lips as I dragged my mouth along his stubbled jaw.

Stooooop.

"Maybe this is a good place to start, then," Wyatt says. "What is it about that story you want to share the most? Find out, and you've found your capstone project." He downs the rest of his coffee and tosses the empty cup into the trash bin next to our bench. "That's what art's all about—vulnerability. Peel your skin off, and let the wolves feast."

He quirks a grin at me and offers me a hand to help me up from the bench as he stands. For a second I'm dizzy in a way that has nothing to do with moving from sitting to standing. My mind just short-circuits, and the whole world reduces down to him, to his hand in mine. I know he feels it too, because in that moment we are—briefly—too close, his eyes widening and my heart beating in my ears. But then his hand slips out of mine, and he clears his throat as he turns away, covering his mouth with his hand. I could keep staring at him forever, but I force myself to look at the ground instead, examining the grimy sidewalk below my feet.

We head back to campus together in silence, but the entire time I'm turning his words over in my head, feeling out the smooth edges of them.

Vulnerability.

Peel your skin off.

Let the wolves feast.

10

Despite picking my capstone focus, I've yet to make progress.

I need to get out of the apartment. I need to do something productive, something that isn't staring at a screen.

Ophelia's the one who ends up saving me. Apparently her ex-girlfriend's new girlfriend (oof) is featuring some of her work at a gallery in Chelsea on Friday night, and it's the grand opening, and "I don't know anything about gallery art, Ely. Please, it's going to be so embarrassing."

I'd texted Wyatt to ask if he knew anything about this place, and to my surprise, he wrote back almost immediately and said he'd gotten an invitation and would be there.

Maybe we'll run into each other, he said, and I keep playing those words in my mind on a loop.

Maybe we'll run into each other. As if he hopes that we will.

It's an obnoxious commute because everything is an obnoxious commute from Queens. Ophelia, next to me, seems anxious somehow—she keeps tilting her head toward her window reflection like she's unhappy with what she finds there.

But when she finally speaks, it's not at all what I expect.

"Do you still write?" she says, turning to look at me instead of the window.

"What?"

She shrugs. "You wrote X-Men fan fiction back in the day. Do you still write?"

"Not really," I say. The answer is actually *not at all*. "I feel like I could only write in someone else's universe with characters that were already plotted out for me. I could never come up with a whole book on my own. Too much pressure. What about you?"

Ophelia catches one of her thin lilac braids in her hand, loops the hair around her fingers and tugs it taut. "I was never a writer. I'm more of an illustrator."

Both my brows go up. "Really? How have we not talked about this? Do you make fan art? What fandom?"

"Not anymore," she says. "I'm kind of . . . doing my own thing now. I've been selling prints on Etsy and doing freelance graphic design work. I actually got this gig to design the new bottle labels for a major liquor company. I've been working on my samples, but you know. . . ."

"Holy shit. That's so cool. Can I see?"

Ophelia laughs and covers her eyes with one hand. "Oh god. I mean. I guess, if you want. I should probably get some second opinions before yeeting this out into the universe anyway. Especially from a fellow artist."

"I don't know the first thing about graphic design," I warn her.

"You still have an artist's eye, though. You know what looks good and what doesn't."

I beckon with both hands for her phone, and after another brief moment's hesitation, she musters the courage to pass it over.

The design is clearly half-finished, the line work all done but the coloring and shading still incomplete. The name of the gin brand is in block letters, surrounded by weaving vines and a burst of wildflowers. My first thought is *Wow, that's a major fucking break*. My second thought is *This is really, really good.*

"I love it," I say, pinching the screen to zoom in closer on one of the flowers, a vibrant pink dahlia. "This is incredible. How did you even land something like this? You must be a really big deal."

She's got her hands all twisted together in her lap, spinning one of her rings—a big opal spider—around her middle finger over and over again. "Not really. It's my first deal. If they like it . . . I mean, if this actually ends up on the special edition labels, it could launch my whole career. But they might take one look and decide they hate it, and then I'm back to square one."

"They aren't gonna hate it."

"You think so?" She finally stops spinning the ring in favor of pressing both hands flat against her thighs, her smile quavering and tremulous. "I've been at it for ages. It was actually due last week, but I just . . . I had to get an extension on the deadline. Which is never a great look."

"I'm sure they understand. Sometimes life happens."

Ophelia doesn't look so convinced. "I'm not so sure about that. I want to make a good first impression. But I couldn't turn in something that I wasn't proud of. You know?"

Of course I know. Just as I know exactly why Ophelia missed that deadline. She wants this so bad it's devouring her from the inside. And so she wants it to be perfect.

As long as she doesn't turn in the work, she never has to find out if her art is good enough.

Analysis paralysis—or at least that's what Shannon called it. When you spend so much time worrying whether something is good enough that you never actually finish it in the first place.

I wonder if Wyatt ever experiences that.

Thinking about Wyatt sparks heat in the pit of my stomach all over again. *Maybe we'll run into each other.* And it's so hard to resist the urge to pull out my phone and text him and ask what time he's going . . . just so I can make sure I'm still around when he gets there.

The gallery is one of the fancy ones, the kind where people are mostly buying the art to launder their money and avoid paying taxes. I'd say I hate it on principle, but let's be real—I'd club a baby seal to have my work displayed in a place like this. (Principles do not, in fact, pay bills.)

Ophelia, seeing the look on my face, rolls her eyes. "It's obnoxious, I know. But apparently Carolina is really good, so I'm trying not to prejudge."

"I believe it. Getting into a place like this is a big deal."

There's an actual, real-life art bouncer at the door. He's not checking names on a list or anything—even schmancy places like this are still open to the public—but he *is* leering at everyone as if to say, *Touch anything with your pleb hands, and I'll cut them off.*

"What, something in my teeth?" I mutter to Ophelia as we sidle past him, which earns me a snicker (Ophelia) and a glare (art bouncer).

The ex-girlfriend's girlfriend's exhibition is a strange one. Mostly paintings, spaced evenly along the ecru walls and perfectly lit. But there are some mixed-media pieces as well, like the green canvas that serves as a vertical platter bearing a collection of ivory bones: *half rabbit,* says the caption, *half hawk*. Or the one that features red paint on red paint, slithering in globs and clots down the canvas. A careless scrap of fabric dangles from one corner, trapped by a wad of near-black acrylic.

"I'm gonna go say hi to Patty and Carolina," Ophelia says, and I nod, too fixated on the gore painting to do much else.

I peer closer, my hands locked behind my back to help me resist the almost-overwhelming urge to touch, to see if the paint is still wet. It looks visceral, like the product of a fresh kill.

"I had a nightmare that looked like this once," says a familiar voice, and I jerk my head up to meet Wyatt's gaze.

I should say something clever and insightful about the piece, but of course my troll brain has other ideas. "You're actually here!" A split second later, embarrassment catches up with me. "Sorry. I mean . . . Hi. Of course you're here. And same."

At least he smiles, even if I suspect he's just indulging me. "Sometimes I exist in places besides campus and gay clubs. Do you know the artist?"

"Only in degrees of Kevin Bacon. She's my roommate's ex-girlfriend's new girlfriend."

"I feel like I need to be better at math to process what you just said."

"Or at least be really good at those riddles where you have to figure out how many daughters a man has based off their eye colors."

"Hate those."

We examine the painting again. It's honestly hard to look away, like trying to ignore someone bleeding to death right in front of you.

"What do you think it means?" Wyatt says.

I tilt toward the canvas. "I don't know. It's giving menstrual blood. Are those actual human *hairs*?"

Wyatt moves closer; his shoulder grazes mine, just for a moment, as he leans in. "Maybe it's a still life of someone having their head smashed open with a brick."

I snort, then quickly press my hand over my mouth and glance around to see if anyone noticed. Big names come to these. Big names like, well, Wyatt Cole . . . although he certainly isn't judging me. He catches my gaze and winks, and my heart does this little flutter that is both expected and completely, damningly inappropriate.

It's getting really hard to stay mad at him.

"Mr. Cole?" someone says, and we both turn to find a slim woman in a pencil skirt and hipster glasses. She smiles and gestures behind her at a knot of people near the bone piece, all of them watching Wyatt with ill-disguised hope written across their faces. "Sorry to interrupt, but I would love to introduce you to a few people, if you don't mind . . . ?"

Wyatt actually hesitates, which I'm tempted to read too far into. But then he nods, says, "Of course," and passes me an apologetic glance before the pencil skirt leads him away. I watch the social climbers envelop him into their nest like magpies who've found something shiny.

I can't keep staring at this one painting all night, no matter how violent it is, so I make myself wander. The rest of Carolina's work is similar, all variations on a homicidal theme. I'm starting to wish I knew this girl, because she seems weird and I like that.

I'm examining another intensely morbid piece when someone steps up beside me, close enough that I can smell their cedarwood cologne. I all but assume it's Wyatt, have already opened my mouth to make a snarky comment about roadkill—only it isn't Wyatt at all.

"Can you imagine hanging this in your dining room?" the man says, nodding toward the canvas. "It'd certainly be a conversation starter."

I stare at him for a moment, trying to figure out if he's someone I'm supposed to recognize on sight. Probably. Feels like this place is full of Big Deals.

"I'm not inviting anyone over who doesn't find possum appetizing," I say. "I have standards."

It earns a laugh, at least. I examine this newcomer, trying to place him. He's dressed as if he just came from a board meeting. Maybe he's an agent or something?

"I don't think I've seen you around before," the guy says, shifting away from the painting—toward me. As if I were the art. "I can't say I have a knack for faces, but I'd remember yours."

Heat flushes up the back of my neck fast and I glance away,

toward the canvas, hoping the fall of my hair might hide the color in my cheeks. Maybe I'm not used to being flirted with. Or maybe it's just the venue and the guy. I'm not used to guys dressed like *that* flirting with me.

"I'm new in town," I say, and finally wrangle my nerves enough to look back at him. "I'm studying at Parker."

Both his brows go up. "Ah. Excellent program. What field?"

"Photography."

"I'll have to be on the lookout for your first gallery opening," he says. Those pale eyes of his are twinkling. My lord, he's good.

I'm tempted to wrap my arms around my stomach, a reflexive, insecure gesture that would say far more about me than I want to confess. I have to concentrate hard on keeping my arms loose and lax at my sides. "Maybe. We'll see. New York standards are pretty high."

"Of course they are. But you got into Parker, so you clearly have what it takes." His smile widens, showing teeth. "I'm so sorry, I forgot my manners. I'm Henrik Andersson."

"Ely Cohen."

We shake hands, and his lingers on mine just a beat too long before finally falling away. "So, Ely Cohen," Henrik says, "perhaps you'll let me take you out for a drink sometime. You can show me your portfolio."

He's standing there, smiling at me and waiting for an answer while I try to figure out whether he's joking. And, if he isn't, whether I should say yes. I don't know this man. He's good-looking enough that he's probably a secret serial killer. On the other hand, escaping a vicious serial killer would be great inspiration for a photo collection.

I'm still trying to figure out how to respond when a hand brushes my shoulder; I turn to find Wyatt there, a pair of seltzers in hand. "Hey," he says, passing me one. "They had mango flavor."

It's somewhat gratifying to see someone as clean-cut and put together as Henrik Andersson on the back foot. Both his eyebrows have gone up, his body language immediately closing off as he takes a step away from me, putting a more collegial distance between us. "Wyatt Cole," he says. "What a surprise. I haven't seen you at one of these in a while."

"Henrik," Wyatt says, smiling as easily as ever. "I try to see other human faces from time to time. I usually regret it."

Henrik laughs even as Wyatt's expression remains perfectly mild and unchanged. "Is Ely one of your students?"

"No. I wish I could take credit for her talent, but . . ."

I cover my own raised brows with a quick sip of mango seltzer. *No? So he doesn't consider me his student anymore? What does that mean?*

"A commendation from Wyatt Cole is as good as gold these days," Henrik tells me with a tiny nod. "Like I said, I'll be on the lookout for your next show. It was nice to meet you, Ely. Wyatt, I'll see you around, I'm sure. . . ."

He wanders off, leaving me standing there next to Wyatt, still trying to decide what I'm supposed to take away from the whole interaction. Because it kind of feels like Wyatt just cockblocked this guy.

Not his student.

Shut up, brain.

"Soooo," I say to fill the silence with something, anything. "Who was that?"

Wyatt lifts his seltzer cup, and I obediently clink mine with his in a mock toast. "That," he says, "was Henrik Andersson. He's a curator at PS1."

Curator of more than just art, seemed like. Because I have a feeling showing him my portfolio over drinks wouldn't have ended with me having my own exhibit at one of the best modern-art museums in the country.

"Did you literally just prevent me from talking to a *MoMA* curator?"

I sip my seltzer. The mango flavor is underwhelming.

Wyatt's face goes as red as the period painting. "I— Oh god. Uh. I can go and get him to come back . . . ?"

I laugh and shake my head. "No. Please don't. I'm ninety-nine percent sure he wasn't interested in my art."

"Ely, how many times do we have to go over this? You're good. You're *really* good. Your work is raw and emotional in a way that a lot of artists are afraid to be. It's what makes your pictures so . . . *consuming*. And if he doesn't realize that, then he's an idiot," says Wyatt.

It's sweet enough that I'm almost willing to forgive him for all the other bullshit.

Almost.

We both drink our seltzers in silence, staring at the painting to avoid staring at each other.

After several seconds have passed, long enough to let the tension thicken to the point of awkwardness, I say: "Maybe I'll do something like this for my capstone project. Instead of taking pictures of people's outsides, take pictures of people's insides."

"Please don't," Wyatt says, and just like that, we're back to normal.

I have the compulsion to try to keep him here with me for the rest of the time we're at the gallery. A terrible idea for a lot of reasons, not least because it'd be incredibly obvious what I was trying to do.

But he doesn't seem that keen to move on either. He lingers by my side as we shift to the next piece, even if we don't say much. I wonder if he's actually paying as close attention to the art as he seems to be, his eyes narrowed slightly as they fixate on a sculpture made out of what looks like skin and fingernail clippings.

The art is interesting enough that I shouldn't get distracted. But that proves to be impossible when I'm standing next to Wyatt. I'm keenly attuned to every time he shifts his weight from one foot to another—every time he takes a particularly deep breath—when he lifts one hand to draw it back through his hair.

I know how soft that hair feels. I twisted it around my knuckles while Wyatt went down on me.

Maybe my capstone project should be a reflection on the subtle embarrassment of being turned on in a public place.

I glance sidelong at Wyatt, half hoping to find him looking back at me. Maybe if I did, I'd murmur something low and provocative and watch him flush. Maybe I'd reach for his hand, or he would for mine, and we'd find somewhere better—somewhere *private*—to discuss art.

But unfortunately Wyatt really does seem captivated by the toenails, so I'm stuck here.

Wanting.

Ophelia finds us a few minutes later, hooking her arm through mine and bumping our hips together. "Hey. You ready to head out?"

"Sure." I turn my gaze back toward Wyatt and offer him a small smile. "See you next week, I guess."

"Remember what I said. No gratuitous gore in the capstone project. I mean it."

"No promises," I say, and then I let Ophelia tug me away, abandoning my half-consumed shitty seltzer on a nearby table.

Ophelia leans in as we head out the door to whisper: "Who was *that*? He's hot. Was I supposed to make you leave with me? Or do you want to go back in there? I'm not trying to pussy block you if you wanted to stay."

Pussy block. Oh lord. Is that actually a term people use now? "That was Wyatt. You know. The . . . guy."

"The guy?" Ophelia starts, but my implication dawns on her almost immediately. "Wait. Oh my god. That's him? *That's* the sexy professor? *Ely, holy shit, go back in there immediately!*"

"*No,* absolutely not, nope. You saved me at just the right time. I was only gonna embarrass myself if you left me there."

"Ely!"

I shake my head firmly. "I can't. I'm serious. I'm trying to respect his boundaries."

"Is he trying to respect his *own* boundaries? Because he looked pretty happy to stick around right next to you the whole time."

Did he? I try to think back over our interaction, teasing apart my memory of his facial expressions, his body language. Was he reluctant to see me go? Or is that my wishful thinking imposing on him what I want to see?

Maybe a little bit of both.

11

Hanging out with Wyatt has clicked something into place in my mind. A determination, maybe, to finally pull my shit together. Or perhaps it's inspiration—like he's just that good at planting himself in my mind and growing there.

I'm still suffering from the paralysis of not knowing how to start, though. *You should take Michal up on her invitation,* a voice repeats in the back of my head every time I see her on Monday. The idea of going to Shabbos still makes me want to slam my head into an anvil. Only I don't have to go to Shabbos dinner to hang out with her. Right?

I sit on the idea the rest of the day, paralyzed by my own indecisiveness. Or maybe it's not indecisiveness. Maybe it's something much more insidious. Something like fear.

But the whole thing turns out to be much more bloodless than I imagined.

"Absolutely" is what Michal says when I actually get up the nerve to ask her about hanging out come Tuesday afternoon, as late in the day as I can get before we all head home. "I'd been hoping you might want to do something sometime. Are you free tomorrow?"

We decide to meet for coffee at this place down in the East Village between classes. It's half bookshop, half café, with full-size windows that swing open so that the place feels like an extension of the sidewalk. I've never been to Europe, but this is what I've always imagined being in Paris might feel like: sitting at a table with a breeze in your hair and a demitasse cup of espresso at your fingertips.

"This is so dangerous," Michal says, eyeing the book-lined walls within. "I'm supposed to be on a no buy."

"They also serve wine and beer, in case you wanted to weaken your impulse control a little more."

Michal gives a dramatic shudder. "Speak no evil. I really need to read all the books I already have before I go off and buy more."

"Oh, same. And I should probably use all the empty notebooks I've bought before buying more, but we both know that's not happening."

"I have that problem but with sketchbooks," Michal says. "But what am I supposed to do? They're all so cute. I found one the other day that had embroidered flowers on the cover. I mean, come *on*."

"That's completely understandable," I say.

"Thank you. Now please tell my wife that."

I have to fight not to show a reaction. I didn't expect a visibly frum woman to casually disclose that she's in a lesbian relationship. It's so far from how I grew up. Sure, there were queer people in my community, but they kept their mouths shut about it. Chaya was a lesbian, but I was the only one she ever told; she knew damn well she was going to end up matched to a nice boy from good yichus just like the rest of us.

I suppose Michal could be a super-progressive form of Modern

Orthodox? I honestly feel a little creepy trying so hard to figure her out, but she fascinates me.

She has everything I always wished I had growing up.

"I didn't realize you sketched," I say instead of tumbling into all the questions quarreling for space in my brain.

She laughs. "I didn't say I was good at it. But yeah, I started with that before getting into photography."

"What made you switch?"

"I went to an arts high school up in the Bronx," she says. "They had a really good photography program, so I took a couple classes and fell in love."

Another surprise. I'd just assumed that Michal—like me—grew up in a religious family. That she went to private school and studied Torah and Hebrew as I did. But she *chose* to become observant. She wasn't FFB, or frum from birth; she walked into that life with her eyes wide open.

I've only met one ba'al teshuva—an observant Jew who was raised more secular—in my life. But my father said that according to the Talmud, a ba'al teshuva stands higher in heaven than even the most righteous scholar because their passion for Torah is greater.

"I can't draw to save my life," I admit. "I can take pictures, and I can paint on those pictures, or cut them up, or use them in papier-mâché, but I can't *draw*. And believe me, I tried. I wanted to be one of those art girls who always have charcoal smudges on their fingertips and a notebook full of floral doodles. Sadly, it was not meant to be."

Michal crumbles the corner of her scone between her fingers. "It's cool that you always knew you wanted to do photography, though. I feel like most young artists aren't nearly that focused."

I smile slightly; I can't help myself. "That was because of my father. He got me a camera when I was ten, and then it was basically over for me. I couldn't stop taking pictures of absolutely everything. My dad had to literally hide my camera on Shabbos so I wouldn't be tempted."

"That's adorable. Do you still have all the pictures you took back then?"

I wish. But I left them behind along with all the other artifacts of my old life. No doubt they're rotting away in my parents' storage space now—if my parents didn't just throw them out. "No. I have no idea where they ended up. Probably for the best, though; I'm sure they're embarrassingly bad. It's cringeworthy enough to look at the stuff I created when I first moved to LA."

"That's right. You're a West Coast girl. What's the scene like out there?"

I feel like Michal is being nice by asking a lot of questions about me and my life, but I would honestly rather hear more about hers. My time in LA is split into two halves: the four years I spent in a haze of drugs and liquor, and the four years since I got clean. I'd just as soon pretend the first four never existed.

"Very different from here, so far. Not that I've been here long enough to judge, really. But it's much more . . . Hmm. I guess you'd say product-focused? Like, sure, you have a gallery opening to show off your work, but you're also hoping to land a deal shooting for *National Geographic* or whatever at the same time. I'm not saying that's good or bad, just . . . different."

And to a certain extent, the way it was in LA was necessary. You had to make a living somehow. I got a job as a barista after I got clean—lots of long days and nights headed home smelling of burnt milk—but I supplemented my income with freelance gigs on the side. Truly, if I never shoot a wedding or maternity session again, it'll be too soon.

The self-consciousness that comes with talking about myself nonstop is too much. I wave a hand and say, "Anyway, I'm boring. What about you? You've always lived in the city?"

"Since I was born. Grew up in Inwood and pretty much stayed there until I got married. My wife's Polish, and she wanted to live in Greenpoint. I suppose the commute could be worse."

"How long have you been married?"

"Six years," she says, holding up her left hand and wiggling her fingers to show off her plain gold wedding band. "We actually met on Yom Kippur. Her kid stole a bagel off my literal plate at break fast, and she had the nerve to defend him."

"What a little delinquent."

"Right? And he still is. Especially when it comes to food. I have to hide the salt-and-vinegar chips if I want any left for myself."

Michal's life seems so far away from mine. She has a wife and a stepkid and clearly has some kind of Orthodox Jewish community that loves and accepts her for who she is. I hate myself a little for envying her. It just seems like it was so easy: She must have had the support of her parents from the start. She never went off the rails. Never blew up her entire life.

I would give anything for just a fraction of what she has.

I would give anything to go back.

TEN YEARS AGO

The party was somewhere in Williamsburg.

I used to know Williamsburg as home of the Satmar Chassidim, a path of Judaism that felt as far from mine as Chabad probably felt to secular people. But in this Williamsburg, people wore wigs that were hot pink and made of polyester; the men's hats looked more like hipster rip-offs of a Satmar flat biber than anything else. I felt like Alice falling into Wonderland there—or maybe that was just the drugs.

I didn't know how long it'd been since I took the pills. I could tell they were Oxy, though, because as soon as I'd snorted them

I'd felt my ears pop and heat flood my chest, my cheeks. And then I was drifting in a seamless dreamland, slipping between the bodies, navigating the furniture like I weighed nothing—like I had no mass but was just a shadow passing through time and space.

A hand closed around my wrist and tugged me down. I went easy, and the sofa opened up to catch me, a patient mother with warm arms. Chaya's nose nuzzled my cheek and her breath was hot, her kneecaps butting up against my thigh.

"There you go," she murmured, and I slid down farther, letting the sofa and Chaya swallow me. Her lap was my favorite place to be. Her fingers slipped into my hair, catching on tangles. "You're okay. Everything's good."

"Everything *is* good," I agreed, and smiled up at her, my Chaya with her starburst halo of curls and her green-ocean eyes. Her lips curved into a smile too; the red lipstick she'd put on was stark against her pale skin, like someone had split her face open with a knife. "You're so pretty."

She wasn't, according to most people. Her face was too pinched. Her mouth was too thin. She was so skinny you could see her spine jutting through her shirt. But other people are stupid and bad at art.

Chaya Mushka Levy was art.

"Shh," Chaya said, and stroked my brow.

I closed my eyes, obedient. I tried to feel Chaya's heartbeat through her thighs, tried to merge us into one beast. Her hand had its own rhythm, sliding against my skin.

Someone came up. I could hear them talking to Chaya, a low rumble of a voice. She answered and there was the click of a lighter, the buzz of something boiling in a pipe bowl. I felt Chaya's stomach shifting when she inhaled, then blew out. The smell of fresh-cut grass was thick like smoke.

"Go away," I mumbled, but I didn't think they heard me.

Chaya shifted, extracting herself from under my weight. I protested, briefly, but then she was back, her head tilted against mine on the sofa cushion, our bodies reaching away from each other like the two hands of a clock. Her skin was slightly damp where it touched mine. I twisted enough to catch a glimpse of her, the edge of the silhouette of her face, her cinnamon-brown curls stuck to her temples.

"You okay?" She asked it softly, like she was asking me to confess.

I hummed. My head felt like it was stuffed full of cotton balls. I had a song stuck in my brain on a loop: "Lecha Dodi," the song we would sing on Erev Shabbos—the night the Sabbath begins—to welcome the Shabbos Queen.

Let us go, my beloved, to greet the bride.

When I pictured her, the Shabbos bride, that sweet evening queen, I pictured Chaya Mushka in white.

I had to pee.

"I have to pee," I told Chaya, and she made a wordless noise and let me get up. The process of standing seemed to take longer than usual; I gripped the edge of the coffee table, hunched there on the floor for a second while the room weaved in and out of focus. Then I pushed myself up, and the world shifted and locked freshly into place.

The bathroom was down the hall to the left. I stood outside of it for forever, leaning against the wall, trying not to stare at the girl in front of me, who was on her phone playing *Candy Crush*. Her score was, like . . . super high. She probably got to play in class. I suspected *her* school didn't confiscate phones at the start of day.

"You can go first," she told me when the bathroom opened up, which was extremely nice of her. She deserved a high *Candy Crush* score.

I pulled the door shut behind me and dropped down onto the toilet, legs stretching out until the toes of my shoes hit the wall. My legs looked awkward without tights. Not like the legs of these other girls with their curves and polished, exfoliated skin. All I could see when I looked at my legs was the gooseflesh pocks where hairs used to be.

Fuck, okay. Focus.

I managed to pee a little.

When I saw my reflection in the mirror as I was washing up, I decided I didn't look like myself. I looked way cooler than my actual self. The makeup Chaya and I had bought at Duane Reade the week before had clearly worked. My hair was as messy as ever, but it looked intentional, like I probably played bass guitar and smoked clove cigarettes and had a boyfriend named Axel. Pretending to be goyish looked good on me.

Perish the thought.

Okay, fine, not goyish. That night I was just a different kind of Jewish girl. The kind that went to parties with really good drugs.

I left the restroom, but I didn't go back to Chaya. I figured, *Let her enjoy herself, find some goyish girl to make out with in a corner somewhere.* I went into the bedroom instead, to find the guy who had given me the Oxy. I asked him if he had more.

"Fuck yeah, I have more," he said.

"I don't have any cash left."

He shrugged. "Venmo me."

I almost told him I didn't have Venmo either, but that would have been a lie. It was just tied to my parents' bank account. They didn't mind me using it to pay back friends for lunch or an Uber ride. Maybe they wouldn't notice this charge. For all they knew, "gregnaut" was somebody's cousin or something.

I nodded and he let me scan his Venmo code and waited as I picked an emoji. I settled on the cheeseburger one because snorting pills off this guy's iPad probably wasn't kosher either. But once they were up my nose I was leaning back, I was falling, I was hitting the pillows with a happy sigh, and I didn't care what my parents might say.

Inject it directly into my veins, I thought, then laughed because that was, in fact, something people actually did with these pills.

I was too heavy to think much past that. I became a filter through which the rest of the world passed—voices, sensations, the throb of the music. I was a bee trapped in its own honey. Everything tasted golden and sweet.

The bedroom door opened again. Gregnaut's voice was a low rumble. "She's good," he said. "She's just sleeping it off."

But then someone was shaking my shoulder—too rough. I groaned and scrunched my face and tried to roll away. The shaking became more persistent.

"Get up," Chaya said. "Ely, get up. We have to go home."

"I didn't do anything to her," said Gregnaut, sounding offended.

Chaya yanked at my arm. "Did I ask, dickwad? Ely, come *on*." She kept pulling and I wanted her to stop, I wanted to yell in her face to let me go, but my mouth wouldn't cooperate. I couldn't even get my eyes open properly.

A sharp heat burst on my cheek, the lance of pain cutting through my honey trap. Chaya Mushka had just *bitch-slapped* me.

"What did you do that for?" I complained, but it was too late. The high was ruined.

"You're a mess," Chaya said. "We have to get you home. Pull it together and let's go."

She had to know that was a big ask. But it didn't stop her from draping one of my arms over her shoulders and heaving me up, her scrawny frame staggering under my weight. I was useless. I couldn't see straight. But I couldn't fight her either; I could only let Chaya drag me bodily out of that party and try to prop me against the wall of the elevator. I promptly slid down into a heap on the floor.

Chaya, standing over me, had her arms hugged tight around her middle. Her face was more pinched than ever, staring straight ahead at the shut elevator doors as the floors dinged past.

"Chaya," I said, but she still wouldn't look at me. "*Cha-aa-ya.*"

"You better apologize to me in the morning," she told me, and even though I never got angry on opiates, that made me angry. Even if the emotion was really just a tiny kernel of frustration burrowing itself into my chest, it still counted.

"You were using too," I muttered, well aware of how whiny I sounded.

She shook her head. "Not like you."

And that was the last thing she said to me for a long time. Her next words were to the Uber driver when he picked us up. Then silence for the whole car ride back to Crown Heights. She kept jiggling her leg against the seat, and I wanted her to stop, but asking wasn't worth the effort. So instead I tilted my face against the chilly window and watched the city lights flash past as we drove away, hipster Brooklyn receding behind us.

Chaya told the driver to drop us off a block away from my place. She let me lean on her for that short walk home, although she kept whispering orders under her breath, as if she thought the neighbors were watching us outside their windows even at three in the morning: "Stand straight. . . . Pay attention idiot, that's a curb."

My keys were in my coat pocket, but I was too useless to dig them out. Chaya had to do it for me, unlocking the door to my building. She paused there, holding the door open with her shoulder, and flipped through my keys till she found the right one.

"This is the key to your front door," she told me, like I didn't already know that. "Don't drop it."

"I don't feel good. I think I'm dying."

"You aren't dying, unless you count dying from stupidity. You're fine. Go take a cold shower or something."

Chaya shoved me gently in the direction of the stairs. I made it all the way to the bottom of them before I realized what the problem was going to be—but when I turned around, Chaya was already gone. I crawled up on my hands and knees, fingernails digging into the winter grime smeared from the soles of twenty people's snow boots. I rested on the landing, leaning my head back against the wall—but it was too much, too easy to slip under the surface of the dark water that rose up all around me.

I couldn't fall asleep there. I had to pull it together.

I squinted open heavy eyelids and lurched forward again, grabbing the banister this time to drag myself up the next flight.

My key fit into the lock. I turned the front-door knob as slowly as possible, free hand lifting to graze the mezuzah on the doorframe, then touch my dirty fingers to my lips. Even though Hashem probably wished I wouldn't; what god wanted the devotion of someone like me?

The apartment was warm and quiet as I slipped inside, shucking off my coat. It puddled on the floor next to our shoe rack, joined shortly thereafter by my hat and boots. I was too numbed out to be scared my parents were still up or even to worry about waking them. Things like that didn't matter when you were high. It was kind of beautiful.

I shuffled down the hall in my sock feet and let myself into the bedroom I shared with my younger sister Dvora. She was a huddled lump in the bed by the window, the streetlamp light casting silvery waves over her form. I tried to be quiet as I stripped off my dress, but it was no good. I staggered into the dresser, and one of Dvora's little wooden horse figurines tipped off its shelf and clattered to the floor.

"Whoops," I whispered as Dvora made a muffled, displeased

noise against her pillow, then twisted around to squint at me from across the room.

"What are you doing?" Dvora's voice was all thick and gloopy with sleep. "Ely, it's like . . . four in the morning. . . ."

The night air weaved around me like silk—beautiful but a little hard to breathe. I thought if I went to sleep right then, I might not wake up. The thought didn't terrify me. Nothing did when I was high. But I was generally aware that dying is something people usually try to avoid.

So I found myself climbing into Dvora's bed instead of my own, slipping under the covers and burrowing in close to the warm knot of her body. She shifted to make room, her hands tucked together between us, fingers worrying each other.

"Are you high again?" she whispered. Dvora was fourteen. My parents probably thought she didn't know what "high" even was. But I was sixteen and had been getting drunk since I was her age. She wasn't that young, so she knew.

I exhaled. My breath wisped through the hair at her forehead, thin dark threads fluttering in the dim light. "Maybe," I said. I closed my eyes. "Yes."

She didn't say anything, but I could feel her breathing faster next to me. God, I wished I could feel guilty. I really did.

Behind my closed eyelids, little bursts of color swam around. "I think I took too much."

"Do you want me to get Ima and Abba?"

I shook my head. "No. Just stay with me. Please?"

Dvora's cold hands insinuated themselves between mine. She locked our fingers together and squeezed tight. "Okay."

"Okay."

We stayed in silence, the exchange of our breaths the only communication. Outside, the recycling truck made its way down the street with the familiar sound of bottles clinking and stacks of folded-up cardboard slapping against each other. The pills leached out of my system slowly, venom draining from a snakebite. I cracked my eyes open enough to see Dvora's face again, her dark lashes like coal smudges against her cheeks. If I were to take a photo of her right now, that's what I'd do. I'd smear soot right there, blacking out a space beneath her eyes, scattering ash like freckles.

"Can't you stop?" Dvora said, and my eyes opened the rest of the way; I'd thought she was asleep.

"Stop what?"

She didn't look at me. She just nestled closer, pressing one hand flat against my chest. I wondered what my heart felt like against her palm, if it was beating too fast or too slow.

"You know what," she said, and I did.

I did know. And it broke my fucking heart, because I also knew that, no, I couldn't stop. I would never stop.

I didn't want to stop.

"Go back to sleep, Devi," I whispered, and I kissed her forehead, and the next morning as we shuffled down to breakfast, two ghosts amid the raucous chaos of a family with five children plus a newborn baby, I wished I could have told her something different. I wished I could have lied.

Instead I ate my cold cereal and made myself sit there and watch her with her young face carefully poised in a mask of innocence that was no longer real, thanks to me. Now Dvora kept my secrets. I'd dragged her down into the muck with me.

And I'd keep dragging her, and everyone, down. I'd bury us, and I wouldn't rest until I'd ruined both our lives.

The least I could do was look her in the eye while I did it.

12

I thought sleeping would get Chaya out of my mind, but it doesn't work. She's still there when I wake up, a specter haunting my steps as I get dressed and tie my messy hair up in a ponytail. She watches me tap my phone at 30th Avenue and hangs on to the subway pole next to me all the way to Union Square.

I believed I had erased her over these past eight years. She didn't occupy all the dark corners of my mind anymore; in fact, I hardly thought of her at all out in LA. Something about being back here has resurrected her.

I just hope this place doesn't bring back other, darker sides of my past.

Back when I was doing drugs, I had no self-control to speak of. I went skinny-dipping at Venice Beach and drove fast cars with no seatbelt and shot strange liquids into my veins without fully knowing what they were. But that's kind of what addiction *is*—a full-tilt sprint toward the mindless void. And if the worst should happen, well, you probably deserve it.

This time when I decide on my next steps, it isn't impulse driving me. It's decisiveness.

At least that's what I tell myself. But the fear that lurches up in the back of my throat every time I think about what I have to do next makes me feel like there's something reckless about it as I walk into my Digital Photography class, slide into the seat next to Michal Pereira, and say, "Is the invite for Erev Shabbos still good? Not this week. But next week, maybe?"

Michal, for her part, doesn't seem surprised at all. "Of course," she says, smiling back at me. "Anytime. But we're ordering in bagels from Russ & Daughters for the oneg this week, if that makes a difference. . . ."

Russ & Daughters? *Say less.* "Okay, fine, this week. Those bagels have been starring in my dreams for eight years straight."

It's all so easy. The entire interaction is over and done with in less than a minute, as the professor shows up and calls the class to order. I doubt Michal has any idea how monumental the moment was for me. And maybe it shouldn't be monumental; maybe it's my nasty ego getting in the way again, still bruised from being shunned eight years ago. But I can't escape the feeling that I've done something that can't be *un*done. Even if I were to change my mind and cancel Friday plans, it's too late.

I can't pretend I don't want it anymore.

I'm proud of me too. Being back in New York hasn't been anything like I thought it would be. I expected to see ghosts everywhere. I thought I would hunker down at Parker and get my work done and emerge from my chrysalis like a beautiful fucking butterfly, a star of the art scene, and I'd never have to actually face the reality of what happened here eight years ago.

But New York refused to hold me at arm's length. It grabbed me with both hands and pulled me in, wrapping me up tight. I met Ophelia and Diego, the best roommates anyone could possibly dream of. I met Michal, who defies all my prejudices about what it means to be Orthodox. And then there's Wyatt, of course. Wyatt, who is both infuriating and alluring. Wyatt, who makes me want to smack him and kiss him at the same time.

I want to be a part of this city. I want to sink my hands wrist-deep into its muck and wallow there.

Only after I get home do I start to regret what I did, just a little. I dump my bag on my bedroom floor, then dump my body on the bed, burying my face in my pillow and muffling my groan against the down. I don't know what I was thinking, signing up for this. It's not as if it's some Reform thing where the women wear kippot and people snap photos of the challah for Instagram. Michal is frum. She's religious—*Orthodox*. I have no idea what stream of Judaism she follows or what their practices are, whether the people at this dinner will be Sephardi or Ashkenazi or—

I text Wyatt.

I just did a stupid thing, I tell him. I'm trying to decide if I should flee the country.

He writes back immediately, which tells me everything I need to know about his evening life.

WYATT: Stupid like drunk sexting an ex? Or stupid like buying an NFT of Baby Yoda in meme glasses?

ME: I agreed to go to a religious thing with someone.

WYATT: You're right, that's worse. What are you going to do? Do you have any uncles who can die last minute?

ME: Maybe I could invent one. But then there's always next week. Or the next. Or the next. . . .

WYATT: How much do you care about disappointing this friend?

ME: She's in my class and about thirty times cooler than I am. I want her to like me.

WYATT: Well then, I hate to say it, but you might have to go to whatever it is. Think of this like an anthropological expedition. You're an intrepid explorer, studying hitherto unknown spiritual practices of the rare and oft-misunderstood New York theist.

I cringe so hard I can basically feel myself disappearing into my own bones.

And then I type the next bit anyway.

ME: Yeah, maybe. Only I wish it was as exotic as going to some Pentecostal speaking-in-tongues revival. But it's just Jewish people, so, you know, I've been intrepidly exploring this particular brand of New York theist since birth.

ME: It's for my capstone project.

ME: don't hate me.

It does take Wyatt a moment to respond this time. Probably because he's punching himself in the face out of sheer disappointment in me.

Then he starts typing. I stare at those three dots.

Finally:

WYATT: I could never. Do it for the bagels.

Well, I can't disappoint Wyatt. So I guess I'm going to Shabbos with Michal.

Just for the bagels, of course.

But when Friday comes, dread rises with it. Trepidation settles like sickness in my gut, and no matter how hard I try, I can't ignore it.

Sorry, I'm not feeling well. I don't think I'm going to make it tonight. Raincheck?

There's not gonna be a raincheck. But still, it feels more polite to pretend.

Michal texts back about an hour later: Of course, no problem. Hope you feel better soon! Let me know if I can bring you some soup or something.

Her kindness only worsens the guilt.

But all I feel as I head home at the end of the day, crammed into a subway car with all the other exhausted commuters ready for the weekend, is relief.

■

Ophelia's there when I get home that day. She's perched on the sofa wielding a bottle of sparkly gold nail polish. Her fingers already glitter—she's hunched over taking care of her toes, although she spares a glance up as I dump my bag on the island and head for the fridge to pour myself a glass of grapefruit juice.

"You good?" she says.

"Yeah." I shove the fridge door shut with my hip. "Why?"

"Because you have this look on your face like you wanna claw someone's tonsils out."

I can't help it—I laugh, because she's probably right. "Sorry. It's nothing. I made plans to hang out with someone, then I chickened out." I down half the glass of juice in one go. "So. What are you up to tonight?"

"Diego's friend Denni is throwing this party. East Village. Sounds like it should be fun. Parties with Diego's crowd usually are; everyone he knows is an actor or a drag queen or some kind of performance artist who only speaks in whale sounds. Occasionally all three. Want to come?"

I can picture it now, some artist's garret on Avenue C with sultry mood lighting and Bowie on repeat. The hazy miasma of weed smoke. Pizza going cold in boxes on the counter. The host's overly affectionate cat crawling from lap to lap. Spilled beer, a stranger's urine speckling the toilet seat. Kissing someone in a dark bedroom while the music thrums—indistinct—just outside.

It's so far from my plans with Michal, so much so that the two experiences feel like they should exist in opposition to each other. Shabbos is candlelight and prayers in Hebrew and challah crumbs down the front of your shirt. It's eating until you feel sick. It's your uncle's tone-deaf and wordless singing to an ancient tune that lives in your blood. It's the Shabbos bride dressed in splendor, G-d turning his brilliant face to gaze on mankind.

And right now, frankly, I'll take the pee toilet.

The place Diego brings us is a sixth-floor walk-up off St. Marks. By the time we make it to the actual apartment I'm already sweaty and out of breath; no place in New York has air-conditioning, not even in the pit of summer, which is a unique brand of awful. Clearly I've been cradled in the slothful embrace of LA traffic too long if an East Village walk-up can defeat me.

Even without the heat, I wouldn't recommend taking the subway from Astoria to St. Marks. The train doesn't get off at a super-convenient station, it's a lot of walking, and the commute takes an hour of your life each way. Drunk tourist city isn't worth it.

Ophelia looks infuriatingly perfect still, not even winded, her violet eyeliner just as crisp as it was when we left Astoria. "I go to a lot of spin classes," she says when I ask.

"Addicted," mouths Diego over Ophelia's shoulder.

Diego doesn't bother knocking. Not that I think anyone would have heard him over the bass of the music or the crescendo of voices talking and laughing beyond the door. Inside, the party is about how I expected, only there's more than just weed smoke overhead—someone is burning sandalwood incense in a little golden bowl on the kitchen counter.

"Want a beer?" Diego offers, heading for one of the coolers sitting at the base of the island.

"Sure," Ophelia says, right as I respond with "I'm good."

Diego digs around in the ice and surfaces with two IPAs. "You sure, Ely? They've got cider too, if you have a gluten thing."

Like I haven't eaten five hundred bagels in front of him this past week. "No, really. I'll get something in a bit." Lukewarm tap water probably, but it's not like I'm expecting craft mocktails. Ask a sober person what they have to drink, and they'll show you a whole fridge full of twenty different seltzer flavors. Last time I asked a drinker for seltzer, they handed me a White Claw.

Diego shrugs as if to say, *Your funeral,* and passes Ophelia both the beers. "I can't open these with my nails," he says, flicking his fingers toward us to show off his rhinestoned talons. "Do you mind . . . ?"

Ophelia rolls her eyes with plenty of gusto, but she does it. "I'm starting to think you just get those things so you don't have to open your own cans. Or wash your own dishes . . . or scrub out the oven . . ."

"Hey," Diego says. "We have a system. You do all that; I clean the bathroom and cook all the food and— Jesus, I'm not gonna list out the whole chore chart. We're at a party. Come *on*."

We delve deeper into the crowd, and Diego finds the host somewhere and introduces us, which turns into offers to roll a few blunts—and I take that as my cue. I slip off and make my way back to the refreshments table, where I pour myself a red Solo Cup of tap water and take a bite of one of the little cheese cubes on display.

I used to be a riot at parties. Chaya and I would pause in the building foyer to roll off our stockings and unbutton the high collars of our shirts enough to show a daring slice of collarbone. We'd fold the waists of our skirts to hitch them up above the knees. And then we'd descend like birds of prey—at college frat parties, boho soirées hosted by someone's online friend's brother, bars that wouldn't look too hard at our IDs.

Going out like that was such a thrill. Because for those few hours, we weren't us. We weren't the weird, frumpy Chassidic girls that goyish people stared at on the subway. We weren't the troublemakers threatening to tarnish our families' good names. And if we drank enough vodka sodas, swallowed enough pills, we kind of forgot we were any of those things ourselves.

Here, at this party, I catch myself staring at the mess of liquor bottles on the kitchen table. I yank my gaze away, but it's too late. I'm already thinking about tequila, nectar sweet on my tongue. About the way getting drunk feels like slipping underwater.

And thinking about being drunk makes me think about being in other, more fractured mental states.

Okay, now I'm just getting melancholic. Time to do something with myself.

I've brought my camera, actually. I feel a little weird having it out, which is different for me—I used to bring my camera everywhere back in LA. It was as much a part of me as a necklace I'd never take off. People in my social circle knew to expect it. Ely Cohen, always there to snap candids, always watching everything and everyone through the lens of a Nikon.

I came to Parker to take pictures, and yet I've hardly done any of that so far. I've been so busy with classes and obsessing over this thing with Wyatt and trying to make friends that I haven't done the one thing that never fails to help me put down roots: taking photos of people in the community I'm trying to be a part of.

I'd tried so hard when I was younger. I took hundreds of pictures a day: the young mothers in their brand-new wigs pushing strollers, old bubbes shuffling down the street to the corner store, the anxious bochur scurrying—late, books clutched to chest—to class. I would develop them in the darkroom at Yeshiva University, where one of the studio-arts professors knew my English teacher and was willing to let me take advantage of the college's resources.

My parents looked at my photography habit the same way they looked at my sister Dvora's ability to speak French: a fun fact to put on your résumé when it was time to find a marriage match but otherwise frivolous. They still hung up my photos around the house, still farmed out my services for all the cousins' b'nei mitzvot, but they never really saw it as a valid career choice.

I lift the camera and focus on a girl who's sitting on the sofa, curled up with her drink perched on one knee, watching the party swirl around her. She seems as if she's a part of this world but not at the same time. As if she knows these people and likes them but is maybe a little tired, already thinking of going home.

I've only been here for five minutes, but I know how she feels.

I check the lighting, the white balance. Looks good, at least for my first time out after a week away from Albert.

That's my camera. I named my camera Albert.

When I lift Albert again, I zero in on two people in conversation, a man and a woman. She has her head tilted slightly to one side, a lock of black hair twisting around her finger. He's saying something with a small smile curving his lips. Flirting, or perhaps manipulating. I snap the photo.

I shift my lens to the left, and it finds a man with curly hair tipping forward to snort a line of cocaine off the coffee table.

My finger stutters against the shutter button, and I accidentally take the damn photo. I close my eyes before I turn away, but it's too late. That image has already painted itself across the backs of my eyelids. And now it's immortalized on film.

I shove my camera back into my bag and stagger away, hardly paying attention to the people I elbow aside. I don't breathe properly until I'm in the bathroom with the door shut and locked behind me, cold water splashing my face.

"Shit," I mutter, eyes squeezed tight. "Okay. Okay, breathe."

I rub the heels of both hands over my forehead and exhale slowly, counting down from ten. I'm flush cheeked when I finally meet my gaze in the mirror again, the edges of my hair wet and stuck to my cheeks.

Someone knocks on the door. "It's busy!" I shout, and put the toilet cover down so I can sit, clutching Albert against my chest.

The music thrums on outside, more muffled now, the lyrics indistinct. I pull my phone out of my back pocket and swipe over to the Messenger app.

I almost text Wyatt. I can imagine the way he'd respond, all comfort and reassurance. I would feel his words like a warm blanket wrapped around my shoulders.

But of course, that's fantasy. Texting him now would just be forcing him to metaphorically rub my shoulders and would probably be weird.

I originally got this phone out to text my sponsor. Or . . . well, Shannon isn't really my sponsor anymore, I guess. I'm supposed to find a new one here in New York. But she's still one of my closest friends, so she's on the hook for witnessing at least 10 percent of my meltdowns.

Not that I've texted her much since moving away from LA. I've gotten plenty of texts from her, but the only thing *I* ever actually talked about was the time I whined to her about the Wyatt situation. I just kind of ignored all the other things she said.

Once again I prove to the universe that I'm the world's shittiest friend. First there was Chaya. Then I ghosted all my dope-fiend friends when I got clean. And now Shannon.

Texting her right now, just to make her help *me,* once again the selfish friend who *takes takes takes* and never gives . . . it wouldn't be a good look.

Fuck. Okay. Fuck being professional; I'm going in.

I text Wyatt instead.

ME: hey. I didn't go to the Shabbos dinner, went to a party. someone's doing coke out there and it's got me a bit fucked up

My heart pounds as I sit there and stare at the screen, anxiety crawling at the nape of my neck. I shouldn't expect a response. I probably shouldn't have sent this text in the first place. *God, if I don't get a reply, it's going to be so fucking* humiliating *come Monday—*

Three dots. *Oh my god. Oh my god.*

WYATT: Are you okay? Do you need me to call?

ME: no, I'll be alright. Just holed up in the bathroom trying to figure out how to be a normal human again.

WYATT: You should leave. I can call you an Uber. What's your address?

ME: I'll be ok. I came here with my roommates, I don't want to ditch them.

WYATT: I'm sure they'd understand your sobriety is more important.

Ophelia and Diego, naturally, have no idea I'm an addict. It's a part of me I'd hoped to leave behind in California. I should have known that four years clean doesn't make me the same as everybody else. They said that a million times in meetings, and I filed it away as information irrelevant to me. After all, I'd reinvented myself once; I could do it again.

ME: i'm fine. seriously

WYATT: Have you been to a meeting in New York yet?

I cringe and bite the inside of my cheek. Honestly, I had kind of hoped to just . . . not go back. NA was helpful. I used to need it every day—sometimes more than once in a day, in fact. But it's been four years. Aside from parties with unanticipated cokeheads presenting themselves in front of my camera lens, I actually do pretty well most of the time.

ME: No. I don't want addiction to become my life, the way it used to be

Wyatt, of course, replies almost instantly to that one.

WYATT: If recovery becomes your life, that's not the worst thing in the world. Have you told anyone else here about your history? Do you have any friends you trust?

The little ellipsis at the bottom of the screen suggests he's typing another text. A part of me doesn't even want to know what he'll say. It's going to be something grotesquely kind and wise, and I don't deserve either of those things from him.

From anyone, really.

It's my own fault for texting him. Now I've gone and made myself look pitiful in his eyes. Now he'll want to *fix* me, and the thought is terrible enough to make me wish I'd stayed home tonight in the first place.

WYATT: Recovery isn't something to be ashamed of. But I get it. And I'm here, if you need to talk.

Oh, fuck me.

My stupid brain can't decide if I'm embarrassed beyond all belief or if it was worth it. My predictions were right, of course. Everything Wyatt says to me feels like a hug, his fingers squeezing my shoulders and the skin of his cheek warm against mine.

But he didn't sign up to be my sponsor. Or my dad.

And I don't want him to be either of those things either.

I shut off my phone and stand, shoving it into my back pocket and facing myself in the mirror once more. I pinch my cheeks; it only serves to make me look feverish. I make a face at my reflection instead and turn and open the door and find myself face-to-face with Ophelia.

"Ely," she says, looking as surprised as I feel. "Hi. Enjoying the party so far?"

She has a beer in hand, so she's already enjoying it far more than I am. "Sure. Yeah. How about you?"

But of course, Ophelia's too smart to fall for that. Her purple-painted lips tilt into a frown. "Are you okay?"

A ragged laugh shudders up from my chest, and suddenly, out of nowhere, I feel like I'm on the verge of bursting into tears.

Ophelia's eyes widen and she reaches for my hand, squeezing tight. "Come here," she says, tugging me after her. "Let's go get some air, yeah?"

I follow her through the stuffy main rooms of the apartment and into the bedroom, which is less busy—just a few people hanging around sharing drinks and chatting in lowered voices. Ophelia pushes open the window and climbs through, out onto the fire escape. It's a warm night, balmy, and smells like smoke. I realize why when I peer over the railing and spot someone a couple of stories below leaning against the rail, the lit coal of their cigarette a glowing ember in the dark.

Ophelia sits down near the edge, her legs dangling out over open air. She pats the spot to her right and I join her, watching my feet hover far above the sidewalk. My socks, the ones with pineapples on them, look childish juxtaposed with Ophelia's pink fishnets.

"You good?" she says, shooting me a quick look.

Outside is better. There's air on my face, even if it's tobacco laced. And I prefer the sound of honking cars and miscellaneous shouting to the white noise of a drunken party. The old Ely would be horrified by how square I am now, but it's true.

"Yeah," I say. "Working on it." I press my palms to my face and blow out a heavy breath, trapping that heat against my cheeks for a moment before I let my hands drop. "Sorry. I know this isn't flattering."

"What do you mean?"

I'm already kicking myself. *This isn't flattering*—who says that? It sounds like I'm fishing for reassurance. "Nothing. Sorry. I just . . . got a little freaked-out for a second. But I'm fine now. It's fine."

But somehow this only serves to make Ophelia look even more concerned. "What happened? Do I need to talk to someone?"

"*No*—god, no, nothing like that." I have to say it. There's no way around it now; Ophelia's already drawing her own conclusions, and they're probably worse than the truth. Not that I could have kept my past hidden much longer anyway. At some point she and Diego were gonna notice that I never drink with their other friends. Or smoke. Or, apparently, do lines of coke.

I dig my fingers against the grate of the fire escape and try to focus on that, on the chilly iron against my skin.

"I'm in recovery," I say. "I used to be an addict." Twelve-step programs would say I still am, but that kind of language has always stuck in my craw. "Opiates, mostly. Heroin. Sometimes other things too." I can't look at Ophelia. I don't want to see the expression on her face: Pity, perhaps. Or disgust. Instead I focus on my words, on saying them as if by rote like I'm reciting a script someone else drafted. "Anyway. I've been clean for four years, but things like this can be hard for me sometimes."

I pretend to be overly concerned with my nails for a second, digging at a cuticle as if I'm the kind of person who gives a shit about my cuticles.

"We could have stayed home tonight," Ophelia says. I'm surprised by how gentle her voice sounds, almost apologetic. I glance up and find her face still close to mine. I don't see pity or disgust there, no matter how hard I look. "It would have been just as fun to do something else."

"I'm usually okay, actually. I mean, it's been *years*. I didn't have any problem when we went to Revel. But sometimes I see something and it triggers me, then I'm all . . ." I flutter a hand in the air, not sure how else to explain the way it's like your mind breaks down all at once, decomposing into disjointed parts. One second you feel like a human, and the next you're a quivering puddle.

I must look even worse than I feel, because Ophelia scootches closer and rests her hand atop mine, her palm warm and heavy. I shift so that she can lock our fingers together, and when she squeezes, I squeeze back.

"Sorry," I say after a moment. "I don't mean to put this all on you. I should probably get a therapist or something." I manage a brittle kind of laugh, one that doesn't sound nearly as lighthearted and dismissive as I'd hoped.

Ophelia's being nice, but I know better than to trust it. Addicts don't get sympathy. And honestly, that's pretty fair most of the time. When we're using, we'll do anything to get our next fix. I must have stolen thousands of dollars from my parents by the time I finally got caught. Addiction makes villains even out of good people, and I was never a moral beacon in the first place.

There's a reason I keep this shit a secret from people I've just met.

"We're friends," Ophelia says. "That's what friends are for."

A flush of heat blooms in my chest. Maybe I should be humiliated that I'm so easy to please. But ever since what happened with Chaya and me, I've felt like . . . well, like the person who's always lurking at the fringes of social groups, *there* but not really there. Just an annoying leech hanging on by its teeth.

But Ophelia called me her friend. And that's pretty much enough to make me ride or die for her.

I smile, the first real smile of the night. "Thanks. You're . . . a very kind person, you know that?"

"It's basic human decency," Ophelia says, "but I appreciate the sentiment all the same."

I look out past the confines of the microworld that is our fire escape, at the yellow window light of the apartments across the street. One apartment has a plant on a windowsill. Next door, a man passes into an adjoining room, and the lamp switches off, casting the scene into darkness. That's one thing I missed about New York. All these people—all these *lives,* each with its own story, its own history and hopes and fears. Millions of people in this city living in their own social webs, silver threads connecting them to friends, lovers, sisters. The tenuous, fragile thread that connects them to me, in this moment where our stories intersect before we depart in our own separate directions.

Makes you feel small. A tiny plankton in a massive ocean teeming with life. Your own problems become small, too.

"How much longer did you say you have on the revised deadline for your illustrations again?" I ask, looking back at Ophelia, who is now sitting cross-legged and barefoot, her pink kitten heels discarded by the window next to my camera bag. "Like . . . two weeks?"

"I wish." Ophelia makes a face. "Try six days. I'm starting to think I'm not cut out for this career. Maybe the stereotype about artists ethereally floating around waiting to be kissed by a muse is valid. Maybe I'm not supposed to work under deadlines."

"I'm pretty sure that's something artists made up so no one will blame us for procrastinating."

"Ugh, shut up. Only say things I want to hear."

I laugh and she laughs back, but it sounds fake.

I might not understand the design industry, but I can understand this: The drive for perfection. The inability to ever let anything be *done*. "This isn't the final product," I say after a moment, as gently as I can. "You still get to work on the actual label. And you'll have plenty of time to do revisions on that."

"I know," she says with a heavy sigh. "I've just put so much time and effort into this project now. And if they don't like it, then I'm back to square one. I've wasted my own time."

"You haven't. You've learned so much from this process already. Think about it—think about all the revisions you've made, the way your eye has gotten keener, how much your vision and technique have developed while you've been working on these samples. You're a good artist. What you've shown me so far is incredible. You just have to get out of your own head and finish the project, no matter what your inner critic has to say about it."

"Yeah," she says. "Maybe."

She doesn't believe me, of course. I don't know why she would; I've been pretty up-front about knowing precisely zero about design work. But Ophelia's a good illustrator. As little as I might know about this kind of art, I can tell that much.

"Art's subjective, anyway," I say. "When you go to most gallery shows, there's a ton of work on display that you're like, *Why would anyone pay hundreds of thousands of dollars for this?* But they do. And there's plenty of art that never got past the gatekeepers that's incredible, and those artists are still out there waiting for the right person to notice them." *Hello, meet yours truly.* "In art you're constantly fighting to convince people your voice is worth listening to in the first place. But you've already done that. You already *won*. You got the gig; the gin people want you. You're so close."

I wonder if it's stupid to even be telling her this, like Ophelia doesn't freaking know. But she finally gives me the first tiny, real smile I've seen since we left the apartment. And—*fuck it*—I reach over and grab her hand, squeezing tight.

"Yeah," she says. "You're right. And maybe that's what's so scary about it. I have that much further to fall."

She's not wrong. Even so, I wonder if she realizes how lucky she is. So many people would kill to be in her position. Yeah, she has a lot to lose, but at least she isn't starting from zero. At least she has some kind of legitimacy in the field. I might have gotten my work into a few shows in LA, but I'm still very definitely an amateur. I'm constantly, unforgettably aware that I'm just two steps up from being back on the Venice Beach boardwalk trying to sell my work to tourists who veer away from me as if I'm visibly diseased.

Maybe some of that shows on my face, because Ophelia twists hers up and says, "I'm sorry. I shouldn't be talking like this. Like, please, I literally won, so why am I over here bitching about how hard it is to be in the spotlight? And you're already going through some shit tonight. Jesus. I didn't mean to make this all about me."

I roll my eyes. "You're allowed to feel what you feel. It's not like you stop being human or having emotions just because you're successful." After a beat, I go on. "Anyway, it's going to be amazing. They're lucky to have you."

"You better be right," Ophelia says, "because if you give me false hope, I'm coming for you."

I grin. And somehow, sitting out here on this humid night with Ophelia's hand still wrapped around mine, I feel like I've put down something heavy that I didn't even realize I was carrying.

I feel like maybe I'm not so alone, after all.

13

WYATT

I wake up Saturday morning to a text from Ely.

It takes me a second to recover from the shock. Obviously, she's texted me before. She texted me literally last night. And yet I still manage to be surprised that she reached out again—and in the middle of the night, according to the time stamp on the text.

ELY: well, I survived. Nobody relapsed, nobody died

I sit there with my thumbs hovering over my phone keyboard. Even though it's too late now, especially considering I talked her off a ledge last night and I probably have some moral obligation to continue the conversation at this point, some brutally scrupulous part of me thinks I still shouldn't respond. Last night was one thing. Last night, that was urgent—that was excusable. She'd needed me.

Am I even allowed to text back right now?

Am I allowed *not* to?

ELY: Still feeling like a piece of shit tbh. Probably shouldn't have gone to a party in the first place

ME: Do you want to talk about it? I'm free this afternoon.

As soon as I hit Send, I wish I could take the message back.

My brain is screaming at me that the line is all the way the fuck back there and I just careened across it. Because I have zero self-control. Because I can't stick to a vow I make to myself for longer than thirty seconds. How hard would it have been to type back something sympathetic and encouraging and end the conversation there?

But on the other hand . . .

On the other hand, she's only here for a summer. And I can't watch another addict suffer and say nothing.

I stare at the three little dots that pop up as Ely's typing, then disappear, then reappear again. It feels like it takes ten interminable minutes, although it's probably more like twenty seconds, before she replies.

ELY: Sure. On campus?

ME: Let's meet at the Met. There's an exhibit there that I think might inspire you.

Of course, making plans for this afternoon means I now have half a day to sit around waiting for the hours to pass. And it's not like I don't have work to do. The anticipation simply consumes any ability I would have had to actually *do* said work. All I can think about is—alternately—how much I'm looking forward to seeing her again and how stupid it was to suggest another one-on-one off-campus hangout in the first place.

I end up leaving my apartment fifteen minutes earlier than I actually need to according to Google Maps. I text Ely once I'm at the museum and buy a hot dog from one of the carts parked on the sidewalk out front. *Oral fixation,* I can hear Ava joke in my head. What can I say? I eat when I'm anxious.

So obviously Ely shows up while I'm still cramming hot dog into my face. I scramble to wipe mustard off my fingers and push up to my feet. She's wearing a dress with thin straps, the kind that shows off the sharp angle of her shoulders and the slope of her collarbones. I remember grazing kisses along those collarbones, the salty taste of her skin against my tongue.

Focus.

"Glad you could make it," I say.

She smiles, squinting slightly against the sunlight. "Wouldn't miss it for the world. I'm desperate enough for inspiration I'd take it from the back of a cereal box at this point."

God, I wish I was that good at banter. I'd kill for something witty and charming to say in response.

I'm not sure if I'm supposed to bring up the party thing or if she will. But probably better to keep my mouth shut and let her drive the conversation.

"I can't help on the cereal box front, but I think you'll like this exhibit. I saw it last week." With Ava, who as it turned out was best friends with the artist, which meant we got a personal tour complete with the artist's own commentary on each piece.

The exhibit itself highlights the work of an Afghan artist based in Atlanta. It features elegant calligraphy on canvases that all but consume the walls they're placed on. The lettering stands out against splattered paint, or smeared charcoal, or pitch-black ink. In one case the calligraphy is stitched, not painted, a mosaic masterpiece of gold filament.

We draw closer, as close as the exhibition will allow. And when you're this near, close enough to see the brushstrokes, you can see that it isn't merely calligraphy that's painted on. The lettering is constructed of tiny scenes: a miniature crowd of people, faceless; a population of millions making up the fabric of an image that only seems uniform from far away.

I want to ask Ely what she thinks, but I bite back the words. I know better than to poison this with conversation. Those first few minutes absorbing a work of art are vital, and they're ones you can't get back. Instead I study her: the way her dark eyes roam the paintings, the slight part of her lips as she peers closer. Her hair falls forward and obscures her profile, a veil of molasses waves.

"What do you think?" I ask, after we've circled the perimeter of the room and she's seen every piece. We've settled on one of the benches in front of Ely's favorite, both of us gazing at a magnificent work of art.

"It's incredible," she says, and I can't suppress the flash of vindication that sparks in my chest at that—the same feeling you get when you recommend a book to someone and they end up liking it. "I know what I read into it, in terms of meaning, but you can also tell that it's not *for* me. And I'll never really understand the nuances of everything the artist is saying, because I'm not Muslim. It's just a small window into a conversation."

There's something faraway about the look on her face as she says it, and I know where her mind is going. She's already thinking about the things she might want to say with her own work: to everyone but also to Jewish people in particular. The way art can say one thing to the world and something else to a community, if you know the right language.

I have the sudden, overwhelming urge to reach out and touch her—as if physical contact could be the key to inspiration. It's not, of course; it's just the closeness of our bodies on this bench getting the better of me. But I still shift my position and brace one hand against the bench between us so that my fifth finger grazes her thigh.

I can tell it affects her as much as it does me. She shivers slightly, her lips parting as she lets out a soft exhale.

"Are you doing okay?" I say at last, once it becomes clear she isn't going to bring up last night on her own. "When you texted me . . . We don't have to talk about it if you don't want to. But I figured I'd ask."

She sighs and stares down at her hands, twisting her fingers together. "It was stupid. I never should have gone."

I shrug. "Sometimes that's true. Sometimes that's what you learn from things like this—that there are situations you can't put yourself in. Or not, at least, until you have the tools to handle them."

"I can't avoid parties forever."

I raise a brow. "Actually, from personal experience, you can *absolutely* become a hermit and avoid all forms of social interaction indefinitely."

She makes a face at me, but she's grinning all the same. "Oh, please. Like you weren't a little social butterfly at that gore-fest gallery show. All wit and suave seltzer-serving."

"With *you,*" I say. "You in particular."

I can't take the words back once I've said them, so I have to sit here and watch her arch one brow, her lipsticked mouth curving into a smile.

Change the subject change the subject change the subject—

"I have a book I'd like to show you," I find myself saying. "What are you doing next week? I can bring it to you."

Ely whips her head around to look at me so damn fast it'd be comical if I didn't feel like I was already on tenterhooks, leaning in toward her, *hoping*.

"Yes," she says almost immediately. "Definitely. I mean . . . yes. I'll be around. We could get coffee after lunch on Monday?"

"Sure. It's a date." *Oops. Shit. Fuck.* "I mean—"

Ely's already grinning so broadly I can't take it back now. She's got to know what I really mean, anyway.

What the hell do you think you're on right now, Cole?

Ely seems to be thinking the same thing, because she nudges her shoulder against mine. A second point of contact, her body heat warming my side. She could shift only slightly, and her thigh would rub against mine. She could reach down and lace our fingers together, perhaps guide my hand to her knee.

I've gotta pull back on this. I need to have some kind of control over myself.

But looking at her, my breath catches in my chest. From this distance I can see the tiny imperfections—the start of fine lines at the corners of her eyes, the pores, the couple of eyebrow hairs she forgot to pluck. It feels intimate. I feel lucky, in a way, to be allowed to see her so plainly. From farther away, I would have said she looked perfect.

This close, she is even more so.

I drag my gaze away, refocusing on the painting across from us in a fierce determination to pull myself the fuck together.

My goal in bringing her here was to get her to think differently about her art, and I accomplished that much.

But if I hoped today would be different—that I'd be able to look at Ely Cohen and see a student, a protégé, and nothing more—well. Judging from the low electric thrum that shimmers beneath my skin when she smiles, when she touches my arm in gratitude . . .

I've failed miserably.

On Sunday, I go to a meeting.

It's the same crew, same faces, I've been seeing every year for the past decade. I've got every one of their stories written on my heart. Even with the people I don't like, it feels like love. Sure, maybe the whole twelve-step thing doesn't really feel like it's for me, but the friendships do.

"Hey, man," Marcus says after the close of meeting, as we're all crowding around the refreshments table trying to steal the last dregs of coffee. "Want to go grab some pancakes or something? I missed dinner."

"Breakfast at nine P.M.? You know me, I'm always down for that."

Our favorite spot is four blocks away, which is a long walk when you're starving but too short when you're walking with a friend. The place is one of those dive diners that has been around forever. The pancakes are kind of shitty, and the coffee is burnt, but for Marcus and me, it's a bit of a tradition.

The best booth is taken, so we settle in toward the back, Marcus all stretched out with his long legs angled toward one side so they don't bump against mine under the table.

"So, tell me," he says. "How have things been? Like . . . for real. Because I know you always hold back in meetings."

From anyone else, that would come across as a scold. From Marcus, it's just a statement of fact.

"It's been an adjustment," I admit. "Busy."

"I bet. I mean, it's been a while since you've had a job with an inflexible work schedule, right? Sounds like that'd be a rough change."

"Easier than you'd think, really. Or maybe I just like the structure. I had worried I'd be less productive if I had to teach classes and grade projects, but if anything, I'm getting more work done. It's like I take my free time more seriously now."

Marcus shrugs. "We expand to fill the time that we have," he says. "Or that's what Ji told me, anyway. Feels like it might be a thing."

I just hope I can keep it up for the rest of the semester and the following school year. I'm also well aware that I tend to distrust good things that happen to me; I'm always waiting for the other shoe to drop. If things go too well, at some point my brain will sabotage me. So . . . we'll see how long this burst of productivity actually lasts.

"What about the girl?" he asks. I should have known Marcus wouldn't avoid that subject for long. I bet he's been sitting on it all week, only just keeping himself from texting me about it. Probably because he doesn't want to feel like a gossip.

And suddenly, of course, I can't look Marcus in the eye anymore. Downside to being friends with someone for nine years:

You start to actually care what they think about you. And I don't want Marcus to hear what I'm about to say and hate me for it. I knew he'd ask eventually, so I've run through this conversation so many times in my head. Half the time he's sympathetic but firm, reminding me of my responsibilities, the precariousness of my sobriety—even after this long. The other half the time he's so disgusted he can't even look at me.

Even imaginary Marcus's disappointment stings.

But I have to suck it up, because what's the point of friends—or recovery, even—if you aren't being honest? So I tell him about Ely. About this joke the universe is playing on us, like something out of one of those YouTube prank videos where any second a guy in a backward baseball cap is gonna jump out from behind the bushes and yell, *Gotcha!*

"Seems like you've only spoken to this girl a few times," Marcus says once I'm finally done. "How do you know she's even worth the risk?"

It's a fair question, and it's not like I haven't asked myself the same thing more than once—usually while I'm lying in bed awake at night running through the laundry list of my personal failures and reliving the most embarrassing moments of my life.

"I guess I don't," I say. "Not really. But we click, you know? There's just something about her. Maybe it's the fact that we're both sober, or both photographers. Maybe it's just her vibe. I can't explain it. When we're talking, it's like the whole rest of the world falls away. And I like who *I* am around her. She makes me . . . funnier. Kinder. I feel like a more complete person, or at least like she sees something in me that I want to nurture. I want to be the person she thinks I am."

Marcus gives me a considering look just in time for the waitress to return with our coffees. He takes a long sip, watching me over the rim of his cup. "And what is the worst possible outcome that could happen here? What are you most afraid of happening?"

"It goes badly," I say immediately. "We don't work out, and we risk both our careers, not to mention our sobriety."

"I think you're catastrophizing, bud. Plus it sounds like she's the one who's pushing for more involvement, not you."

"I mean . . . yeah. With her project. She wants my help."

"And you agreed to give it to her. You're both grown-ups here."

I shrug. "I guess I'm not sure which is worse: continuing some kind of professional relationship with her after what happened or punishing her by refusing to teach her when half of why she came to Parker was to study with me."

And this is exactly why they say not to get into relationships with students. This exact kind of predicament. Because no matter what I choose, I'm choosing badly.

"Maybe there's not a best choice," Marcus says. "She's only here for the summer program, right? It's hard to imagine how you could mess up her career so badly in a single summer just by helping her out with an art project. And you said she's been clean for four years. It's not like she's some newbie with a one-month chip hunting for validation. You know, some might argue that being with another person in recovery is the best move. You can build each other up, not tear each other down."

It's so different from what I thought he'd say that I blink twice in quick succession and sit back in my chair, turning his words over in my head. It's also pretty much the opposite of the feedback I got from the other guys in NA, which I fully expected Marcus to echo tonight. Isn't that what sponsors are supposed to do—tell you to get your baser impulses in order and control yourself?

"I guess. . . ." I say.

"It sounds like you don't believe me."

"No," I say quickly. "No, I do; I get what you're saying. And maybe you're right. It doesn't have to go beyond that. But . . . yeah. Yeah."

Wow, Wyatt. Great conversational skills. Really a pro there.

"If it *did* go beyond that, it'd be okay, you know. No one's gonna smite you."

I'm not 100 percent sure I believe that. But maybe that's paranoia. Or fear of fucking up somehow, of turning into one of those assholes like my father, who used people and then threw them away. Who prioritized his own wants over everything and everyone else.

I've spent my whole life trying to get away from that shit. I've built everything I am today from the ground up—from underground. I've come so far. I've got walls, and they're fucking *great* walls.

I don't want to risk anything that might compromise them.

"It's such a cliché, isn't it?" I mutter at last, after the silence has stretched on long enough for Marcus to take two more gulps of his coffee. "Guy with childhood trauma fears meaningful relationships because he's afraid of turning out like villain dad. That's pretty much me."

Marcus has the grace to look sympathetic. "You talked to your brother lately?"

I snort. "You ask me that every time we hang out. Answer's still *no*."

"Be honest," Marcus says. "You're still stalking his social media."

"Shut up."

"I know you do."

He's not wrong, to my great humiliation. I've spent way too many nights scrolling through Liam's page from my dummy account—the one with no name and no profile pic. Liam's still in North Carolina. Different town, same state. Married now. He seems . . . happy.

Just looking at that makes me angry.

It's not fair that Liam should get to go on and have a normal life—find himself a cute blond debutante, get married, white picket fence with two perfect kids, fucking . . . fucking seashell collecting on the beach with his gorgeous wife. The bitter core of me thinks he ought to have been cosmically punished somehow. I'm not sure why I think that. Liam never did anything to me. He didn't bully me. He wasn't cruel. He wasn't even home the night my father lost his shit and kicked me out for good.

So why do I want him to suffer so damn badly?

Jealous, a voice murmurs in the back of my mind. I shove it down.

But isn't it true? Liam's living the life I might have lived if I'd been born a cis guy. Watching him is like watching a sneak peek at some alternate-universe version of my life. Where I never got hooked on dope. Where my family actually loved me and wanted me around.

Liam got it all. He won.

"You don't always have to compare yourself to him," Marcus says, more gently than I would have said it to myself.

"Yeah, right," I mutter.

"It's not a competition."

But it is, of course. The competition started the day we were born, a screaming, red-faced supposed girl and a chubby monster of a baby boy. It continued every day after that, the pair of us dressed in our cute matching twin outfits: pink and blue, hair bow and bow tie. Ballet versus soccer. Etiquette lessons from my grandmother, but *boys will be boys.*

Yeah, it's a competition. And my brother's been winning from the start.

14

ELY

Sunday, I take my camera into Manhattan.

In the late afternoon the light is perfect, golden and filtering down between the buildings like molten amber. I walk through Greenwich Village, all the winding streets I used to explore in secret. Not because the Village was in any way forbidden to Chabad kids, but because I worried that if anyone saw me here, they might see the truth—that I belonged here, in front of Stonewall kissing a girl with glitter in her hair, far more than I had ever belonged in Crown Heights.

I trail my fingers along a wrought-iron fence and turn my face toward the sky, toward the silhouettes of the rooftops against blue. I take a photo of a man on a balcony leaning against the railing with a cigarette dangling from his fingertips. He's in a white shirt, barefoot; another man behind him slides a hand up his spine and kisses the nape of his neck.

I capture that moment, just as I capture the girl in the bubblegum-colored dress smiling at her phone as she nearly walks into traffic; the children coloring with chalk on the corner, tracing rainbows into concrete; the tattooed old woman on a café patio scowling at the newspaper and tearing her croissant to pieces.

This is the kind of day I used to dream about back when I was a teen. Nowhere to be, no one expecting me home. Just me and my camera and the city opening up before me like a map.

I'll see Wyatt tomorrow. But this space stretching out between yesterday and then feels infinite. I wish I had just texted him and asked him to meet me today too. Then again, that probably wouldn't be fair considering he lives all the way out in Bushwick.

But it'd be nice to stroll by his side, his warm hand finding mine and his low voice narrating the architecture around us—because in this fantasy world, of course Wyatt knows about architecture. Knowing about architecture is hot.

I wander out of the West Village and head east, meandering past NYU and Parker—apparently I can never stay that far away, as if the school has its own magnetic pull—with no particular destination in mind. At least, not consciously. But when I find myself on Broadway staring up at the red flag of the Strand Book Store, I know exactly why I'm here.

My mother and I had this tradition. We used to come here together every Sunday afternoon, after I got out of my Bnos Menachem weekend classes. She'd give me a crisp twenty-dollar bill and tell me I could buy whatever I liked. Naturally, I tended to treat the Strand more like a library than a store—I'd spend hours curled up in a corner reading until my mother would finally come get me, her own books in one of those plastic baskets slung over her arm, and make me pay for the book instead of devouring it for free.

It didn't occur to me as a child, but it occurs to me now how impressive my mother was. How much love she had—how even with all those children she would still carve out time to spend with each of us. Me and the bookstore, Dvora and her obsession with geology. My mother had whole universes she built with each of us, castles that belonged to Ima and me alone.

The sense memory of being here punches right into my gut. And all at once I'm twelve years old again, effervescent with excitement, mind jumbling between options: Will I get another fantasy? A romance? Or maybe one of those photography books with glossy pages and an editor's interpretation of each picture's meaning typed in clean Baskerville font.

I can't help myself, of course; I go in.

From the moment you enter the Strand, it's overwhelming. The ground floor doesn't just have more books than anyone could read in a lifetime. It also has T-shirts and postcards and tote bags and stickers and enamel pins and all other kinds of nonsense that no one actually needs but that you'll still drop a cool fifteen bucks on. There are more rooms upstairs: young adult, art, nonfiction, rare books. But I like the stacks in the back of the first floor, where they keep all the used books. I like the way they feel in my hands, like old paper wilted by spilled tea. I like finding the little scribbled notes in the margins. All evidence of books well read and well loved.

I choose an aisle at random and peruse the spines. There's a ragged copy of *Sabriel* by Garth Nix that I find hard to resist. When I open to the title page, I see that someone has written: *Property of Dara Shirazi, return to owner.* I bury my nose in the open pages and breathe in; it smells like cigarettes and someone else's life.

I'm tempted to buy it, but I don't really have room in my tiny coat closet of a bedroom. So I return the book to the shelf and move down the rest of the aisle and into the next. That's where I suddenly stop short, all the air crushed from my lungs.

It might have been nearly a decade, but I'd still recognize her anywhere. The knowledge is stitched into my blood and bone.

My mother looks the same at fifty as she looked in her early thirties. She even wears the same sheitel, a straight-haired wig that is modestly cut just below her chin.

Even as quickly as I turn my back, hiding my face, I can't help worrying that she saw me.

And if she saw me . . .

If she saw me, would she even say anything? Or would she turn and walk briskly away, as if I were nothing and no one—as if I were anyone but the little girl who sat next to her other children at Passover, eating matzo and getting crumbs all over the floor? She loved me once upon a time, back when I was just a chubby thing making friendship bracelets with Chaya Mushka Levy and reciting my prayers in a thin, high-pitched child voice. Then, of course, it all went wrong. If she doesn't recognize the face of her little girl, she will certainly recognize the teenager I became. The heretic daughter who dragged that sweet, innocent version of her little girl off the derech. The teenager she used to find nodding off over her half-finished homework. Who stole money from her mother's purse and, when she got caught, screamed at everyone and threatened to slit her own throat with a kitchen knife if anyone tried to take the heroin she held crushed in her fist.

I can't stay here.

I slip out of the aisle and dart through the stacks, heading for the front door so fast I half worry someone will stop me and accuse me of stealing. When I burst out onto the sidewalk, it feels like I'm finally able to take a breath after being trapped underwater. I grab on to one of the used-book carts out front and hold on for balance as I try to exhale, exhale, *just relax.*

But the memories are too thick, too hot. They rise up like magma. They overtake me.

NINE YEARS AGO

Rosh Hashanah was, to me, the pinnacle of fall.

Maybe in the rest of the city, fall was pumpkin spice lattes and UGG boots and tossing leaves in the air in Central Park, but for me it was cleaning honey off my sisters' sticky faces and the crisp bite of a Gala apple and the sound of the shofar blowing. My mother would make honey cake that filled the air of our apartment with a rich scent that clung to your hair and coat. School was out and so the streets were full of kids running wild, shrieking as they darted between the more orderly sidewalk procession of scholars and strollers.

Chaya was over again, hiding from her father, who always got in a bad mood around the High Holidays. We'd taken some Percocets up in my bedroom and were sitting down at the kitchen table slicing apples for my mother and fighting not to nod off. I cut too hard at my apple and the knife grazed my thumb instead, spraying a little bouquet of blood across my skin.

"Whoops," I mumbled, and Chaya giggled as I stuck my thumb in my mouth to suck it clean.

My sister Dvora glared at us from across the table, where she was elbow-deep kneading challah dough. Always a bucket of cold water, Dvora was. Chaya and I couldn't even enjoy our secret without Dvora there to remind us that the things we did in private weren't that secret at all.

"Has anyone seen Bubbe's pearls?"

My mother had appeared in the kitchen doorway, half-dressed for that night's Erev Rosh Hashanah festivities. Her hair was covered by a messily tied tichel, not the shiny wig she would typically wear around guests like Chaya.

My stomach immediately twisted in on itself. Because, yes, I'd seen Bubbe's pearls. I'd last seen them on the pawnbroker's glass counter as he peered at them through a loupe to examine their quality. That $400 had gone to financing the Percocet swimming in my and Chaya's veins.

I dropped my gaze to my apples, but too late; I'd already caught the accusatory glance Dvora had sent my way. Even Chaya shifted uncomfortably in her seat. Because it was that obvious where Bubbe's pearls had ended up.

"I haven't seen them," said Malka. "Have you asked Abba? He might have taken them to get cleaned."

Thank Hashem for Malka and her naïveté. The truth hadn't even occurred to her. I guess she still saw me as a child, too innocent to do any intentional wrong. The four years between us might as well have been an ocean.

"I haven't seen them either. What about you, Ely?" Dvora might not have been willing to outright turn me in, but apparently she wasn't above twisting the knife.

I shook my head and reached for a fresh apple. It was difficult to feel guilt, or shame, or any negative emotion really on opiates—but right then, somehow, I managed it.

I jumped at the first opportunity to get out of the apartment that afternoon, insisting that I walk Chaya Mushka back to her house, even though the Levys lived just two blocks over. Chaya nudged me with her elbow as soon as we were out in the chilly late-September air, her brows knotted together. "You did it, right?"

"Obviously. Shit. I really hope they haven't sold yet."

"And you're planning to buy them back with what money?" Chaya said, lowering her voice to a whisper as we passed too near a woman carrying groceries—anyone in this neighborhood was likely to be a gossip, given the opportunity. "Pretty sure we snorted all of it."

She was right, of course. "What am I supposed to do? I have to try. I can beg him for mercy. I'll promise to pay him back with interest in two weeks. It's a holiday."

"Like that goyish pawnbroker gives a shit. It's a random day in

September for him, Ely. And he has a freaking job. He can't just *give* you your grandma's pearls back and trust your word."

Right again. Particularly since it wasn't like my word was worth much. "Fuck," I muttered, and beside me Chaya just sighed.

I considered it, of course. I entertained the idea of just . . . stealing the $400 out of Chaya's dad's wallet. He always kept it in his coat pocket, hung up on the rack next to the front door. It would have been easy. Chaya took money from there all the time.

But I also knew what he'd do to Chaya once he realized the cash was gone, and I couldn't justify being responsible for those bruises. Not even for my grandmother's pearl necklace.

My brain drew the stupidest ethical lines sometimes. Because if I were such a good fucking person, I wouldn't have stolen the pearls to start with. Even when Chaya stole the money from her dad herself, it was still my fault, ultimately.

After all, I was the one who'd dragged Chaya down into this hell in the first place.

15

As promised, Wyatt finds me in one of the common areas Monday right after lunch, sliding into the seat across from mine and handing me a coffee.

I raise my brows. "For me?"

"They're free in the faculty lounge. Hope you like doughnut shop blend."

It tastes burnt, like most of those coffees brewed in the little pods, but it's the first caffeine I've had all day, so I gulp it down all the same. "I feel special."

"You should. I only steal coffee for people I like."

"I thought you said it was *free* coffee."

"There's a little sign on the dispenser that says, *For faculty and staff use only*."

"Oh, well, in that case." I finish off the cup. Probably the best worst coffee I've had in my life. "Slumming it with the students today?"

Wyatt makes a face, one that looks almost pained. "You aren't my student."

"Technically," I say.

"Technically."

Wyatt shifts in his chair, tugging out his satchel from where it was stuck behind him. "I brought something for you," he says, and passes me a book.

I glance down at the cover, which is still glossy, even if the spine shows the familiar cracks of being well loved. *Hannah Wilke: A Retrospective.* "I love Hannah Wilke," I murmur, flipping past the cover and front matter to get to my favorite set of photographs, stills from Wilke's *Intercourse With . . .* film piece, in which the viewer listens to recordings meant for Wilke from her answering machine before Wilke reveals her nude self covered in the names of the message leavers and slowly, methodically strips the names from her skin.

Her work was so focused on the self, almost a commentary on societal attitudes about female vanity. Narcissistic, the way people say selfie culture is, but a sort of feminist reclamation of the sin: a fierce and unrelenting presentation of herself, her presence in the world, her own ambition. She continued to document her body even as it deteriorated before her death from lymphoma in the early nineties.

"If you want to study mixed media, there's no better place to start," Wyatt says. "Wilke was a genius. Not just with photography and film, but watercolor, sculpture. . . . She pushes boundaries, but I figured you would like that."

He's right. Hannah Wilke's the kind of artist that makes me feel like I don't have any excuses. I mean, she made sculptures out of *chewing gum,* for fuck's sake, and said it was a metaphor for how we as a culture treat women. Meanwhile, I get pissy if I don't have the right lens cleaner for my camera.

I let the pages riffle against my thumb, back to the title page, then pause. The book is signed. The book is freaking *signed.*

"Where did you get this?" I gasp.

Wyatt laughs. "Um . . . my apartment?"

"No, I mean . . . you met her?"

He scrubs a hand back through his hair. The ultimate effect is like a sudden punch to the throat: He looks just how he did back at Revel. Messy around the edges, like a good man who will ruin you. I swallow hard and look back down at the book, at Hannah Wilke's signature in black ink.

"How old do you think I am?" he says. "I was a toddler when Wilke died, so no, I haven't met her." *Oh.* Right. Obviously. "It was a gift."

"Some gift," I say.

He blows out a heavy breath, half a laugh. "Yeah. No shit. Wish I knew who it was from."

Both my brows go up. "For real? Someone sent you a signed Hannah Wilke book and didn't even include a greeting card?"

"I didn't believe it myself. It arrived shortly after I moved here, to New York. No return address. I almost thought . . ." He trails off and I wait in silence, letting the seconds stretch out until he shakes his head and forces himself to finish. "I could tell it was sent from North Carolina, though. I've talked about liking Wilke in interviews. . . . But there's no way the book came from her."

"From . . . ?"

He swallows visibly. "My mother."

He talks like he hasn't spoken to his mom in years. Or like she's dead. I don't know how to respond. I don't know what would be right here.

"Why not?" I say eventually. "Did you ever ask?"

I do in fact regret the question as soon as it's out of my mouth because it's clear from the way Wyatt's lips twist that he doesn't want to talk about it. Too late now, though. My mouth is faster than my brain.

"Sorry," I say. "You don't have to answer that. I—"

"It's okay. I just don't talk to my mom much. Or . . . at all." He rubs both palms against his thighs, then grips his knees, fingertips digging into the denim of his jeans. At last, he manages a grim smile. “My family didn’t want much to do with me after I came out.”

The admission hits me like a bullet to the chest. Wyatt isn’t meeting my gaze, and I know why. I know that feeling too well—the sickly blend of shame and anger, even after all these years still not being sure who to blame more: them or yourself. The deadly undercurrent of hope that one day, just maybe, they might change their minds and come back for you.

“Shit,” I whisper. “Wyatt, I’m so sorry. I shouldn’t have asked. We don’t have to talk about it if you don’t want.”

But he shakes his head, and I swear I can see the exact moment he pulls bravado over himself like a coat—slim protection against the cold. He looks at me again, at least. “No. I’m not the one who ought to be embarrassed. Honestly, even now I’m not sure if it was being trans that did it, or the fact I got kicked out of the military when my commanding officer found out. My dad was a marine too. I think that was the only reason he was ever proud of me. I might have been a good-for-nothing girl, in his mind, but *Semper fi* or what the fuck ever.”

I sit there on that sofa, trying my best to process what Wyatt just said. It’s similar to how I used to feel in shul when we talked about G-d, like I was trying to comprehend something that defied comprehension.

“I didn’t know you were in the Marines” is what I end up saying.

Wyatt shrugs. “It was kind of the only option in my town. Nobody in my family had ever gone to college—hell, some of us never graduated high school. Where I grew up, there weren’t that many options for kids like me. And since my granddad served, and my dad, my aunt, all my cousins . . . Even my brother was planning to enlist. It just seemed like the best choice. Besides, at least if you joined the military, you could see the world, make something of yourself. I thought maybe I could be happy—like maybe if I was a girl in the Marines, I wouldn't mind the whole *girl* part. Idiotic, I know."

"That's not idiotic. You made the best decision you could with the options you had."

He arches a brow. "Is joining the US military ever a good decision?"

"I don't know. You would know that better than me."

He gives me one of those looks that say, *You aren't gonna trick me into talking about politics.* I'm only too familiar with it; it's the same look my sister used to give me across the dinner table every time I tried to rile my parents up. A feat that was usually disappointingly easy to accomplish.

"Well, I guess that's another thing we have in common," I mutter. "Both our families fucking hate us."

That earns me a laugh, which feels like a step up from bitter smiles, even if Wyatt quickly hides it behind a sip of his coffee.

"How did you get into photography anyway?" I ask after a beat. I don't want to let this conversation shrivel up and die, not after I just got Wyatt to talk to me properly. To talk to me like a friend, not like a student.

He makes an ambivalent gesture. "It was kind of a slow evolution, I guess. I was having issues with drinking already, and that turned into . . . well, you know. I don't have to tell you the kinds of shitty things you'll do to get a fix. A buddy and I held up a tourist one night who'd stayed out on the boardwalk a little too late. I'd like to say it wasn't my idea, but I'd be lying. We just wanted the cash. Took it straight to my guy and spent the rest of the night nodding off on my friend's ratty old couch."

He keeps searching my face, no doubt looking for the reaction we always expect: disgust, revulsion, disappointment. The same emotions we usually see painted over everyone's faces when we confess our darkest moments—the stolen credit cards, the used needles, the blow jobs in back alleys that you swore you'd never trade for dope until you did.

I hope he doesn't find any of that there when he looks at me.

I hope he knows how deeply I understand.

"Anyway, one of the things we grabbed off him was a camera. Nothing super fancy, just your basic tourist Canon. We could have gotten decent cash for it at a pawnshop, but I started messing around with it. Taking pictures of my friends at first, but then it was more. Fishing boats heading out of the harbor at dawn, the cats roaming around the herb garden belonging to that crazy lady who took in fifty strays, the sun going down over the trash littering one of the beaches that isn't all cleaned up for tourists. Nothing super artistic, but I liked it. It made my world feel just a little more permanent, you know? As if life wasn't just crawling from one fix to the next. As if there were beautiful things, if you knew how to look."

There's a soft smile on his face, small enough that I'm not sure he even realizes it's there. For a second he looks across the room, unfocused, like he's gazing off into the past.

"Of course," he adds a second later, "I ended up pawning that camera after all and spending the money on dope. But the seed was there. And after I got out of detox I got a cheap phone and started taking pictures again. Once I'd moved to New York and could afford it, I bought a camera of my own." He clears his throat and shakes his head, like he's trying to get fog to clear. "Anyway. I didn't mean to get all . . . Sorry. We were talking about you."

"I don't mind," I tell him honestly. "I like to hear about you."

He avoids looking at me, staring at one of the pieces of student art hanging on the wall opposite instead.

I press stubbornly on. "Listen, I was thinking I might try again and go to that Shabbos dinner thing this Friday night, with

Michal. I think if someone came with me, I might stick to the plan this time. So . . . maybe you want to come with me?"

He's still staring at the student art even though I'm 90 percent sure he isn't really seeing it. No doubt he's ruminating on all the reasons he should say no. But when he opens his mouth, something else comes out.

"Sure. Yeah. That sounds fun."

And just like that, it's a date.

Sort of.

16

Friday comes too quickly and yet, at the same time, not quickly enough. It's like the universe can't decide if I'm more nervous or excited—because as much as I dread the dinner itself, I can't stop thinking about Wyatt. Who said yes. Who is going with me. On our sort-of date.

It's not really a date, of course. This dinner falls well within the purview of *instructional content*—I'm only going for my capstone project, which Wyatt is helping me plan. And because Michal invited me. So I probably shouldn't be reading too much into things.

I'm definitely reading too much into things.

Michal, when I tell her I'm coming, lights up immediately. "You're going to love it," she says, already flipping through her notebook to find a scrap of paper, scribbling down the address. "We have a really good group of people. Everyone will be so excited to meet you."

I'm not so convinced.

"Um . . . listen," I force myself to say because not saying would be a dick move, "I kind of invited Wyatt Cole. Is that okay?"

Both Michal's eyebrows shoot up. "Like my professor Wyatt Cole?"

Ugh, die now. "That's the one."

She barks out a laugh, and instead of rescinding the invitation as I expect, she goes, "I mean, yeah. Bring him. I'm definitely not saying no to feeding challah to Wyatt Cole. He seems like he'd be fun once he got the stick out of his backside."

I mean. She isn't wrong.

"And is it okay if I take pictures?" I ask. "I'm doing my capstone project on different spiritual paths within Judaism and—"

She doesn't even let me finish. "Yes, of course! That sounds like an amazing project. We'd be thrilled."

So I guess that's that, then.

My last class of the day ends at six, which is almost but not quite early enough for me to make it back to Astoria, get changed, put on makeup, and then fight either traffic in an Uber or the absolute mess of train transfers required to get from Queens to Brooklyn before sundown. I'd just stuffed a black dress and some Glossier in the pit of my backpack and hoped for the best.

But as I'm swiping mascara onto my eyelashes in the fluorescent light of the Parker bathroom, I'm not really sure why I'm so concerned. I don't think anyone at this dinner will care what I look like. Michal's seen me looking worse. And Wyatt . . . well, I might care what he thinks, but he's seen me in a variety of humiliating states, so the shine has probably worn off there.

I find him in his office at six-thirty, backpack slung over one shoulder. My lips feel weird and dry beneath their layer of red lipstick. "Hey. You ready?" I ask.

Wyatt glances up from his desk and meets my gaze. For a moment it's almost like he doesn't recognize me—a moment that stretches on long enough for me to wonder if he's already forgotten that he agreed to come to dinner tonight. If this, the dress and the lipstick and the shoes with metal studs on them, is all just a bit too much.

Or if maybe, just maybe . . .

A coal flares in the pit of my chest, and I stare right back at him, refusing to look away even as that heat spreads like liquid through my entire body.

He clears his throat, one hand rising to grip the back of his neck. "Yeah. Sure. Ready whenever you are. Just—hold on." He clicks at a few things on his computer, then finally pushes away from his desk to rise to his feet. His cheeks are slightly flushed, despite the healthy rattle of the window unit blowing cool air into the office. "Where is this place again?"

"Greenpoint."

"Ah yes, the most inaccessible part of Brooklyn. Love it. How do you get there from here again?"

The answer is a route that involves more effort than any trip to Brooklyn is worth, in my mind, but I also understand I'm biased. You have to take the W or the R to the L and then switch to the G train, which is—in fact—the *only* train that goes to Greenpoint. Like, at all.

Greenpoint sits at the northern tip of Brooklyn, cut off from Long Island City—and the rest of Queens—by a slim creek, crossed by the Pulaski Bridge. It's an old Polish neighborhood, the kind with short, narrow streets arranged in alphabetical order and little bakeries selling luscious marbled babka for prices half what you'd pay at Orwashers. It also has what might be the best pizza in New York. Hence it being an exception to my "never setting foot in Brooklyn again" vow.

It's rush hour, of course, because rush hour is really like rush *three* hours in New York. That means Wyatt and I are crammed together on the train, shoulder to shoulder, his hand gripping the gross subway pole just above mine. I'm hyperfocused on that point of near contact, on how easy it would be for him to slide his hand just an inch downward and cover mine. The way it would feel illicit somehow, in public like this. My whole body aches to just . . . lean back against the firmness of his chest and let him envelop me.

Okay, be cool be cool. Look at something else. Someone else.

Only, fuck, no, don't do that either. Awkward. It's an unspoken rule that you don't look at other people on the train. You're supposed to just gaze blankly into space, absorbing without seeing, as if in a trance, until your stop. And even if you might talk to someone you know on the train during normal times, when it's this busy, it doesn't feel right. It'd be like clipping your nails in public—doing something that everyone does but that's weird in this context.

I shift away from the rest of the train to turn toward Wyatt, not that staring at Wyatt's broad chest improves my predicament. He's wearing a navy-blue shirt that puckers slightly at the base of his throat. The color is heathered, intertwined with threads of gray and gold. One of them has come loose just over his heart. I stare at that thread like I can cauterize it with the heat of my gaze alone.

This close, even on the train, even surrounded by the stench of body odor and urine and someone's McDonald's fries, I can smell the low, warm scent of Wyatt's shampoo.

Ahhrgjgjgjhgsd. I'm going to die here. I am going to perish, and on my grave they will write, *Died horny for teacher.*

Two transfers later, we emerge onto street level, and I take in several steady breaths of air that doesn't smell like Wyatt. And I immediately dig out my phone and pull up the address on Google Maps.

"Okay," I say at last, once I trust my voice to remain steady. "It should just be a couple blocks from here, if we head south."

"This isn't weird, is it?" Wyatt asks abruptly. "Michal's my student. I probably shouldn't be here."

"It's *fine,*" I insist. "I told you, I already talked to her about it. She's excited. She wants to make you eat challah."

He laughs weakly, but then we pass by a bakery, and his gaze tracks over to the plump gold pączki in the window. "Should we bring something? Aside from the . . ."

He means the grape juice I have stowed away in my bag. I don't really anticipate that our hosts will have anything nonalcoholic for kiddush, so I brought our own.

"Probably," I say. "Sure. Just not this bakery, though; I don't think they're kosher. Do you like babka?"

"Can't say I've ever tried it."

"Oh, man. Okay. Well. Come on. We're gonna fix that."

When we finally make it out of the adjacent kosher bakery, we're laden with far more bags of baked goods than we intended to come out with—kołaczki and babka and rugelach and apple tart and a steaming-hot Americano for me because these things can go late. Really late. And I'm old now.

"Is this extra?" I ask, lifting one of our brown bags of pastries.

"Where I come from, this is the bare minimum. If you really want to impress, we could pick up flowers from the bodega on our way."

I flap the fingers of the hand that holds my Americano, waving him off. "Okay, I clearly would not survive in the South. My idea of a host gift is a six-pack of nonalcoholic beer."

"See, personally I would love that host gift."

"It's really more of a gift for me. I mean, nobody else drinks it."

We turn the corner onto a side street and I pause, glancing back down at my phone. I'm not used to being back in a neighborhood where streets have actual names.

"Is that it?" Wyatt says, peering over my shoulder, then pointing at the brick building on the corner.

I double-check the address. "Yeah. I think so. Hopefully we aren't too early."

"Unfashionably prompt."

The nerves are back. They scratch at the inside of my sternum as we cross the street. Wyatt rings the bell, and we stand on that tiny stoop, my knuckles going white around my Americano and my heart in my mouth.

What am I even afraid of? That Michal's friends will take one look at me and declare me *not a real Jew* and kick me out? That it'll be the opposite—that they'll somehow smell the Chassid on me and declare me *an extremist Jew* and kick me out? Because now I'm out here imagining that total strangers can tell intimate details about my past just by looking, and that's what my therapist back in LA would call magical thinking.

I should probably chill.

My anxiety must be rising off my skin like heat, because Wyatt shifts his bag of pastries to the other arm and reaches over and squeezes my shoulder once. Some of the tension drains out of me at that single, simple gesture, his touch warm and miraculously grounding. I glance at him, surprised, and he offers a tiny smile.

"You got this," he says, right as the door buzzes.

I exhale and try to breathe my panic out with the air. Wyatt's hand falls away, but I can still feel the heat his touch left behind, steadying me as we enter the foyer and head for apartment 1B.

I hear laughter inside, the clink of cutlery and glassware. The low thrum of music playing on a record player. This could be anyone's house, anyone's party. Wyatt and I could be two people who met anywhere, a couple who fell for each other normally and now brings Polish pastries to friends' dinner parties.

Then the door opens, and I'm greeted by the smiling face of a woman with bushy gray hair and purple cat-eye glasses. "Hel*lo*," she says, beaming even wider at the pair of us. "You must be Ely. And who's this? Your boyfriend?"

Heat floods my cheeks. "This is my—um—"

"Wyatt," Wyatt interjects smoothly, stepping forward and shaking the woman's hand. "Thank you so much for having us. We really appreciate it."

"Of course, of course," she says. "I'm Kinneret, one of Michal's friends. I'm just so happy you could both make it. Please, come in."

We step inside. My hand twitches reflexively toward the mezuzah on the doorframe, but with my arms full of coffee and pastry, the gesture is abortive.

A sidelong glance at Wyatt reveals his anxiety is back too, despite his smooth introduction. The skin around his mouth is vaguely green—and I can't help thinking back to that night I first met him, the strange and intriguing juxtaposition of confident Revel Jamie and the softer, sweeter Wyatt I met in the hotel bedroom.

The interior of Michal's apartment is what I always fantasized *my* house would look like, if I grew up to be rich and became the kind of person who, like, donates to art museums. There are musical instruments I don't recognize leaning against the wall, next to sculpture pieces from cultures I've never visited and paintings by artists I've never heard of. The whole place smells faintly of myrrh, and I spot an incense cone burning idly by the record player. Is Michal secretly an heiress or something? Because damn.

The other guests are here already—at least, I assume this is all of them. My brain reflexively wants to try to categorize them—Modern Orthodox, yeshivish, Reform, Chassidic—but this group defies categorization. There's a man with a black hat and peyos deep in conversation with an androgynous person with dyed-pink hair. A woman in a straight brown wig carries challah to the table while Michal, in a violet tichel, moves dishes to the sink to be washed before Shabbos officially begins. A little boy around twelve years old, who I assume is Michal's stepson, darts around vrooming his model rocket ship. All in all, viewing this scene feels like watching a movie where the director did some research but not quite enough.

Michal catches my eye from the kitchen, and a huge grin splits her face. She immediately abandons the dishes, drying her hands off on a tea towel as she hurries over to greet us. "You made it!"

"Always with the tone of such surprise," I tease, even though we both know I almost didn't come.

Michal's gaze flicks to my left, toward Wyatt. If she's intimidated by his presence here, she does a great job of hiding it. "Professor Cole," she says. "Wow, I'm hosting a legend."

"I come bearing gifts," says Wyatt, lifting the bags of baked goods and grape juice. I wonder if I'm supposed to make some clarifying remark about how we're *just friends* or something, if Wyatt will think I'm taking advantage of the fantasy if I don't.

But then again, it's not like he's said anything to explain his presence here either.

"Oh, you didn't need to do that," Michal says, but when she peeks inside and spots the babka, she goes, "*Hell* yes, good choice. People are going to fight over this bread."

She introduces us to some of the other people who have gathered here, including her wife, Shoshana, an adorable five-foot-nothing woman wearing a blond wig and a gauzy kerchief who ignores my extended hand in favor of outright hugging me—one-armed, since the other arm holds the fattest baby I've ever seen.

"Gut Shabbos," Shoshana says. "Michal's told me so much about you."

I feel my cheeks pinken. I can only imagine what Michal had to say. I mean, how would I describe me to someone else? Especially after I flaked on the last Shabbos dinner?

"It's so nice to meet you," I say, falling back on politeness. "And who is this?"

"This is Hadas," Shoshana says. "She just turned six months."

I grin and hold out my finger for Hadas to latch onto. She gives me a gummy smile, just two little teeth sticking out above her bottom lip. "She's adorable. I had no idea Michal had a daughter." She'd mentioned the stepson, but that's it.

"She'd tell you she's glad you missed her awkward pregnant stage," Shoshana says.

"Valid." I glance around at the apartment, its gorgeous art, and I'm overwhelmed by the sense that I ought to be here. Or at least, if not *here,* then someplace like this. Someplace warm, with someone I love. A future with a family, even if that doesn't involve children. Not for me.

I want it so bad it's like a sailor's knot twisted rough and tight in my stomach.

You gave up this life, a voice murmurs in the back of my mind. *You left.*

"You have a beautiful home," I say at last, although with my dry mouth it seems to come out scratchy and raw.

"What?" Shoshana says. "Oh, no, this isn't ours. This is Kinneret's house. We're just borrowing it for tonight. We switch around—someone new hosts each time. And sometimes, if the weather's nice, we'll meet in a park for Kabbalat Shabbat instead."

Somehow it had literally never occurred to me that you could celebrate Shabbos outside. But I guess there's no real prohibition against it, at least for the evening services. Usually those just involve a few prayers and songs, followed by dinner—or at least an oneg with snacks and wine. I just—still—can't put my finger on this group. Kinneret seems to have materialized a mechitza from somewhere and is erecting it in the space between the living room and the small fenced-in backyard. Which I guess means we're going to have a service at Kinneret's house, the way you might with a Chabad couple on shlichus. The mechitza cloth is meant to separate men and women during prayers and is very much an Orthodox thing. But on the other hand, I've never been to an Orthodox service quite like this.

"Would you like to do the honors?" Michal asks me when it's time to light the candles, offering me a box of matches. They're the long kind, the sort that can be used for decoration or to light fireplaces.

"I—" I glance sidelong, hoping for Wyatt to step in and save me. But he, traitor that he is, just nods and smiles encouragingly. "Well, I was hoping to get a photo of someone else doing it. For my project. If that's still okay."

"*Ah,* right, of course," Michal says, tossing both hands up as if to say, *Silly me.* "How could I forget! Shoshana, it's all you, my love."

Her wife takes over, and I lift my camera, focusing the lens so that the flame sparks like magic as she bends it toward the wick. I want to capture the glow of gold light in the air, the warmth that bathes Shoshana's face as she folds her hands around the flames and draws them toward herself once, twice, three times. Here, only Shoshana is performing the mitzvah—but in Chabad every girl lights candles, even as young children. Every Shabbos I'd light my little votive next to my sisters and my mother. We'd murmur the blessing together. I wish my lens could immortalize the feeling of standing there whispering the bracha and knowing you're carrying on the same tradition as your mother, and her mother, and her mother, all the way back for thousands of years.

A tradition I broke.

One of the men starts singing "Lecha Dodi," and I snap another photo, another, as other voices join in.

If I were to close my eyes, I could be back there again. I could hear my father's voice coursing over the notes like cool water over stone. See my mother's cheeks amber in the candlelight, auburn strands glittering in her sheitel and falling across her face as she tips forward in prayer. My sisters and I lighting our own candles and murmuring brachos under our breath. Dvora with her secret smile just for me, our hands lacing together as our mother prays for us. For our family.

I wonder if she really believed that would be enough.

I lower my camera and glance down at the screen, flipping through the last few shots I've taken. Wyatt peers over my shoulder, his breath a warm gust against the curve of my ear.

"These look good," he says, low enough that only I can hear him over the song. "You've captured the magic."

I don't know if that's true or if it's even possible. I feel strange right now, disembodied almost. Similar to the way I used to feel when I was high—as if flesh and bone were just constructs. My skin tingles where Wyatt's breath touched it, and I sway on my feet. I imagine him wrapping his arms around me and pulling me close, holding me like Michal is holding Shoshana, her lips grazing Shoshana's temple.

Too much. I whisper my thanks and step back, letting Wyatt join the stream of men heading into the back garden for prayers.

This part is familiar. I've been to a thousand Chabad services just like it—the murmur of baritone voices reciting Hebrew, the women whispering among each other, one lady bouncing a baby on her knee while Shoshana and Kinneret fawn over its tiny chubby hands. The only person not separated out is the nonbinary person I'd spotted earlier, whose chair is positioned exactly halfway between inside and outside, one foot in the women's space and one in the men's.

I was worried about how we were going to get away with skipping the wine at kiddush without making things awkward, but I shouldn't have been. Wyatt is smoother than I give him credit for; I've just finished snapping a fresh photo as the mechitza comes down before he's there, passing a cup of grape juice into my hand. I don't think anyone even notices.

Not that I'm ashamed of my sobriety. But.

Some of the tension has leached out of me by the time we're seated properly at the dinner table. The food is a mix of things I'm used to—typical Ashkenazic cholent and kugel—and more Sephardic things, like golden-brown kibbeh stuffed with mint and lamb. I help myself to a stuffed pepper that oozes spicy tomato sauce onto a bed of couscous and tastes better than a lot of meals I've had in Manhattan restaurants.

"Oh my god," Wyatt comments between mouthfuls, pointing down at the borscht with his spoon. "This is incredible. Can I convert?"

"Nope," I say. "But I'll send you my grandmother's recipe."

Shoshana smiles at us from across the table. "So, how long have the two of you been together?" she asks, punctuating the question with a sip of her wine. Next to her, Hadas smashes some mushy carrots against her mouth. "Am I allowed to guess?"

I almost choke on my bite of kibbeh. I'm still struggling to clear my throat and fumble up some appropriate words to say when Wyatt—thank fuck—steps in.

"We aren't," he says, easy as anything. "We're friends. I'm helping Ely with her photography project, so she invited me to tag along."

One of Shoshana's thick brows goes up. "Aha. Friends. Yes. Michal and I used to be 'friends' too."

"*Shosh,*" Michal interjects, covering her eyes with both hands, but I can't help it—I laugh. Which earns me a predictable kick in the ankle from Wyatt.

"Sorry, sorry," Shoshana says, waving her fork through the air like a conductor's baton. "I'll stop. I just can't help myself. I watched too many Disney movies as a child."

"Same," I say. "Holding out for a suitor on a horse."

Wyatt quirks a smile and gestures toward himself, almost self-deprecatingly. "Horseless."

If I thought I'd be ready to flee the premises by this time in the dinner, I was mistaken. That is, I don't fully want to yeet myself out the window just yet. Reserving the right to change my mind in the future.

But this is easier than I thought it would be. Maybe that's the Wyatt effect.

"So what made you decide to do this project in particular?" Kinneret asks later in the evening, once the main course is just bone and sinew on our plates and everyone (aside from me and Wyatt) has gulped their way through at least three glasses of wine.

"What do you mean?" I ask.

"You're doing a project on Judaism, right?" she says. "You said you're taking photos of different ways people approach Jewish spiritual life. What got you interested in that?"

She has no idea what a loaded question that really is. I find myself glancing toward Wyatt, as if he could answer in my stead—but of course he just looks back at me, opaque as ever. The fucker probably sees this as a learning experience. Like I'm supposed to take this opportunity to practice what I'd say at my hypothetical gallery opening or some shit.

I take another bite of now-cold food to buy myself time. A mistake, frankly; room-temp meat never tastes great.

"Um . . . well . . . I guess I'm still trying to figure out where I fit. Spiritually." I had hoped that would be enough, but everyone's still looking at me like they expect there to be more information coming. "I grew up Orthodox. My parents are Chabad." I'm not sure how much anyone here even knows about Chabad or if they just think we're the guys in college towns who host Seders for religiously confused freshmen. "But I left the community . . . obviously . . . and now I'm just . . . I don't know."

"Well, you're still Jewish," Michal says, punctuating her words with a gesture of her fork. "That never changes."

"Do you believe in G-d?" asks Shoshana, because why not cut right to the real questions.

My palms are sweaty; I scrub them against my thighs under the table and laugh awkwardly. "Yeah. I do. I guess that never changed either."

I can feel Wyatt looking at me. His gaze is like a hot coal boring into the side of my face. Suddenly I'm too keenly aware of the effort it takes not to look back—to keep my eyes fixed forward on these strangers across the table. My heart is beating so fast I can almost taste it like blood in my mouth.

I don't know why I'm scared. And I don't know what cosmic fist I expect to come crashing down on me right now.

But I know it's coming.

17

"Do you have an easy way home from here?" Wyatt asks once dinner is over and we're back out on the curb, loaded up with more than our fair share of leftovers (including the remaining grape juice).

I make a face. "I mean . . . sort of. I can take the G to the 7 to the N." Wyatt raises his eyebrows at me. "On second thought, I might call an Uber."

Although now that I've said it, this tiny voice in the back of my brain keeps wondering if this was Wyatt's way of offering to escort me home. Only that can't be right. Because that would be, in his universe, inappropriate. People only take other people home when they wanna . . . you know . . . *take them home.*

For somebody who's only drunk off grape juice, I sure am getting ahead of myself.

Wyatt shifts his load of Tupperware in his arms. "How much of this do you want?" he asks. "I'm happy to split it fifty-fifty. Or I can take it all, but . . ."

"But you'd devour all five boxes in one sitting. Yeah, I bet."

From the sheer volume of brisket Wyatt consumed at dinner, it seems like he is a bottomless pit. "I have no idea where you put it."

"Excuse you," he says. "I am very bulky and manly."

"You're like a culinary Mount Doom. Or the ghost character in *Spirited Away* who eats the entire bathhouse worth of baked goods. It violates the laws of thermodynamics."

"His name is No-Face, and the laws of thermodynamics are overrated. Besides, that's why I became an artist, not a physicist."

"The laws of physics don't apply to artists?"

"Well, I wouldn't know, would I? That's the point!" He winks at me—freaking *winks*—and I dig out my phone so I can stare at the Uber app while I call a car instead of letting him see the way my cheeks go pink.

I'm still hyperconscious of him standing next to me. I wish I could shut off the part of my brain that seems to be custom tuned to the presence of Wyatt Cole.

This is one of those moments where you'd usually start waiting for one of you to offer to take the other person home. And then you'd have the whole scene lingering on the sidewalk outside until *do you want to come in* and the inevitable cascade of touches that follows.

I could spark that flame, if I wanted. Or I could at least try. I could reach out and drag my fingertips along the line of his hipbone and tell him it was too late to go back to Queens. That he'd better take me to his place instead.

"Hey," Wyatt says, and I look up, maybe a little too abruptly. Some weird, paranoid part of my brain immediately worries he can somehow psychically tell that I was obsessing over the smell of his laundry detergent.

He's standing so close, near enough that I could draw constellations in the scattering of faint freckles across the bridge of his nose. His gaze is dark and soft where it meets mine. The way he's looking at me feels like someone squeezing both hands on my shoulders, massaging out the tension.

"You did really good in there," he says. "I know it wasn't easy."

Whatever I was expecting, it wasn't a compliment. "Oh. Thank you. I thought . . . well. I felt like I was a little awkward." Then I laugh, which is *definitely* awkward.

"Not at all. And you were the perfect candid photographer. You kept everything discreet—you let the photographs become part of the background noise. You were part of the night, not an intrusion. That's the kind of skill that takes years to perfect." One corner of his mouth quirks up. "But I have a feeling you have always been good at that. You make it very easy for people to be around you."

No one has ever told me anything like that before. Or at least not in that tone of voice, low and wrapped in the warmth of sincerity.

"I'm good at blending into the background," I say, a bit dryly, but he immediately shakes his head.

"That's not what I meant. You could never blend in."

I can't rip my gaze away from his. I feel like his eyes are searing into my skin, tearing past all the onion-paper layers I've constructed between the outside world and my soft and vulnerable underbelly.

"You're blushing," he murmurs, and god, that only makes it worse. I stand still, so still, hardly dare to breathe as he lifts one hand and grazes the crest of my burning cheek with the backs of his fingers.

He draws closer, the pair of us listing in toward one another as if we're caught in some sordid magnetism. The humid New York City summer has nothing on what simmers in that negative space between us. Or the heat that's bloomed between my thighs.

In that split second, my heart hammering in my chest and his lips parting, slightly damp from the outward flicker of his tongue, I almost think—

But then he pulls his hand away and roughly drags it through his hair, his gaze dropping to the asphalt. "Sorry. Um. I shouldn't— Anyway. I'll let you . . . Your car is probably almost here, right?"

"Right," I say, before I've even glanced back at my phone. Suddenly the only thing I want in the entire universe is to become Kitty Pryde from the X-Men and develop the mutant ability to sink down into the ground and out of sight.

Wyatt gives this brittle laugh, still not quite looking at me, and says, "Right. Okay. I'll . . . I'm just taking the subway, so . . . I'll see you back on campus. Bye then."

Of course, once he's gone—once I'm sitting in the dark back seat of the Uber driver's Toyota Corolla and trying not to get sick as we lurch from light to light—all I can think about is how stupid it was for me to let him go.

Because in that moment, I think . . . if I'd been brave enough . . . if I'd kissed him, he wouldn't have stopped me.

Stop thinking like that, I snap at myself. He's trying so fucking hard to be respectful, and I need to try at least half as hard to respect him back. Especially in a professional environment. Which this was. He came with me to Shabbos as my mentor because I was psychologically incapable of going alone. The last thing I owe him, after all that, is bulldozing his *very fucking clearly communicated boundaries.*

But telling myself that doesn't do much to stem the tide of anxiety that wells up in my gut alongside the carsickness-related acid reflux.

Maybe I shouldn't have gone tonight in the first place. Maybe all of this was a mistake. I got good photos, I think—editing will reveal all—but was it worth it? Michal and her friends are perfectly nice people. Generous. Hospitable. That's not the problem.

The problem, as usual, is me. Because I'm pathologically incapable of not overthinking things, and it fucks me over every time.

Right now, less than ten miles away in Crown Heights, my family might still be having their own Shabbos dinner. My father singing, pounding the table with his fist in an imaginary rhythm, several wines in. My brother Gedaliah is boring everyone to tears asking for another retelling of the story about Yaakov and Esau. Gedaliah's twin, Sholom Ber, will have figured out a way to sneak undiluted Bartenura while no one is watching—although our oldest sister, Malka, got wise to that around the time I left. My mother will have put the youngest children to bed—only, god, Levi Yitzchok must be ten now, old enough to stay up. Did my parents have more kids since I left? Do I have siblings I've never even met?

I wonder if my sisters are there or if they're having their own dinners at their own houses with new families.

Dvora must be married now. She must have at least two kids—it's been long enough. Possibly more.

I suck in a shaky breath, and shit, I'm about to cry in this cab. Which is worse than crying on the subway, because at least on the subway no one gives a shit about you. I can't cry in front of Sergey the Uber driver.

I fumble with my phone, flipping to the Messenger app, and text Wyatt.

ME: Let me know when you get home safe okay?

The ellipsis shows up almost immediately. I stare at the screen waiting for his reply to appear, like a freak. Luckily it doesn't take long.

WYATT: Almost back. What about you?

ME: Ten more minutes. Or at least it better be. I'm getting carsick.

He sends the wastebasket emoji as a response. At least I can count on Wyatt to make me smile, even when I feel like trash.

There's music playing when I make it back to the apartment. I can hear it from the landing below our floor, which means either my roommates are hosting a party I wasn't invited to or Diego is having another emo breakdown. (The last breakdown was because he rewatched *Sailor Moon R* and was driven to the edge by the tragedy of Tuxedo Mask's star-crossed love with that alien who was being mind controlled by an evil flower.)

But when I open the front door, it's not to a rager or to Diego crying on the sofa.

Ophelia and Diego are both standing on the furniture, Ophelia with a bottle of champagne in hand and Diego's glass sloshing over and spilling wine all over the rug as they screech out the lyrics to Queen's "Don't Stop Me Now."

"That's why they call me Mr. Fahren-hay-yaaaa— *Ely, you're home!*" Ophelia jumps off the sofa and hurtles toward me like an incoming missile. She collides with me hard enough that I rock back on my heels, both arms lifting to wrap around her reflexively.

"Wow, I feel special," I say. "What's going on?"

"Ophelia has good news," Diego says with an eyebrow waggle.

"*Really* good news," Ophelia says, and she finally breaks the hug to look me in the eye. She's smiling so wide it looks like her face might crack in half. I haven't seen her like this in . . . well, ever. Her happiness is like a lantern illuminating her from the inside out. She looks even more beautiful than before.

"Okay," I say, "well, don't keep me in suspense—"

"They liked it!" Ophelia exclaims, answered by a whoop from Diego. "The gin people! They liked it! They actually liked my shitty sample pictures!"

Her joy is contagious. I find myself grinning just as wide as she is, and before I can stop myself I've flung my arms around her again, squeezing tight. "That's the best news," I tell her. "I'm so freaking happy for you. Oh my god!"

"Thank you," she says, her fingers digging into my shoulders briefly before we separate again. "I seriously didn't think it was going to happen. I thought they'd take one look and be like, *Ugh, this shit,* but they really— I'm going to be in *stores*. People are gonna have my art in their houses!"

"You deserve it," I say. "More than anyone. You've earned this."

She laughs and wipes the heel of one hand over her cheek—there's glittery eye shadow streaked down her face, presumably from crying. "Thanks. I can't believe it. I keep waiting for them to email and take it back."

"Absolutely not. They would never. They know what a good thing they've got."

Diego bounces on the sofa again, waving the champagne bottle in the air. "Okay, you two, stop crying and come celebrate! This is a party, dammit!"

"Did *you* just tell *us* to stop crying?" Ophelia says, but she goes and I trail after her, dumping my camera bag on one of the armchairs.

Diego scrounges up an empty water glass and dumps a solid eight ounces of champagne in there, then shoves it into my hand. "Bottoms up," he says. "We're toasting the next Banksy here!"

Ophelia's gaze catches mine before I can even start thinking of a response. I can see the worry in her eyes—like she thinks I'd throw my sobriety away on a whim.

The thing is . . . The thing is, I've been clean for four years. That's a long time. That's two black chips in a row. And the goal isn't always abstinence; sometimes the goal is to approach normalcy. It's moderation.

Maybe it's been long enough. Maybe I should let myself breathe a little.

One sip won't hurt me.

I hesitate, my palm gone damp against the glass. But Ophelia has already looked away, practically wriggling out of her skin with excitement, and Diego's eyes are big and glassy with pride, and I'm not gonna be that person. I'm not gonna be an asshole.

I'm gonna be normal.

So I drink.

18

I wake up the next morning curled up in the center of my bed like a cat, the covers kicked down to the foot of the mattress and my arms draped over my face to block out the sunlight. My phone alarm keeps beeping in my ear like it thinks I haven't heard it already, and I groan, fumbling to press the Mute button.

It's been a long time since the last time I had anything to drink. Four years, five months, and sixteen days, to be precise. And it's not like I got drunk last night or anything—I just had a glass. No big deal. But my mouth still tastes like something crawled in there and died.

I feel like a part of me died.

I'm such an idiot. I can't believe I deluded myself into thinking a few sips was no big deal. Of course it's a big deal—I literally went four whole years without breaking my streak. And it was so goddamn easy to let the whole glass castle shatter around me. And for what? Because I thought I could make myself normal for a night?

I've never been normal.

I push myself upright and lean against the wall, swiping open my phone to scroll through my latest notifications.

The top one is from Wyatt, a text I'd missed last night.

WYATT: I'm back. Hope you made it home okay.

Guilt seeps in like water through rotten floorboards. One glass. One stupid glass into the mouth of one stupid Ely. The fucked-up part of my brain wants to say that it's a good thing that I was able to just have the one glass and then cut myself off. It used to be that I couldn't. If I had a single sip, I'd drink and drink and drink until I wished I were dead.

I scrub both hands over my face, squeezing my eyes shut tight.

No going back now. I made my choice last night, such as it was. And who knows? Maybe it really *is* okay. Maybe four years clean has knocked me out of whatever rut I was in before, fixed whatever was broken in me. I certainly have no desire to drink more. Or worse, to go out and find someone behind a dumpster somewhere to sell me smack.

Still, my hands are a little shaky as I open up the messaging app and text Wyatt back—like he'll somehow sense what happened through the phone screen.

ME: Hey! Sorry I forgot to text back last night. Made it back. Hope you're alive and didn't eat all the leftovers in one sitting.

I shove my phone away from me before I can see if he replies. A part of me hopes he doesn't. I don't know if I can stomach his kindness on top of everything else.

Diego is a bundle of blankets on the couch when I emerge from the bedroom, either having fallen asleep there or having nested there, hungover, when he woke up. He doesn't stir as I move around the kitchen making coffee and grabbing breakfast, but I leave him a mug—black, four sugars—on the coffee table before I go, just in case. At least Ophelia is gone; I don't have to face her cautious concern and try to explain myself.

The train into Manhattan is running slower than usual today. We keep stopping in between stations, and the normally rocket-fast journey under the river is reduced to a drudging forward rumble. I find myself staring at the scars along my left forearm. They're barely visible anymore, just off-white smudges against my skin. I remember when they were angry fissures stretching along the lengths of my veins like portals to hell.

That was so long ago now.

Wyatt has texted me back by the time I get off the train: **Two sittings. I finished the brisket for breakfast.**

A beat, and the phone shows he's still typing. I climb the stairs out to street level still staring at my screen like the perfect stereotype of everyone my age.

WYATT: Could probably go back for more.

I grin and have to make myself stick my phone in my back pocket so I'm not tempted to text back too quickly. I wonder if he's at Parker, if he bothers to go in on Saturdays. Perhaps he's on a train somewhere headed here now. He might ascend those stairs minutes after me or be just a couple blocks ahead, tapping out a text while he sips his morning coffee.

So what if I walk a little quicker these last four blocks to campus? Sue me; I'm human.

Although once I'm there, I am faced with the reality that it'd be incredibly awkward for me to just show up at his office demanding attention for no reason. So I have to actually do something with myself, and of course there's no class on weekends.

I end up in one of the computer labs, uploading my photos from last night to Lightroom and sorting through them. Most of them are kind of shit, but that's standard. Digital photography has some upsides over film, and one of them is that you can take a million pictures of a scene that is constantly in flux. You aren't beholden to the number of film cartridges you have on hand—you don't have to try to freeze time, to capture a moment perfectly in as few slides as possible.

It's pretty easy to rule out the bad photos and get to the good stuff. But even then, I usually have way more options than I actually need. It becomes a matter of looking more closely at the scene, especially the exposure and focus. Some things, like crop and even lighting, to a degree, can be fixed in editing. Other things are unchangeable: Either the distribution of figures to negative space is good or it isn't. Either the exposure is good or it's hopeless, the light having burned away any data you might have recovered in post.

These particular photos turned out better than I expected. Last night felt like a fever dream at times, like I was existing in some liminal space between the past and the present. But onscreen, it's easier to see those moments as what they are. I'm not afraid of colors and shapes in a photograph. I'm an artist. This is what I love more than anything in the world.

As I fiddle with my favorite photos, I find myself wondering what Michal is doing today. It's still Shabbos but late enough that she might be home from shul by now. I find it hard to envision her life outside of what I've seen of it so far, both last night and at school. I try to picture her curled up in an armchair, reading a book while her wife and kids play on the floor. But even that simple scene is impossible to visualize. I keep catching myself imposing relics of my own experience onto hers, putting her into a wig instead of a tichel, hanging a portrait of the Rebbe on her wall.

Through my camera's lens, she is luminous.

"Are these from last night?" a voice says from behind me.

Heat flushes the nape of my neck before I turn to meet Wyatt's gaze. He's leaning against the doorframe, cup of La Colombe in hand. His hair is sticking up in an awkward fashion, as if he forgot he put pomade in it this morning then ended up raking his fingers through it one too many times on his commute. And suddenly I can't stop thinking about how he looked that night we fell into bed together, his cheeks flushed pink and his hair askew, his skin warm and supple beneath my hands as I touched him.

It's been like a solid ten seconds since he asked the question. *Shit.*

"Yeah," I say, and it comes out husky, like I haven't taken a sip of water in ten years. I clear my throat and try again. "Just doing a first pass."

Wyatt comes closer, setting his coffee down on the desk next to me and leaning in to peer at the images on my screen. He's near enough that I can see the stubble on his jaw and throat. One of his hands grips the back of my seat. All I can hear, for one reeling moment, is the pounding of my own pulse in my ears.

"Do you mind?" he asks, gesturing toward the mouse. I shake my head.

He scrolls through some of the images I've selected, pausing on two or three to take a longer look. Of course, now that he's watching, all I can see in my photographs are the mistakes.

"These are really good," he says after a while—long enough that I'd begun to contemplate faking a doctor's appointment or something just so I could leave. Which is stupid, because I'm the one who begged him to help me with this project in the first place. "I like how you've balanced the light. It makes the scene seem dreamlike almost, like this moment exists in a space between worlds."

"Thanks. I—I guess I wanted to make it feel . . . private, maybe? The way you feel when you're praying. There are other people in the scene, and you can feel their presence, but at the same time you're alone. Just you and G-d."

He nods. "You did that very well, then. It's definitely coming across. You have such an eye for light—the way you capture it . . . everything in the photo feels ethereal somehow. It's your focus on the *people* in the portrait that grounds the viewer in reality, but it makes that reality so much more beautiful. I think this could be a very powerful body of work, in the right hands," he says. The softness of his voice wraps around me, sends a thrill down my spine. "In your hands, specifically."

I stare down at those hands. I know what he's trying to say. Or at least what he wants me to infer from this.

To do this properly, I'd have to actually go back there. Not to Crown Heights, not literally, but . . . it might as well be the same thing. I have to stop holding this project at arm's length. I have to let myself *feel* it, let the memories well up like pools of silver nitrate solution. I have to stare directly into the past. I have to face it.

I have to face *her*.

Wyatt reaches over and grabs my shoulder, squeezes. He leaves his hand there a beat longer than he should—but not nearly long enough. I can still feel his phantom touch even after he pulls away. "What are you thinking about?" he asks.

"I don't know," I start, even though I do. "I guess just . . . It's a lot. It feels like undressing in front of someone you don't know. The exposure, you know? If I do this project right, I'll be making myself vulnerable."

He hums out a wordless sound of agreement. "I know what you mean. All the best art is like bleeding in front of strangers. It's terrifying. 'Vulnerable' is a good word for it. Someone could slip in while you're raw and aching and twist the knife right where it hurts the most."

I shift in my seat to look at him properly—how had I not noticed how close he is? If I'd leaned back just a little farther, his knuckles would have grazed my spine. I have to forcibly drag my attention up to his face.

"Is it worth it?" I say. My voice comes out scratchy. "After all the fear . . . I can't stand the idea of doing all this for nothing."

He nods slightly. "Yes. It's worth it. It hurts, but it's worth it. That's why we do this, isn't it? We want to say something important. But in art, you can't just say what you want to say outright. You have to wrap it up in layers of meaning and symbolism and trust that your viewer will be able to unwrap them. Even when it's scary. Even when it hurts." A pause. "Especially then."

He's right. You can't just say what you want to say outright. Not in art and not in life either. Not really. Because if you could, I'd open my mouth right now and tell him the truth about why I can't face my past. I'd admit my sins and he'd recoil, and all that gentleness in his voice and hands would vanish into steam like water thrown on a hot pan.

Maybe that's what I've been trying to do with my art all along. Beg for forgiveness over and over in as many languages as I can speak.

But I've spent so long trying *not* to think about my past that I can't imagine letting it overtake me, pull me under like a tidal wave. Even now I feel like I'm drowning. Like if I opened my mouth, I'd find it full of seawater.

Art should scare you, someone told me once. Someone from an art residency back in LA whose name I can't even remember. But their words have stitched themselves into my brain permanently.

Art should scare you.

I'm scared all right.

I haven't told him what I did last night, and I don't intend to. I'm used to keeping my mouth full of secrets. But something must show because a crease of concern forms between Wyatt's brows.

"What is it?" he says. "You're shaking."

His hand catches my jaw, his thumb rubbing a soft, warm pattern just below my lower lip. And if I wasn't shaking before, I sure as hell am now. That single point of contact smudges heat into my body, and a shudder unfurls down my spine.

He feels it too. He must. His eyes, initially wide with shock, have gone heavy. The dark fan of his lashes brushes against his cheeks as he draws in close, as I reach up to grasp his wrist, to keep him there.

"Careful," he murmurs, but it's not clear if he's saying that to me, or to himself.

Either way, he doesn't move. He stays right where he is with his hand on my cheek and his hips tilted in toward me. I don't want to breathe in case it scares him off. But I couldn't have, anyway. My chest is utterly empty, all the air squeezed out to make room for the all-consuming, the pounding *need need need*.

Wyatt's thumb shifts toward my mouth, exploring the terrain of my lower lip like he still doesn't believe he's kissed it before.

That thumb presses in against my damp lower lip until my mouth parts, ready to let him slide his finger into my—

"Is that you, Wyatt?" a voice says from behind us, by the door.

I almost topple out of my seat, but Wyatt—thank god—is a little bit more in control of himself. He straightens so slowly, as if he wasn't about to kiss me right then, a cool little cucumber in comparison to the way my brain has become a helpless *skree* of alarm bells.

"Hi, Ava," Wyatt says, just as slowly.

Shit. I thought he had it under control. But nope. He's only taking things slow because he's desperately trying to figure out what to say.

"I'm surprised to see you in on a weekend," she says.

"Haze wanted me out of the house," Wyatt replies. "Some kind of secret cat thing."

The moment of silence after that makes me want to curl up and hide beneath one of the desks. I still feel the phantom of Wyatt's would-be kiss on my lips. Why couldn't Zhu have walked in ten seconds later?

Only that would have been *way* worse, so. Maybe my hormonal fantasies can take a little break.

"I was about to head out," I venture at last, because Ava and

Wyatt are having some kind of silent conversation next to me, carried out in nothing but eyebrow raises and head tilts. "Um. I'll see you in class next week, Dr. Zhu. And . . . um. Thank you, Wyatt. Professor Cole."

"Wyatt," he says.

"Wyatt."

I can't look Zhu in the eye as I slip past her out the door, but I can feel her watching me.

And I can tell that she knows.

19

WYATT

"What was *that*?" Ava says with a raised brow as soon as Ely has vanished down the hall, the far door having opened and firmly shut behind her.

"It's not what it looked like," I plead. "Ava. Nothing's going on. Or I mean—well, obviously *something* is. But we have it under control. It won't interfere with her work."

I'm so stupid they should name some kind of satirical prize in my honor. If the whole plan is to hold my weaker instincts at bay and behave like a mentor for the next month or so, I'm doing a really shitty job of it.

One more month, Wyatt. One more month, and we could have done whatever we wanted, and here I am with no self-control.

Being unable to restrain myself is up there with my most loathed personality flaws of all time.

Losing control never got me anywhere good. I mean, it got me into a couple overdoses. It got me to do things for drug money that I still hate myself for.

Losing control turned my father into a monster.

I've built a whole life out of getting that control back and never, not once, ever, giving an inch.

Until, apparently, now.

"Wyatt," she starts, but this is already so humiliating I want to die, so.

"Please don't," I say, holding up a hand before she can finish. "Seriously. I want to hide in a cave right now. Please just let me go hide in that cave."

She's silent for long enough that I dare to steal another glance at her face. She's got a little quirk to the corner of her mouth, half a smile, and I have no idea how to interpret that.

"Stop whatever look that is you're trying to give me."

"I'm not trying to give you anything. Anyway, I think you said something about a cave you had to go hide in?"

This time I don't let myself mess up my exit. I'm out of there before she can change her mind.

I dig my phone out of my pocket as I head for my office and tap over to the messaging app. Ely's third on the list of most recent texts, behind Marcus and Ava but above the Uber Eats guy.

ME: I'm sorry about that

ELY: Oh don't you start

ME: Start what?

ELY: Start pretending like you didn't want to kiss me back there!

ME: I wasn't going to say that.

I save the next half of that text for once I'm safely in my office, the door shut. And locked.

Even then my hands are shaking a little as I turn back to my phone, thumbs hovering over the screen for a long moment before I finally type.

ME: Because I did want to kiss you back there.

Ely replies in an actual second, so fast she must have had the response pretyped in.

ELY: Knew it.

ELY: Don't you think maybe you should have?

I'm struggling to figure out how to respond to that when another notification pops up at the top of my screen: a message from Marcus.

I can't decide if his timing is incredible or piss-poor.

MARCUS: So I was on the train just now and this one guy was selling prints of his photos car to car. They were pretty good, too. Reminded me of you.

I know Ely's probably staring at her screen waiting for my response, but I tap one out to Marcus instead.

ME: The good photos, or the selling them on the F line for drug money?

MARCUS: I think you're being a little unfair with the last bit, man. On yourself and on subway guy. He's just trying to catch his break.

In case I needed reminding that I'm an asshole. Here I am, supposed to be clean but still seeing addicts everywhere I go. Even when I'm not physically there.

MARCUS: I bought one of his pieces. I'll show you next time we hang out. Maybe you'll like them. Or maybe you'll tell me they're derivative pieces of trash, who knows. It'll be a party!

He's trying to make me feel better in that weird Marcus way of his, but it doesn't really help. Today already feels like it's gotten fucked up in so many ways that I'll never disentangle myself from all of them. The only way out would be to cut the lights and start over from 12:01.

The one part of this I don't regret is her. Ely.

No matter how idiotic I might act around her, I never regret a single moment I spend with Ely.

20

ELY

The humiliation of almost being caught kissing Wyatt by Ava Zhu is at war with the elation of realizing that *I almost got caught kissing Wyatt by Ava Zhu*. Which would mean that I was almost kissing Wyatt again.

Which would *meeeeaaaaaan* he has decided not to be weird about the whole student thing after all.

His texts certainly seem to suggest as much.

I literally have the song "Walking on Sunshine" stuck in my head for the rest of the day as I keep editing the photos. Wyatt's words echo there too. *I think this could be a very powerful body of work.*

Like this moment exists in a space between worlds.

I'm light-headed by the time I finish and log out of my account at the end of the day, the kind of dazed feeling you get after staring at a screen for too long. I float out of the computer lab and down the hall, intentionally drifting past Wyatt's office—but his door is shut, the light dim in the crack against the floor. He already left, I guess. *Without* saying goodbye.

The dreamlike feeling ends by the time I'm on the subway

headed back to Astoria, crammed into an orange plastic seat between a cluster of gossiping high school students and a thirty-something-year-old man who still feels the need to play music without headphones. But all that's an excuse to tip my head back and close my eyes and try not to think of anything at all . . . at least until the train barrels out of the tunnel beneath the East River and rises to the elevated platform at Queensboro Plaza.

Back home, I'm alone. Diego and Ophelia are still out, although one of them has left a bottle of tequila open on the kitchen counter. I wipe sticky residue off the fake marble and am about to screw the cap on the tequila when instead, on impulse, I tip forward and inhale.

The aroma is just as I remembered—sweet but with a steel wire cutting through the sugar. Like poisoned honey.

That smell is laced through so many of my best memories. And my worst. Drunken nights with Chaya Mushka, the both of us a tangle of limbs on a bed somewhere, giggling over some stupid boy (or girl). Sitting on a stranger's dirty floor next to a smashed bottle of the stuff, my hands trembling as I slide the needle into my wrist. The acrid way tequila smells when you've thrown it up, my sister Dvora scrubbing it off our bedroom floor as I moan and roll uselessly around in my own misery.

I lift the bottle and take a tiny sip. I hold it in my mouth for one second, two. I could spit it out. I should, probably. But two seconds turn into three, then four.

Nothing happens. The world doesn't implode. G-d himself doesn't descend from the mountain to smite me. I just screw the cap back onto the bottle and put it away in the booze cabinet and clean up the rest of the mess.

I spend the rest of the evening sitting on my bed tucked right beneath the window, the curtains drawn so the streetlights don't wash out the colors on my screen as I edit the remaining photos from Friday night. The bodies of the people in the pictures shift, and there's my mother, her head bent over the candlesticks. A man's face blurs, and then he's my father, smiling in the flickering light next to Michal and her wife. There's Dvora, still fourteen, distracted by the dog pawing at her shin.

I clench my eyes shut and shake my head to clear my mind. *Focus.* I have to stay present. It would be too easy to let myself put my laptop away and bury myself under the cover of the duvet, hide in the dark until I forget how to feel again.

That's the problem with making yourself vulnerable: It might be necessary, but it also makes you want to hide from your own art. To just . . . never finish.

It's nearly dark by the time I'm done and all the photos are neatly labeled and organized in their own folder in my Dropbox. I close my laptop and let it slip off my thighs as I tilt back, letting my head rest against the window frame.

The world is draped in violet dusk, the buildings and people outside gone blurry as the light falls. It's a new day by Jewish reckoning. Shabbos is over. All over the East Coast people are lighting braided havdalah candles and sipping wine, smelling sweet spices in reverence to the departing bride.

I wonder if there's something interesting there, some contrast I could draw between beginnings and endings, openings and closings.

Eight years. It's been eight years.

The world can change a lot in eight years.

I shove the sheets back and tumble out of bed, grabbing my bag and phone off the desk. I'm out the door and halfway to the subway stop before I can let myself think too deeply about any of this.

It just feels like the next step, somehow. Like I'm on a downhill slope picking up speed, careening toward this inevitable conclusion.

Wyatt's right, after all. I have to face it. I can't hide.

Even near dusk the air is still hot and humid, summer beating down on the nape of my neck and sweat prickling at the small of my back. I dodge the clusters of friends on Thirtieth headed out for a late dinner, their heads tilted together and their mouths laughing. I try not to let my gaze linger on the people with their dogs' leashes looped around their chairs as they pick at their appetizers, oblivious to the way their pets' eyes grow big and hopeful every time a stranger passes close by. I wonder what it'd be like to snip myself out of my own life and insert myself into one of their lives instead. Somehow it's impossible to imagine any of these people having regrets. Guilt doesn't live in their stomachs like it does in mine, festering like an open wound. They spin glittering nets of friendships that come easily; they aren't constantly wondering how they'll poison them.

I swipe into the station and stand on the platform to wait for the train, the evening breeze picking up and tangling itself in my hair.

Time to rip my heart open and spill out the gore.

Crown Heights is both exactly and not at all as I remember.

This deli is the same deli that has been on this corner since I was a little girl. But the video store next to it is a smoke shop now. The kosher supermarket still uses the same font to announce its weekly sales, but the awning is green when it used to be blue. I find myself peering at the faces of the people I pass by, trying to tell if any of them are people I knew from my old life. Would Yaakov from next door look like that if he had a beard? Is that Bracha, her vibrant red hair obscured under an auburn wig?

If they recognize me, it doesn't show. Turns out my past isn't written indelibly on my skin after all. No one stops me on the street and accuses me of being Elisheva Cohen. No one seems to realize I'm anyone other than one of the goyish hipsters who's moved into one of Crown Heights' newly renovated, gentrified apartment buildings.

I know the walk from the Kingston Avenue stop to our old place so well. Even after eight years, the path is ingrained in my muscle memory. There's the bakery where I used to buy doughnuts with my pocket money every Monday. There's the boutique where Chaya and I used to say we'd shop once we were grown-up and fashionable and rich. There's the kosher pizza place where I nodded off in the bathroom and woke up to find like five different pizza delivery boys staring at me, the door hanging off its hinges.

Our building looks the same from the outside. I assume my parents still live there. But maybe they don't. Maybe they've moved on and some other family has taken over the apartment—some other kids' heights marked on the kitchen wall, someone else's shoes scattered by the front door.

I still have Dvora's number saved in my phone. I have no idea if it's the same—although I suspect it is. I suspect she still has that same shamelessly Luddite Motorola flip phone she had when we were teenagers, the one with the scratched paint on the side from the time I got angry at her and drunkenly threw her phone at a dumpster.

This is such a bad idea. This probably rises to the peak of bad ideas I've had since getting clean—the crown of "worst idea ever" having previously belonged to the time I tried to go off-roading in Shannon's Toyota Camry. But I tap Dvora's name and hit Call.

The phone rings and rings again, and I should hang up. This was such a stupid idea, embarrassingly masochistic—

"Hello?"

Dvora sounds just how I remember—soft, like she's telling you a secret. I could close my eyes and let that voice soothe me to sleep.

The back of my throat has gone wrinkled and dry. My breath feels like it sticks to my tonsils.

"Hello?" Dvora says again, and I clench my eyes shut and my free hand into a fist.

Fuck it. "Hi," I say back. "Um. It's me. It's . . . Elisheva."

The silence that hangs in the following seconds feels like a blade waiting to fall. My nails dig into my palm and I count heartbeats; my pulse is pounding so hard I can feel it in my temples.

"What do you want?" she says at last.

I feel like I've been stuck with a live wire. My mind scorches to white static, and for a moment I almost want to laugh—because what did I expect? I should have known. After everything I did . . . after I left the community, left my *family* . . . of course she wants nothing to do with me.

My mouth opens and closes a couple times, abortive little efforts to speak. Finally, I manage to say, "I—I'm sorry. I just . . . I wanted to . . ."

"Do you want money?" Dvora says crisply.

I flinch. The worst part is, I can't even be offended. I don't deserve to be hurt. She's right. I used to call all the time with one sob story or another, begging for cash. Making wild promises we both knew I'd never be able to keep about things I'd do if only she'd send money, if she'd talk to our parents, if they'd let me come home again.

The morning my parents finally kicked me out, I remember standing on this same curb with my one suitcase, the goyish taxi driver waiting impatiently in the street, my fist closed tight around the money my parents had given me for travel—money that taxi driver would never see, because I would spend it all on heroin and walk to the bus stop instead. Dvora was on the steps, her cheeks shiny with tears and one arm clutching our little brother Gedaliah's skinny shoulders. She kept crying my name, begging me to stay—to apologize, to be a better Jew, a better person.

But I walked away.

Dvora isn't crying anymore. The Dvora on the other end of the phone sounds more like our father: laden heavy with anger and disappointment.

The phone slips in my sweaty hand, and I blow out a hard breath.

I wish I were someone else. I wish I were literally . . . anyone else.

"I'm sorry," I say again. "Sorry to bother you." And I hang up before I can make things any worse than they already are.

EIGHT YEARS AGO

The worst day of my life began in an ice storm.

The power had been out since the night before, which Chaya and I had spent bundled up together in my narrow twin bed, sharing warmth. In the morning my breath made little frozen clouds in front of my lips. Even my Cheerios felt like they came straight out of the freezer.

"Are you sure your parents are okay with you staying here?" my mother asked Chaya for the third time. "Do you need to run home and check?"

"They don't care," Chaya assured her. "Promise."

I couldn't tell if Chaya was lying, but I wasn't about to press her on it. Selfishly, I wanted her there. With school canceled, the hours stretched out long and empty before me, ready to be filled with menial chores and demands to watch my younger brothers.

"We have to study anyway. Big test coming up," I added for good measure, in case my mother was entertaining notions of having me and Chaya take the boys somewhere to get their energy out.

It worked like a charm because there was nothing my mother cared about as much as grades, and mine had been slipping lately. Chaya and I stole some blankets from the chest in the living room and escaped back upstairs, bundling ourselves into the fortress of my bedroom.

"Maybe we *should* study Hebrew," Chaya said, her head the only thing poking out from her chunky knit blanket. "Didn't you get a C- on the last exam?"

"Ugh, don't start." I pulled open the top drawer of my dresser and shoved aside socks and underwear until I found what I was looking for. My stash was hidden away in a little carved box my grandmother had given me. She'd said her mother had brought it here all the way from Poland. Whatever it used to hold, it made a good home for my colorful collection of Percs and Oxys and the tiny bag of brownish powder that I'd bought the week before, because it was cheap, but was still too chickenshit to try out.

"M&M's or Skittles?" I asked, spinning around with the box in hand to give Chaya my best cheeky grin.

"Skittles. And by Skittles I mean Oxy, please."

"A woman of discretion and taste, I see." I shook a couple of pills out into my palm and put the box back into its hiding place. We settled in together on the floor, close enough that our crossed knees bumped together. I crushed the Oxy under the weight of an amethyst crystal I'd bought after visiting the natural history museum and divvied up the powder into several slim lines. "Ladies first."

Chaya dipped forward, accepting the rolled-up piece of paper I gave her, and the first line vanished up her nostril. Two more, then she offered the paper to me and sagged back against the side of my bed, her head tilted against the mattress and her eyes half-lidded.

"I wish I took the Benadryl," she mumbled as I leaned over and did my own lines. "I always forget to take the Benadryl. I get so itchy."

We settled in side by side, cuddled up under our respective blankets. I stared across the room at the ice that had crystallized on the window glass over Dvora's bed, tracking the shape of the fractals.

"Hey," Chaya said after a while. "Do you have any more? I'm not really feeling it."

I couldn't relate. My brain already felt boggy, weighted down by the drug. "Sure," I murmured, flapping my hand in the direction of my dresser. "Help yourself."

I closed my eyes, tracking her movements only by the sound of her body shifting around, the open-shut of my sock drawer, the grind of the amethyst.

"These are Percocets, right?" she asked. "They look a little crumbly."

"They're probably just old," I said without opening my eyes. "Hey. Give me a little too."

Chaya's finger slipped between my lips to rub some of the powder onto my gums. I hummed out my thanks and let the honey-sweet sea rise around me, drawing me under.

The next thing I heard was the sound of my sister screaming.

At first my eyes wouldn't open. My lashes felt glued to my cheeks, all my reflexes slow, as if I were trying to move underwater. At last I squinted against the overhead light. Dvora was pressed against the wall by the bedroom door, both hands over her mouth.

"What?" I mumbled. "What's wrong?"

Dvora didn't answer, but she didn't have to. I followed her gaze to Chaya, who sat next to me against the side of the bed. Her skin was the waxy color of old seashells. A thin dribble of vomit crusted the corner of her mouth. Her eyes were open and still as glass.

21

I wasn't planning on relapsing.

Not when I first went out, anyway. My *plan* was to get some air. To fling myself into the city and blind myself with the lights illuminating strangers' windows, forget who I was between the shoving elbows and screeching car horns.

But there are five billion different metaphors about good intentions for a reason. And that's why I'm in a bar at midnight, staring at the bottom of my empty whiskey glass and wishing cellphones had never been invented.

Addicts are selfish. They tell us that in twelve-step programs all the time. We're selfish, shitty people, right down to our rotten and gooey cores. You can't trust us. *We* can't trust us. There's a little gremlin that lives in our brains that's constantly trying to ruin us, and it'll devour anyone who gets in its way.

I kept that gremlin at bay for four *years,* but it's found me. It was always going to find me.

Because you can run from your problems, but you can't run from yourself.

And I'm the biggest problem I have.

"Another, please," I tell the bartender when he comes by. I wonder if he can tell by looking at me. Like, maybe bartenders have some secret sixth sense for when someone's fallen off the wagon.

I get a fresh whiskey in hand and down it. This isn't the good shit. This is the swill they mop up off the bar floor at the end of the night: rancid, sour, and all too good at doing the job. By the time I put down my empty glass the room has started to sway. Every time I blink it's a little bit harder to focus my eyes again.

I bet Dvora has already forgotten about me. I bet she's gone back to her perfect life and her perfect family. I bet her husband asked her who was that on the phone, and she said, *Nobody*, and when he pressed, she said, *Just my useless addict sister.*

Fuck, now I'm crying. I'm crying in a bar like the awful navel-gazing main character of a TV show about rich, quirky white women in Brooklyn written by rich, quirky white women in Brooklyn.

I fumble my phone out of my back pocket and swipe clumsily at the screen until it unlocks. I'm not gonna call Dvora again. I'm not. I'm *not.*

I do something even stupider.

"Hello?" Wyatt says. His voice sounds too awake, too goddamn *perky* for how I'm feeling right now.

I sniffle and swallow another sob, the heel of one hand pressed to my damp mouth. I don't even know what I'm doing or why I called him. Maybe I wanted to hear his stupid perky voice. Or maybe I just wanted to torture myself.

"Ely?" Wyatt says after a moment, a little softer now. "Are you there?"

My next breath shudders out of me. "Yeah," I say. "I'm here."

"Are you okay?"

What a question. I feel like I haven't been okay in years—even if I know that can't actually be true. I was happy the other day, when Ophelia landed that job. I was happy standing outside that Polish bakery in Greenpoint with Wyatt. But those things feel like they happened a long time ago, all of a sudden. Or like they happened to someone else.

I shake my head, a tremulous smile pressing across my lips. "I— No. Not really. I . . . fucked up, Wyatt. I really fucked up."

There's a moment of silence that answers that. It lasts just long enough for me to start to wonder if he's hung up on me. If he, like my sister, wants nothing to do with me anymore.

But then he says, "Where are you?" And it's only another half hour—and another guilty drink—before familiar hands slide along my upper arms and Wyatt is guiding me off the barstool and onto unsteady feet. For some reason the gentleness of it just upsets me even more.

"I'm sorry," I mumble, and his hand tightens on my arm slightly.

"It's okay," he says. "It's okay. Come on. Let's get you out of here."

I can barely walk, a discovery that would be more embarrassing if I had two brain cells to rub together. I list to one side, my weight dragging against Wyatt's as he pays my tab and navigates us out of the bar and onto the balmy sidewalk. I'm crying, because of course I am, wet gulping sobs that make me feel like I'm drowning in my own snot.

"I'm sorry," I say again, the hand that isn't latched onto a handful of Wyatt's shirt swiping tears off my face. "I'm so . . . so stupid . . . fucking . . . the worst. I'm sorry."

"Shh," he murmurs, and his arm circles properly around my shoulders, drawing me in close. "The Uber will be here in a second. It's okay. You're going to be okay."

"'M not. I fucked up. I'm . . . It's so . . ."

I give up talking. What words are there, anyway, to describe how I feel right now? The only way to make Wyatt understand would be to plunge my fist into his chest and start shredding organ meat. I can't even blame Dvora for wanting nothing to do with me. Turns out she was right, anyway. All it took was this one setback, and here I am again, a drunken shit show. Back on my bullshit.

Taking bets on how long until I'm injecting smack between my toes in a grimy subway station somewhere.

The car pulls up at the curb, and Wyatt hustles me forward, holding open the door while I slide in across the leather back seat.

"She's not gonna puke, is she?" says the driver.

Wyatt glances at me, one brow raised, and I shake my head. "She won't," he says. "But I brought a bag, just in case."

I wish just one thing about this night would be less than 110 percent humiliating. I never should have dragged Wyatt into my mess. I should have called Ophelia, or Diego, or even Michal—anyone else. Instead here I am, needing him to baby me and pat my shoulder and take me home because I'm too much of a wreck to take care of myself.

"I'll pay you back," I mutter. "For . . . for the car."

"Don't worry about that," Wyatt says firmly. He leans across me and presses the button to roll down the window. The fresh air feels good on my face but not as good as that one moment felt, where Wyatt was so close, bracketing me in against the car seat, warm and safe.

I doze off at some point during the ride, blearily aware of the different sound the car tires make when we cross onto the bridge, the briny scent of the East River assaulting my nostrils as we leave Manhattan. And then Wyatt is gently shaking me awake, and I'm blinking myself back to reality. The bright city lights are gone, replaced by the dimmer glow of the outer boroughs.

"We're here," Wyatt says, and he offers me a hand, helping me crawl across the seat. "Careful—don't rush. You got it. There."

The solid ground feels strange under my feet. I'm like a sailor who's been aboard ship for nine months straight for whom dry land is now vertiginous and uncertain.

"Where are we?" I ask eventually, once I've reoriented myself enough to realize I have absolutely no clue where we've ended up. This street isn't like the streets in Astoria. It's got fewer trees, for one. And the buildings are taller.

"Bushwick," he says. "I took you back to my place. I hope that's okay. I just don't think it's a good idea for you to go home alone right now."

God, sober me would be delighted. Drunk me, however, can only muster a weak mental fist pump.

Wyatt lives in a third-floor walk-up, which normally wouldn't be too bad, but drunk me also needs an elevator. The banister does a lot of the heavy lifting in getting me up to Wyatt's floor, where I slump uselessly against the wall while he unlocks the front door. I swallow down the urge to apologize again. I'm pretty sure he knows how sorry I am at this point.

I wish I were clearheaded enough to appreciate the interior of Wyatt's apartment once I'm in it. As it is, I can detect a blur of hardwood floors, furniture upholstered in dark colors, a bunch of books scattered around the place. Normally I'd be cataloging all this the way I do whenever I go home with someone, judging them by their reading taste and how clean they keep their water glasses.

Wyatt helps me over to the sofa, where I gratefully collapse against his array of fluffy throw pillows. Wyatt, perennially too good for me, brings me a glass of water with a little lemon slice floating happily among the ice cubes.

"Fuck, you're bougie," I say after I take a sip—because it is, of course, *sparkling* water.

"We could have the great Sanpellegrino-versus-LaCroix debate again, but I don't think you're in the right headspace to argue your points."

"I'm sober enough to know this isn't Pellegrino," I say.

There's something tight about the set of his smile, but I'm too out of my gourd to know what it means. I sip my water and try to focus on something solid in the room, something to anchor me against the way my head feels like it's pinned on a merry-go-round.

"We don't have to talk about it right now," Wyatt says after a moment, his voice so carefully soft, so gentle, like I might shatter. "But if you want to . . . at some point . . ."

And that gentleness is what breaks me, really. My chest clenches and a fresh heat swells in my eyes: another humiliating round of tears. I tip forward and bury my face in both hands so Wyatt won't see. Ridiculous, of course. He's already seen. And I'll never be able to look him in the eye again after tonight.

His hand finds my back, rubbing soft circles against my spine. I only wish I'd done anything to deserve this kindness.

"I've ruined my life," I mumble against my palms. "My family hates me. My friends are . . . are better off without me. And now I've gone and fucked up and—and—and made it even worse. Because that's what I do. I make things worse."

Wyatt is silent, the motion of his hand on my back the only rhythm I can cling to.

My next breath shudders into my lungs. "I don't even have a good excuse. I don't. . . . It's not like I had a terrible childhood or I was abused or horribly traumatized in some way. I have no reason to be the way I am. I just—I'm broken. Something in my head isn't right. But I have no excuse."

"There's never an excuse," Wyatt says. He touches the crown of my head, and his fingertips are light, so light, like birds resting on my skull. "You don't need one. Addiction is a disease. It's . . .

chemical. Your brain doesn't work like other people's brains work."

"You're damn right about that," I mutter, and manage a wet little laugh.

Other people have excuses, though. Chaya was a lesbian living in a culture that would never accept her. My first sponsor was horribly abused as a child. I used to get high with a girl who had grown up in foster care and been homeless since she'd turned eighteen. Shannon got addicted after a back injury.

Me? Nothing. No sob story. I was the blueprint for every fucked-up antidrug propaganda piece about not giving in to peer pressure. I had no self-control.

Have no self-control.

"It's not a race to the bottom," Wyatt says, as if he can read my mind. His fingers loop through my hair, and I wish he would keep touching me like this forever. Even if I don't deserve it.

But instead he pulls away, carrying my half-empty water glass to the kitchen counter and refilling it. I take advantage of his absence to scrub my face against my sleeves and try to pull myself together. Not that it works. The room is still spinning far too wildly for me to even pretend I'm not a goddamn mess.

"Come on," he says when he's back, offering me his free hand. "Get some rest. You'll feel better in the morning."

"I doubt that."

"Well, let's test it and see."

I sniffle and take his hand, letting him pull me upright. The change in position makes me dizzy all over again and I stumble; Wyatt catches me, an arm sliding around my waist, fingertips pressing in at my ribs. He helps me, just like that, the pair of us picking our way across his apartment to the bedroom. He doesn't turn on the light, so I can't catalog the room—it's all dark shapes and edges as Wyatt settles me onto the bed and places my water glass on the nightstand.

"I'll be in the other room if you need anything," he says. "Bathroom is through that door. . . . Try to get some sleep, okay?"

He closes the door softly behind himself, and I curl up in the middle of Wyatt's bed, burying my face against the pillow that smells like him, and try to pretend I am someone else, anyone else in the entire world.

22

When you go four years without a single hangover, you start to forget how god-awful they are.

Or maybe the hangovers just get worse with age.

Either way, waking up the next morning is awful. The sunlight streaming in through the windows falls directly on my face, I have the headache from hell, and my tongue feels like a slab of dryer lint. I fumble on the nightstand for my phone before remembering that—*right*—I'm not at home. I'm at Wyatt's.

My hand hits the sweaty side of a glass of ice water. I crack my eyes open just enough to see; Wyatt's left the water and a bottle of aspirin next to the bed. *Bless this man.*

Also, there is a black cat sitting on my chest.

"Hey, buddy," I mumble. Opening my mouth feels like a gamble, but you can't meet a void cat and not say hi. It's extremely rude. "Sup?"

I manage a clumsy scratch behind its ears, which only sends it leaping off me and tottering off into another room on three legs. *Great. Even the cat hates me.*

I down two of the aspirin and then embark on the slow, agonizing process of getting out of bed.

By the time I make it out to the main part of the apartment, the pounding in my head has escalated to a constant throb right between my eyes. Worse is the humiliation that coils in the pit of my stomach, hot and nauseating.

Wyatt is in the kitchen pouring pancake batter into a skillet. The smell of frying butter makes my gut curdle; I try to breathe through my mouth.

I wish that I were here under literally any other circumstances. There are so many versions of this morning I could have spent watching Wyatt's strong muscles shift under his white T-shirt as he flipped pancakes. In another world I could have come up behind him and slid my arms around that firm stomach and kissed the nape of his neck. And he'd have been happy to see me. He would have shifted in my arms to catch my mouth with his, still smiling.

Why did I have to call him? Of all the people on planet Earth. *Fuck you, past Ely.*

"Hi," he says, setting the spatula down on a spoon rest as he turns to face me. "You're up. Did you sleep okay?"

He looks so cautious, so . . . *sympathetic.* I wish he wouldn't. The kindness is worse than disappointment or even anger would have been.

"Yeah." I slide onto one of the leather-padded barstools at Wyatt's kitchen island, both hands still gripping the water glass he brought me. "Thanks for letting me stay here last night. Really."

He nods. "I didn't want to just take you home. I was worried you might . . . well. You know."

I do know. It would have been only too easy to spiral further—to think, *Well, I've fucked it up now; might as well fuck it up worse,* and go out and find something that would well and truly wipe my mind blank.

"I'm sorry," I say. "For putting this all on you. You aren't— This isn't your responsibility. I can get out of your hair. . . ."

"Don't be ridiculous. I'm glad you called. You reached out for help. You did exactly what you were supposed to do."

He's not wrong, technically. But I should have called Shannon instead. Or Ophelia. Or Michal. Calling Wyatt was the equivalent of drunk dialing an ex. My memory of last night is blurry, but I'm pretty sure I didn't throw myself at him. He wouldn't be acting this normal if I had, right?

"You're such a good friend," I say, and if I wish I could use a different word from "friend," that isn't our current reality, so. "Seriously. Thank you."

Wyatt offers me a small smile, then turns to plate the pancakes and sausages he'd been preparing. The pancakes look too sunny, too happy, with their little pats of butter swimming on top—like they're mocking me. A liberal dose of raspberry sauce takes care of that problem; now they look rather more like a crime scene.

"So I guess I'm fucked, huh?" I say after we're both a couple of bites in, Wyatt standing on the opposite side of the island with one elbow perched on the counter. I wonder if he always eats breakfast standing, coffee mug in hand, like he's ready to rush out the door at a moment's notice.

"What do you mean?"

I drag the tines of my fork through the remains of my half-demolished pancake. "I mean, I relapsed. I have to start over now. Day zero. Four and a half years, all for . . . for fucking nothing."

"Not for nothing," Wyatt says, cutting in so firmly that I glance up. "That was four and a half years of your life when you weren't actively trying to kill yourself. You built an entire future in that four and a half years. You grew as an artist. You became independent. You moved out here. None of that would have been possible if you weren't clean."

"I guess. . . . But still. I threw it all away. One night. That's all it takes." It's so goddamn easy for me to destroy everything.

"No. Stop saying that. You don't have to start over. You slipped up, that's all. It happens. And now you get back on the horse, and you keep doing what you've been doing for four and a half years."

I shake my head. "That's not what my sponsor would say."

Wyatt sighs. "Listen. I like NA as much as the next addict. It does great things for a lot of people. But in my opinion, that's one thing twelve-step programs get wrong. You don't have to be defined by your addiction, and you don't have to go back to square one just because you messed up. You still have all the tools and skills you've developed this whole time you've been clean, and you can use those to *stay* clean. One mistake doesn't mean you have to turn in your chip." He shrugs one shoulder. "But hey, that's just my opinion."

The smile that tugs at my mouth feels fragile, but at least it's real. "I like your opinion."

"Me too. Generally speaking, I think my opinions are pretty good."

The three-legged black cat takes that opportunity to reappear and try to walk across what's left of my pancake breakfast.

"Oops! Hi, little buddy," I say, gently picking it up and redirecting it onto my lap. "Sorry, that food's not for cats."

Wyatt laughs and tilts forward, scratching the cat behind one fuzzy ear. Wyatt's abrupt proximity makes my stomach lurch, even if his attention is focused exclusively on those of the feline persuasion.

"This is Haze," he says. "I've had him for three years. He's the most annoying cat on earth."

"Isn't every cat the most annoying cat on earth?"

"Yeah, but mine actually wins."

Haze rubs the side of his face against my palm, thrumming out a low purr. "I can't believe he's really sitting here, doing this. Most cats I know stay as far away from strange humans as they can get."

"Haze might be the most annoying cat on earth, but he's also the best." Wyatt's giving him this big soppy grin, like he's an absolute idiot for little void cats, and I love him so much more for it.

Wait. Love?

Nope don't go there nope nope nope. Especially not right now.

I turn my attention back to my plate. The pancakes have gone cold and slightly mushy now, but it's for the best; my stomach is still uneasy from last night. I take a tentative bite of sausage instead. "Okay," I say after I've swallowed. "Okay. I'm telling this to you, Haze, so you can hold me to it. Last night was . . . a blip. That's all. I'm not starting over. I'm *continuing.*"

"I like that. A blip."

I do too. Although a part of me worries, as I keep one hand moving at a slow and steady pace down Haze's lavishly undulating spine, that this is still the wrong way to think about it. Am I making excuses if I let myself believe that one slipup does not make a relapse? Is that just giving myself permission to slip up again—and again—and again?

I can't afford to keep doing this. I can't go back to how I was. Never.

But the idea of starting over . . . it makes me feel like something's been carved out of me. It makes me feel hopeless. And that feels even more dangerous.

"I was gonna go to a meeting today," Wyatt says after a while, once I've made nibbling progress through half my sausage. "Maybe you'd like to come with me?"

"Yeah. Yeah, I think that's a good idea."

And it is. As much as a part of me resents the idea of being back there, sitting in one of those hard folding chairs in a church basement, picking away at stale doughnuts, it's where I need to be right now.

I just wish I could reach inside myself and excise the shame that has taken root in my gut, growing like a tumor.

Haze mraows loudly and smashes his face against the underside of my chin, a gesture of pure adoration that I do not deserve, not even from a three-legged black cat.

I wish I could see myself the way Wyatt sees me.

But I can't.

23

I've been to my fair share of NA meetings. For the most part, they're all the same—they follow a very specific formula, even if who's there and the content of what they have to say changes. I know Wyatt said I don't have to start over, but I feel like it chisels away at a piece of my heart every time someone gets out of their chair to receive a chip. Especially the black ones for two or more years. That's what I had, before I fucked everything up.

"How are you feeling?" Wyatt asks me after, once we've settled into our seats at the diner next door. The waitress was quick about bringing coffee; I cup my hands around the warm mug and tip my face toward the steam.

"I don't know," I say honestly. "Disappointed in myself. Annoyed. I keep wishing I could rewind and make a different choice, but that's obviously impossible. So I guess I'm just stuck here with the consequences of my own stupid decisions."

"It's going to feel that way for a while," Wyatt admits. "When I had my first relapse, I hated myself for weeks. Ended up spiraling, started using again for a few months before I was able to get myself checked in to another detox."

I glance up from my coffee, meeting Wyatt's gaze across the table. "I didn't know you relapsed."

"Oh yeah. Three times. Everybody does." He shrugs one shoulder. "Or a lot of people, anyway. If you managed to stay clean after your first go-round in rehab, you're a unicorn."

"I did. I mean . . . I had a great support system. I had Shannon—she's my sponsor, or she was, anyway. She was basically my best friend back in LA. And I had gotten involved in the art scene right around that time too, so I had those friends. Had to ditch a few of them because they were still using, and the rest I kind of . . ."

That was one of the hardest parts about getting clean. My first connections to art people had been through other users. People who could, it seemed, just do a little casual coke on the weekend and be perfectly fine afterward. I mean, maybe not. I didn't know their lives; maybe they were just as broken as I had been. But I always felt like I was different. There was a section of my brain hell-bent on killing me, and the rest of my brain was more than happy to let it try.

Of course, now I'm thinking about how I still haven't texted Shannon since the slipup. I don't even know if I can. How can I admit to her what happened? After everything she has done to help me get—and stay—clean? It feels like a slap in the face.

And now that I think about it, I haven't texted her at all, period, about anything, in like . . . weeks.

It's a classic Ely move. My brain loves sabotaging friendships. Every time I get a good one, my shadow self is right there to be, like, *lol, bitch, you thought.*

"You have support here too," Wyatt says. His voice is soft, gentle, as if he thinks I need convincing. "You have Michal, and your roommates. You have . . . well. You have me."

All at once it's like he can't meet my gaze. He stares down at his napkin, shredding the corner of it between his fingers.

"*Do* I have you?" I ask.

He tears a long strip off the napkin. Then, at last, he looks up. "Yes," he says. "You do. For whatever that's worth."

Something warm tightens in the pit of my stomach. He means he's here to support my sobriety, obviously. But some part of me refuses to read it that way. Because he's still watching me, his eyes big and doe-like, and I keep mentally circling last night, how he took me home, the way he was this morning—like I meant something to him. Like I was worth protecting.

The moment lasts just a beat too long. I have to tear my gaze away under the guise of taking another sip of coffee and examining the menu. I'm almost relieved when the waitress shows up again to take our order. I ask for eggs Florentine, even though I don't like hollandaise sauce. I can't fucking think straight around this man. It's a problem, and my taste buds are about to pay for it.

"I should have seen this coming," I say once the server has gone—dragging the subject back to safe(r) ground. "I had a few mistakes leading up to it. A glass of champagne, a few sips of tequila, that kind of thing. I just kept telling myself it was okay."

Wyatt shakes his head. "People think it gets easier the longer you've been clean. And it does, obviously, but . . . there are different challenges. Like you start to forget how bad it used to be. You start lying to yourself, thinking how things might be different this time."

Pretty much. And I wish I'd been right. I feel like I've been fighting my whole life just to be *normal*—the kind of person who can handle herself. Handle shit going wrong. Instead I'm *intense,* like Chaya told me during the worst of our fights. I feel things too much. I don't know how to tone it down, or shut it off, or whatever it is other people do to keep their minds sailing along on an even keel.

"I volunteer at a place in Midtown every Tuesday," Wyatt says abruptly. "It's a harm reduction organization. They have a needle exchange, counselors, you name it. It helps me remember why

I'm staying clean. And it lets me give back. You should come sometime."

"Yeah. Yeah, sure. I'll try to make it next week."

Wyatt reaches over and finds my hand, curling his fingers tight around my palm. And suddenly that heat is back, flushing beneath my skin. "Listen. You got this. Okay? Don't let yourself get stuck here. You can choose to keep fighting. And I'm not gonna let you give up. All right?"

I don't know why, but right now, this feels like the nicest thing anyone has ever said to me. I press the heel of my free hand against my eyes, trying to scrub away the tears threatening to slip free. Wyatt rubs his thumb against my knuckle and squeezes my palm.

"Do you want to talk about it?" he asks softly. "What happened?"

"I told you," I mumble. "I slipped. It just . . . spun out of control."

"It's usually more than just that. It might not be obvious what, but something made you feel like this was a solution. You wouldn't have made it four years clean if it was as simple as giving in to temptation."

I wipe another wave of tears off my face and meet his eyes across the table. I feel like I'm desperate for that life vest he's offering: An excuse for why I'm such a shit show right now. Something sympathetic. A sob story that makes me more than just an addict who fell off the wagon.

It'd be so easy to blame it all on Dvora, but the truth is, I lost control before I made that phone call.

"I don't really have an excuse," I say. "I'm just a piece of shit."

"Don't say that. You're not. You're one of the strongest, stubbornest people I know." Wyatt's leaning in across the table, clutching my hand between both of his now, as if he could press his brow against mine and *will* me to believe him. "You don't deserve what you are doing to yourself."

The waitress chooses that moment to reappear with our food. I take the chance to discreetly scrub my face with my napkin; there's nothing less attractive than dripping snot into one's side of hash browns.

"I do, though," I say once the server is safely out of earshot. "I'm not a very good person. I've . . . I've fucked up. A lot."

One of Wyatt's brows goes up. "And you think that isn't everybody?"

"I killed someone."

There's a part of me that grimly relishes the way Wyatt's expression falters. It's not about trying to sound shocking—or okay, maybe it is, a little bit. But of course Wyatt never thought I'd ever actually *hurt* anyone. He thought when I said I did bad things, I meant stealing my mom's credit card or cutting class or getting into stupid fights over drug money. And I let him think that. Because I couldn't stand the idea of him knowing the truth. Because if he knew the truth, he wouldn't want anything to do with me.

"What do you mean?" he says at last, carefully, as if using the wrong words might shatter me.

"My best friend, Chaya. I got her into drugs. I made her use with me. She fucking . . . she died. She overdosed. Because of me."

"Ely . . ."

"It was my fault," I press on. I'm crying again, but this time I don't bother trying to wipe the tears away. I grab my fork and stab at my eggs Florentine, puncturing one of the poached eggs and splattering its yellow contents across my plate. "I bought some cheap Percocets. Turns out they weren't Percs at all. They were laundry detergent laced with fucking fentanyl, and she . . . she . . ."

Wyatt passes me his napkin, and I take it with my shaking hand only to ball it up in the pit of my fist.

"If she'd never met me," I whisper, "she'd still be alive right now."

"You don't know that. You can't possibly know that. And even if it's true, that doesn't make it your fault. She made her own choices, just like you did."

Did she? Did any of us really? Maybe if I'd let Chaya go after we had our biggest fights, things would have turned out differently. If I'd gotten clean, if I'd never had those pills in my room to begin with . . .

Did she really *choose* to use, or did I make our friendship dependent on it?

"Anyway, that was kind of it, for me. Chaya's parents never forgave me. Everybody in the community knew what happened. So my dad told me it was probably best if I went away. He gave me a thousand bucks, which I spent on bus tickets to LA and a shitload of heroin."

Wyatt hasn't touched his waffles. They're starting to go soggy under their lake of syrup, but he doesn't even seem to notice. He places his hand on the middle of the table, palm up, and after a moment I reach over and let him lace our fingers together. That simple point of contact is grounding. My heart rate gets a little slower; my chest feels less like it's caving in on itself.

"We've all done things we regret," he says. "But you don't have to let your past define your future. I know it's a little trite, but when they say, 'One day at a time,' that means something. Every day you can make different choices. Every day is another step away from that person you used to be. Eventually you'll look back and see how far you've really come. And those who love you will be there waiting for you, no matter what. There's always a way back."

I don't know if I believe him—or if it takes ten years to get to that point—but I'm still glad he said it. I wrap those words up and keep them safe in the corner of my heart, where they might take root and maybe—one day—have a chance of becoming true.

In a perfect world, I wouldn't live in a house that had alcohol in it at all. I'd have my own apartment, completely scrubbed clean of everything that might tempt me off the straight and narrow. I'd go to NA every night. I'd keep in touch with my sponsor. In a *perfect,* perfect world, I might have even checked myself into rehab after this last slip.

But this isn't a perfect world, and I'm not a perfect person. So I go to NA the night after my slip, and when I get home I bake Ophelia and Diego a really nice quiche, and over what essentially amounts to egg pie, I tell them the truth. I tell them I'm an addict and an alcoholic, and I cannot be trusted, and that if they ever see me sneaking swigs of bourbon in the bathroom, they should probably knock me out with the bottle before I do anything worse.

Ophelia knows already, of course, but she does a good job faking otherwise, and Diego takes it surprisingly well. It turns out Diego's brother has substance abuse issues too, and Diego is pretty empathetic for someone who had his college savings stolen to fund someone else's drug habit. He pulls me into a hug, the kind of bone-crushing embrace that makes you feel like the other person is trying to *smoosh* their affection into your visceral organs.

Sometimes I realize that I am the luckiest person in the world.

Wyatt texts me every few hours over the next couple days, always the same thing: **All good?** And I text back, **All good.** It's a small ritual but it feels important. Like if I can just keep texting back that "all good," then it'll be true. It'll *stay* true.

24

WYATT

Ely: Can you come over?

The text appears on my phone when I'm midway through washing dishes—another gourmet meal of boxed mac and cheese—and I pretty much immediately give up on cleaning. (Not that I wasn't already looking for an excuse.)

Of course, I start typing, but this doesn't feel like a texting sort of situation. So I hit Call instead and listen to the phone ring twice, three times, before Ely picks up.

"Hey," she says. Her voice is a little shaky. Maybe someone else wouldn't notice, but I'm listening for it, and I know her. I know the sound of someone trying to sound cool, sound *normal,* even when they're falling the fuck apart inside.

"Hey there," I say back. "What's going on?"

Her exhale is low and somewhat ragged. "I just . . . Rough night. I feel like my mind keeps circling the drain and I can't shut it off. I don't . . . I can't be alone right now."

I check my watch. It's 9:00 P.M.—late but not middle of the night. Haze will be fine parkouring off the furniture without me.

Not that I think the time of night would have actually made a difference in the end. I knew what I was going to say before I even picked up the phone.

"I can be there in an hour," I say. "Are you going to be okay until then?"

"Yeah. Yeah, I'll be fine. I can . . . watch *Schitt's Creek* or something. I'll be okay."

"Okay. If you're sure. I'll head out right now. Text me if you need to talk while I'm on the way."

The commute from Bushwick to Astoria is terrible, and I find myself furiously staring at my phone every time we pull into a subway station, waiting for the little signal bars to pop up, bracing myself for a text from Ely. I should have taken a cab. An hour is an hour, but it's also a long damn time when you're fresh out of a relapse. Anything can happen in an hour.

You can't be a helicopter parent. Or a helicopter . . . whatever Ely and I are.

This is kind of a thing of mine, though. A couple of weeks after I adopted Haze, he got sick with some kind of respiratory virus. I could hear him wheezing with every breath. The vet seemed okay about it, but I stayed up all night for two nights in a row just watching that cat breathe. Making sure he was still alive.

I want to stare at Ely all night and make sure she's still breathing too.

The bus drops me off, and I ring the bell at Ely's building and stand there for the world's longest twenty seconds waiting for her to buzz me in. But even after she does, as I stride up the stairs to her floor two at a time, my shoulders still don't descend from their tense posture up by my ears.

I know better than anyone that *alive* isn't always the same thing as *okay*.

But then Ely opens the door, and my gaze reflexively skips down her whole body, looking for signs of—of I don't even know what. But whatever I'm looking for, it isn't there. She looks normal, her dark hair drawn up in a messy bun, the bluish smudges under her eyes no more pronounced than usual.

"Sorry it took me so long," I say.

She musters half a smile, at least. "You literally came from Brooklyn. I'm impressed you got here on the same calendar date."

I've never been inside Ely's apartment before. And maybe this isn't the time for it, but I can't help a quick, surreptitious glance around . . . even if the pink velvet sofa and baby-blue credenza probably speak more to her roommates' tastes than to her own.

"Back here," she says, and leads me through a door across the living room.

Ely's bedroom is tiny, about the size of a moderate-to-large suburban bathroom. The bed itself takes up most of the space, with a rickety desk crammed into what remains, its chair facing the window that peers out over the street below.

She kicks the door shut behind me and drops down onto the edge of the bed. I choose the desk chair, even if it—frankly—looks like it may not hold my weight.

Being here, shut in a bedroom with Ely, feels illicit. I can't quite figure out where to rest my gaze; it ends up settled on Ely's hands, watching her fingers clench and flex against the duvet fabric.

I remember how she gripped the sheets as I drove into her that first night. Our only night. The perfect shape her mouth made as she moaned. The line of her arched throat, her thighs tightening around my hips.

Think about cats think about cats think about cats—

"Thanks for coming," she says eventually, which—thank god—puts a halt to my obsessing over her hands and everything they remind me of. I drag my attention back up to her face, but she's looking away, staring at an empty spot on the opposite wall. "Seriously. I know this is probably . . . a lot. It'd be a lot for anyone, but you're in recovery too, so . . . If this is too much, I understand. I don't want to trigger you."

"What? No. No, don't even worry about it. I'm fine." I had no idea she was even concerned about that. "I've been clean for years. It's a lot easier for me to just not think about it, most of the time. You aren't triggering me at all."

Her lips twist into a sad facsimile of a smile. "I wish that were me. I wish I could just not think about it."

"It will be, if you stay clean long enough. Recovery takes time."

She nods slightly. "I felt like I was getting there, maybe. This past year or so . . . I was able to forget. It felt like I was just like anyone else. And maybe that made me cocky, because I swear, I thought . . ."

I know what she thought. It's the same thing I thought before my relapses: *I can do this. I'm better now. I can handle it.* But I couldn't handle it. And Ely is no different.

I just wish it hadn't taken this slip for her to figure that out.

"Remember what you told Haze the other day. It's just a blip, and you're *continuing*. That cat will hold you to it. Trust me."

It earns me a brief, muffled laugh, which is something.

My hand is on her wrist. For a moment I tense—*I should move; I should stop touching her*—but then I curl my fingers around those delicate bones, and she draws back just enough to press our palms together. Her fingertips rest light atop my veins. Against my will, I shiver.

This is it: This is the point where I always pull away. Every relationship, it feels like. They open up, they become vulnerable, and the pressure to reciprocate that vulnerability makes me want to run.

I don't want to run this time.

"When I was first starting out," I say, "I had a really hard time breaking into the scene. I felt like I was pouring everything I had into my work and no one cared. I was telling people who I was, and they were looking right at me, looking into my soul, and rejecting it. I mean, that's what art is, right? It's personal. So when people hate it, it's like they're saying they hate you."

Ely is watching me with her big dark eyes, and right now it feels just like that: like she's looking at my art. Peering past all the layers I have wrapped around myself into a part of me I haven't shared with anyone.

"I thought about quitting. So many times. Honestly, I'm surprised I didn't. I was barely holding it together at that point. I was just a few years out from everything that happened with my family, and I just . . . my head went to a dark place. Too many times. My dad was an asshole. The violent kind. I guess that left a mark on me in more ways than one—I kept thinking maybe this was what I deserved anyway. Kept hearing his voice in my head saying I was a piece of shit, better off dead. And then out of nowhere my work got noticed by the right people, and suddenly I had a gallery show, and I was selling work, and I'd finally fucking made it—or at least I was well on my way."

It felt like a dream. And my first instinct—god, I hated this—my first instinct was to call my mom.

Instead I called everyone else I knew. Maybe it was spiteful in part. I'd been the last person to succeed. I'd been the one they'd all pitied. But here I was, and my gallery was better than theirs had been, my art was selling for more, and a fucked-up part of me wanted them to know it.

I hope I'm a better person now than I was back then, but sometimes I'm not sure.

"So after the opening night, some people took me out to celebrate," I say. "Important people. And I figured . . . why not, right? I had earned it. It was worth it. And it wasn't a big deal just this once. So I had a glass of champagne, which turned into a few, which turned into shots at the bar. And that one night turned into a relapse that took me months to claw my way out of."

Ely's hand tightens around mine. I hadn't realized we were still holding hands. After a second, I squeeze back.

"I guess what I'm trying to say is . . . you aren't alone. And you aren't the first person this has happened to, not by far."

Ely attempts a smile, but it comes out tremulous. I wish I could squeeze her hand tighter, but if I did, I'd worry about breaking fingers. "I just feel stupid. I should have known better."

"If you're stupid, then I'm stupid too. Maybe we can just be idiots together?"

The smile is still shaky, but it widens slightly. She lets out a shallow breath and says, "I'd like that."

"I'd like that too."

It's too far. It's way too far.

It isn't far enough.

She's the one who shifts in and slides her nose along my cheekbone with a soft sigh, her exhale hot on my skin. I can smell the clean-linen scent of her detergent—or maybe it's her shampoo, as a lock of her hair drifts forward to graze my jaw.

We are held together in a castle of our own making, an existence of breath and skin and the marvel of Ely's lashes skirting her cheek.

I kiss her, and I don't regret it.

She makes a soft sound against my mouth, as if she didn't think I'd actually go so far—but then she kisses me back, parting her lips for me. I've leaned in so far that I'm in danger of falling out of the desk chair and right into Ely's lap. And that seems to be her idea too; both her hands are on my back, dragging me in closer, and god, I want to go there. I want to go wherever the hell Ely Cohen takes me.

The chair finally tips me out and I stumble forward, half

knocking Ely back onto the bed. My self-control gives in about as easily as the chair and I follow after her, pushing her the rest of the way down. She hums against my mouth, dragging one knee up along my side to curl her leg around—

Shit, stop, stop, fuuuuuck.

I yank my mouth away from hers. Even if I can't quite make myself stand upright yet, I can do this: stay here half-crouched over her body on this tiny twin bed with my face turned sharply away from hers, gasping.

"Sorry," I manage at last, around the time I gather the ability to slowly push myself away from her and back into the precarious-feeling desk chair. "Wasn't really supposed to end like that."

Ely is still half-reclined on the bed, propped on one elbow with almost-black hair tangled in front of her face and a flush of color high on her cheeks. "You can end it like that anytime you want, mister."

Jesus *Christ.* Even looking at her feels sinful.

"Yeah, no, rules, et cetera; you've heard the lecture before. Good *lord,* I've got to get out of here. You just relapsed. I shouldn't be doing this right now." I let out a fragile laugh and wonder if I sound as terrified as I feel. "Are you going to be okay without me?"

Her brows lift and she says, "I mean, if I say *no* . . . ?" But then she sighs and nods. "Yeah. Sorry. Not trying to play the woe-is-me, I'm-vulnerable card. You can go. I'll be all right. I'll just be lying here *wishing* you'd stayed."

Probably thinking, *What the hell happened to his boundaries?* because that's what I'm thinking right now. I still feel overheated, as if the radiator's on even though it's late June. I scrape both hands back through my hair and blow out hard. "You don't make it easy, do you?"

"Would you like me any better if I did?" she says with a sly grin, and as always, I'm the one left on the back foot.

I don't even have anything to say to that; I just shake my head and fumble around to find my phone and shove it in my back pocket as I stand. She still hasn't moved. Because why would she? She's got me right where she wants me. Right where *I'd* want to be too, if only I weren't so infuriated with myself for losing control. Again.

I do finally make it out, but I text her from the bus and again from the train just to check that she's still okay.

Looking, maybe, for an excuse to go back.

25

ELY

As with most things, the timing could not possibly be worse. I'm less than a week out from my mini-relapse when I get an email back from Nechama Rubenstein, the rebbetzin of the Chabad House in Astoria. I'm in desperate need of more content for my capstone, so I can't exactly blow her off.

I scoped her and the rabbi out carefully before writing them and asking if I could photograph one of their events. Chabad is big but also, like, not really. I had to make sure they didn't know my family. Which meant—with a young couple like Moshe and Nechama Rubenstein—I had to make sure *their* family didn't know my family. Because otherwise I could imagine how things would go: me, the Cohen girl with drug problems, lurking around Chabad House events as if she didn't run off and break her mother's heart. It would have been a bad look.

But neither Moshe nor Nechama is from Crown Heights originally. They're both children of shlichus families—that is, their parents led their own Chabad Houses in other cities, little outposts of Orthodoxy reaching out to Jews who didn't know how to light a Shabbos candle or pronounce a Hebrew prayer.

So I'm pretty sure it's safe.

"Is this a leech thing to do?" I ask Wyatt over the phone as I walk from Thirtieth toward Broadway. A part of me wanted to ask if he could come with me, but that felt childish, as if I were a little girl afraid to go to camp on her own. But that hadn't stopped me from calling him as soon as I left my apartment. "Like . . . isn't it a little parasitic of me to impose on them like this and use them for my project, and the whole time I'm just, like . . . masquerading as this random secular Jew who doesn't know anything about being Orthodox?"

"You *are* a random secular Jew," Wyatt says. "You aren't practicing now, are you?"

I chew my lower lip and sidestep a pile of dog shit that someone considerately left right in the middle of the sidewalk. "I mean . . . I guess not. Not really. I don't know that I'd say I'm *secular,* though."

I still don't know how I feel about G-d. I'm pretty sure he exists. But I thought I was done with all this. I *was* done with it before I went to Shabbos with Michal and felt that magic lighting up inside my chest.

I used to believe in Hashem the way everyone else did. Somewhere along the way I lost that. I wish I could have it back. I don't *want* to be one of those people who say things like "G-d is chaos" or "G-d is a universal constant" or a "cultural legacy." Those are all perfectly fine things to believe. A lot of Jews believe them. But those beliefs don't fill my cup the way religion used to.

I want the feeling of arms wrapped around me, holding me tight. I want the structure of halacha and mitzvot, the rules and commandments all Jews are bound to follow as part of our covenant with Hashem—even the silly ones.

I *want* to believe in G-d, but I gave all that up. I threw it away.

I don't know what I believe now.

"You'll be fine," Wyatt tells me. The sound of his voice is low and soft, and if I closed my eyes, I could imagine him murmuring those words in my ear, the two of us in a dark, quiet place. Alone.

In that universe, I imagine him saying that would immediately relax me. I'd uncoil to bask in the warmth of it. Instead I hover at the edge of the sidewalk, craning my neck to watch for oncoming traffic, waiting for a break between the cars long enough to let me dart across the street. Tension is a live wire strung down my back. And Wyatt's words don't do much.

"I hope you're right," I say. "Otherwise this is going to be really embarrassing."

Maybe I should have just asked him to come. The asking would have sucked, but the having him here would have made it worth it. *Oh well.*

The Astoria Chabad House is located near Thirty-sixth Avenue. It's brand-new; Astoria didn't have much of a Jewish community until recently. I mean, you can't even find a decent Jewish deli in this neighborhood to save your life. I once saw someone ask on the Astoria subreddit where to find good challah, and everyone told them to just suck it up and take the train into Manhattan.

But I guess enough new people have been moving in lately that the demographics have changed, or else someone in charge decided that if they had the money to fund Chabad Houses in Wyoming, then they had the money to fund one in northwestern Queens. I ring the bell and take a step back, my hands laced behind my back and fingers twisting together, sweaty and awkward as fuck. My camera bag suddenly seems too heavy, the straps digging into my shoulders. I feel a lot like a wayward middle school student waiting to be let in for her piano lesson.

The woman who opens the door is short, with a long brown sheitel and a modest navy-blue dress. She smiles the second she lays eyes on me, a bright smile that shows teeth and crinkles the corners of her eyes. I can hear the chaos of raucous children somewhere behind her, all screeching voices and thunderous footsteps.

"You must be Ely," she says. "Please, come in!"

She steps aside to let me move into the entryway. I toe off my shoes next to the collection gathered by the door, my dusty floral Doc Martens taking their place amid the neat line of sensible flats and sneakers. The pair of men's dress shoes is identical to the ones my father used to wear, to the point that I almost wonder if Moshe shops at the same shoe store.

"I'm so glad we were able to make this work. So sorry about the mess, by the way. The kids have been going crazy all summer. Maybe I feed them too much sugar." Nechama touches the back of my elbow, guiding me deeper into the house, chattering away the whole time. "They're very excited to meet you. My daughter Menuchah especially. She loves taking pictures. I'm sure she'll want to hear all about your studies at Parker."

I wonder if Menuchah is like I was, lurking at bus stops and snapping photos of the ladies with baby carriages as they pass by, trying to get the shutter speed *just right* so that the traffic is a blur behind them. If she wastes her allotted computer time developing new presets in Lightroom and could spend hours in the photography exhibits at MoMA.

Or maybe that's egotistical of me. Maybe we're nothing alike at all.

Nechama leads me back into the kitchen, which is large considering this is New York. She even has an island, already laden with dry-goods canisters and a carton of eggs. My mother would be so jealous.

"Have you made challah before?" Nechama asks, so unassumingly I kind of want to die because here it is: my first lie by omission.

"A few times," I say. "But it's been years. I don't remember much."

I remember some, though. I remember the sensation of warm dough pillowing up between my spread fingers, the way flour clouded the air as my mother dusted it over the countertop. But I don't remember how many eggs to use or how to form the intricate braids that my mother always accomplished so easily.

I used to imagine my future standing in a kitchen of my own, braiding challah with my small horde of offspring running around underfoot. I can't admit it to anyone I know now, because they'd think I was bananas, but I still like the idea. Or maybe I just miss the version of myself who craved that future more than anything.

"It's easy enough once you get the hang of it," Nechama says, just as an army of children races into the kitchen. There are six of them, all dark haired and barefoot and sharp elbowed. One flings both arms around Nechama's thighs and she laughs, patting his head. "I had a feeling we wouldn't make it long without company. This is DovBer, Menuchah, Chaya Mushka, Batsheva Tikvah, Bentzion, and the little one is Yehuda Simcha."

"Hi," I say, waving at them, already certain there's no way in hell I'm gonna remember all those names. Dvora was just as bad as I am. She used to jokingly call every little girl Chaya Mushka and every boy Menachem Mendel. And since pretty much every Chabad family we knew named a kid after the Lubavitcher Rebbe or his wife, odds were that she was at least part right at least 20 percent of the time.

I've met a hundred Chaya Mushkas in my life, but hearing the name still makes me flinch.

"Hi," says one of the girls. "You're here to take photos of us?"

"Well, not specifically . . . but, yeah, I'm here to take some pictures—and to braid challah with your ima," I say. "Are you going to help us?"

She nods fiercely. "I always help Ima make challot. Can I try your camera?"

I'm abruptly very glad I brought both my DSLR and my film

camera, because the thought of trying to figure out how to politely inform a ten-year-old that no, they can't waste my precious film makes me want to punch myself in the nose because it's so obviously an asshole thing to say. "Sure," I tell her, and set my camera bag down on the nearest stool to dig out the DSLR and a lens. "You must be Menuchah, right?"

She nods and takes the camera when I pass it to her, turning it on and peering through the viewfinder with the practiced ease of someone who has done it a hundred times before. "Is this the D850?"

"Good eye."

"I have a D3500," she says, almost morosely, swiveling the focusing ring and snapping a photo of her mother.

"That's still a really good camera. Especially for beginners."

She makes a face and takes another picture, then pulls back to stare down at the screen, examining it. "It's okay. I've had it for like two years, though."

You're like ten years old, I want to tell her, but having been ten years old myself once, I know about how well that'd go over.

"Give Ely her camera back, Minni," Nechama says. "I have no idea how much it would cost to fix that if you broke it, and I don't want to find out."

Menuchah hands me the camera reluctantly, and I pack it away again, getting out my SLR instead. It's a hell of a lot lighter in my grip than the bulky D850 and didn't cost nearly as much—and thank god for that, because after buying my digital I had to spend the rest of my precious money on developing if I was gonna shoot analog.

And of course I was gonna shoot analog. For all the photos I can take on digital, scrolling through a million shots of the same scene to find the one that's exactly right, nothing will ever beat the magic of film. Of having to trust yourself to find the perfect shot, the perfect frame, and the perfect focus.

"What is that?" Menuchah asks.

"It's a range finder," I say. "For shooting on film."

Menuchah has that hungry look in her eyes, but I can't trust a ten-year-old not to use up all my film on art shots of her kitchen island, so this time I don't hand it to her.

Nechama disperses the children, or at least the male ones. The girls get to stay, to become part of this tradition that is supposed to carry them into their adult lives as wives and mothers. I find myself thinking about that second universe again, the one where I'm in Nechama's position, baking challah with my daughters. I wonder who this fantasy version of me would have married. Where I would have met him—because it would, of course, be a him.

That version of me might still shoot photos, but only as a hobby. If she had a career, it would have to be something that paid more consistently, especially if she'd married a scholar whose time was to be spent reading Torah instead of toiling behind a counter somewhere.

Nechama assembles the ingredients we need and I draw back, making room for her daughters to join her at the counter, some of them kneeling on chairs to reach. I do my best to be discreet with my photos—especially with film, I don't want to waste any shots on a scene that is too overtly influenced by my presence. Things can change when people know they're being observed—something I luckily learned early while I was shooting exclusively on digital. I have had to throw out far too many shots of rictus smiles and taut shoulders.

Maybe it's the children's presence, but Nechama doesn't seem afflicted by the same problem. When I take a photo of her hands—just her hands, deftly weaving together the long strands of challah dough—I can almost imagine they belong to my mother. I can almost be there, all those years ago, standing at our own kitchen counter and weaving my own small loaf.

My phone buzzes midway through the challah making. When I check, it's Wyatt's name that has popped up on the lock screen.

WYATT: hope it's going well. I'm eating bread and thinking about you.

I type back: **does your bread have a six-stranded braid or is it boring**

WYATT: how would you categorize limp whole grain that's still plastic-wrapped from the grocery store?

"Do you want to try?" Nechama says, and I jerk my head upright a bit guiltily, like I'm betraying her by spending time texting instead of just betraying my own project.

"Oh. . . . Sure," I say. "Why not? Like I told you, though, it's been a really . . . really long time."

"It's okay if your bread is ugly," one of Nechama's daughters pipes up. "Ima says Hashem didn't command us to bake *pretty* challah."

I laugh. "I suppose that's true."

"It's a mitzvah," Nechama says, as if I still need the encouragement. "A good deed. I'll help you. Come on."

She helps me roll out six long strands of dough. And as much as I claimed not to remember, it turns out braiding challah is all muscle memory. I know on some ingrained level how to weave the ropes together into their tapestry. Nechama doesn't even have to help, in the end. And when we're sliding the loaves into the oven, our two adult challot surrounded by their smaller fellows, it's impossible to tell which one was mine and which was hers.

"I grew up in Chabad," I confess while we wait for the bread to bake. "In Crown Heights, actually."

I'm not sure if I should take her clear surprise as a compliment or not. But Nechama schools her expression into submission with remarkable alacrity and says, "Really? You should have said! I wouldn't have done nearly so much lecturing on Judaism 101."

I should probably drop it. This is such a nice note to end on—*oh, look, we have something in common; how nice, la la la*—but as usual my traitorous mouth doesn't know when to stop talking.

"I left the community when I was eighteen. Well. I guess you could say I was kicked out. Everyone decided it was better for me to be off the derech than on it." I fiddle with the corner of the still-damp washcloth. "It was my fault, really. I had a drug problem. I hurt a lot of people."

"I'm so sorry," Nechama says softly. "That must have been so difficult for you."

I force a laugh. "It was a long time ago. I'm sure they're happy to be rid of me. They probably never want to see me again."

But Nechama's hand finds my wrist, curling lightly around my arm and squeezing once. "I'm sure they miss you very much. Ely . . . you must know the doors of our community are never closed forever. Even if you caused a great deal of pain . . . there is still a place for you here, with us. If you want it."

I'm not so sure Dvora agrees. But when I meet Nechama's kind brown gaze, I can tell she really means it, down to the word.

I want to say she's being naïve. I broke my family's trust in me. I broke *everyone's* trust. My family are *Kohens,* descended from a long tradition of rabbis and scholars going all the way back to the actual town of Lubavitch that Chabad Lubavitch is named for. That yichus, that lineage, is half the reason why I'm not welcome back. Maybe other sects would shun you for life if you went off the derech, but Nechama's right—not Chabad. I knew so many kids when I was growing up who had an aunt or a cousin who lived in Boston and didn't believe in G-d anymore. They'd still come back for Seder every year. They knew they still had homes to return to, if they ever changed their minds.

But they probably didn't steal thousands of dollars from their parents' credit cards before leaving.

"You don't have to let your past define you," Nechama goes on, her hand still rubbing a gentle pattern against my wrist. "There is nothing you could ever do that would erase Hashem's love for you. *Or* the community's. If you don't think there is a place for you with us anymore, that's your decision. I won't tell you how to live your life. But it isn't because Judaism doesn't want you anymore. Your seat at our table is always open."

I duck my head but not quickly enough to hide the way tears suddenly prickle at my eyes. Nechama doesn't know me. She doesn't know what I've done. But even so, hearing her say this . . . it means everything.

The door isn't open, but it isn't shut anymore either.

Maybe Wyatt was right.

There's always a way back.

26

There's something heady and disorienting about the smell of those chemicals as I wash my prints and clip them to drip-dry on the line. I always get light-headed in the darkroom. Maybe it's an effect of the strange red light, but most likely it's just the developer killing off my brain cells one by one.

The photos are turning out better than I expected. In black and white, they seem almost timeless. Nechama could have emerged from any era between now and the 1940s, a composite of all our mothers and grandmothers and great-grandmothers. And I understand now why these traditions are so important to people, why the community I grew up in clings to them with both hands—they're like a thread strung through time. If you tug, you'll feel your ancestors tugging back.

I dip another print and watch the image emerge beneath the developer fluid, the smiling faces of Nechama's daughters smudged with flour, Nechama herself wrist deep in a mound of dough and watching them with fondness crinkling the edges of her eyes. Film either softens its subjects or makes them stark; with Nechama, it's the former.

There are a couple of digital photos of me in there too. I'm impressed by Menuchah's eye; for such a young girl, she really has an instinct for how to frame a subject. I almost don't recognize myself. I fit into the scene more easily than I would have thought. All that time away from Crown Heights, but I still look right at home kneading challah dough, a tiny smile settled on my lips as if I couldn't be happier doing anything else.

The door to the darkroom swings open and shut again. There's not that many people using analog at Parker, so I look on reflex.

"Nice to see someone's focused today," Wyatt says. His smile always makes me stand a little straighter.

"Unlike yourself, I'm guessing?"

Wyatt ducks under one of the lines of drying prints and moves closer to me, peering over my shoulder at my own photographs. "For the record, I am very busy and important."

"Oh, right. And that's why you've stalked me into the darkroom. Just doing your mentoring duty."

"Absolutely."

He reaches past me to pluck one of the images off the line. The sudden proximity makes me stand too still, like if I move, the moment will splinter.

The photo is one I took of Nechama standing behind her youngest daughter, Batsheva, Nechama's hands gently cupped around Shevy's as she shows her daughter how to knead the dough. A puff of flour has been caught in the air, frozen forever by the snap of my camera lens.

"This one," Wyatt says. "This is perfection."

At least it's red in here; my blush blends right in. "Not perfect. But it's . . . okay."

Wyatt shakes his head. "Nothing's ever perfect. But nothing has to be. And you shouldn't doubt yourself like that. You should take pride in your work."

I can't keep looking at him when he's saying things like that.

The eye contact makes me feel too unsettled, hyperaware of my position in space relative to his. The air between us feels as if there's an electric current running through it. So I turn away to look at the other photos myself, scanning from one shot to the next without really seeing them. Maybe Wyatt's right. Maybe there's a part of me that can't stand to be observed, even by him.

"You're talented," Wyatt says from behind me. His voice is soft but close enough that I can almost imagine his head tilting in toward my neck, his breath ruffling through my hair. "Acknowledging that won't hold you back. It won't keep you from learning. I wish you could see yourself the way everyone else does. The way I do."

I turn around and he's so close all of a sudden, close enough that I would have stepped back on reflex if not for the table behind me, pressing up against my thighs. Wyatt seems frozen too, his eyes widened slightly and his lips parted but unbreathing. It would be easy for him to step away. But he stays where he is. And if before I found it impossible to look at him, now I can't look away. The red light casts strange shadows about his face and shimmers in his dark eyes like lights moving beneath the surface of a lake.

Any minute now, I think. *Any minute now he's going to move back.*

But he doesn't, and I stay where I am, and my heart is pounding so fast I wonder if he can hear it.

The words I want to say are trapped on my lips: *I wish I could see anything the way you do.* But speaking has become impossible. Wyatt shifts closer, just slightly, and when his fingertips skim my hip, I almost shiver right out of my skin.

The loud droning sound of Wyatt's phone vibrating in his pocket cracks the amber of that moment, and reality crashes in like an unexpected wave. He flinches and takes a sharp step back. I turn my face away, pretending sudden interest in the tray of developer fluid on the table behind me. But really, I just don't want Wyatt to see my face. I don't want him to see that I can't quite hide how hurt I am that he just . . .

It's like he regrets it already.

"I'm sorry. I have to get this," he says, and I nod without looking up. I stare at the developer and listen to the sound of his footsteps walking away, the subsequent open-shut of the darkroom door.

I exhale and tip my head forward, bracing myself against the table for a moment. *Shit.* If that phone hadn't rung when it did . . . I feel like I know what would have happened next. And it was time. Wasn't it? We both want this; we both have tried so hard to keep things professional. It seems so stupid to keep fighting it. We're both adults. I'm not even Wyatt's student anymore. For fuck's sake, I've spent the night *at his house.* If there was ever a boundary there, it's clearly shredded to bits by now.

I wonder if Wyatt is relieved we got interrupted. Maybe he's out there thanking whoever is on the other end of the phone for saving his ass from the student throwing herself at him in the darkroom. Maybe he's already castigating himself for even considering going for it, making a brand-new list of all the reasons we can never be together. A list I'll probably get the privilege of hearing recited as soon as he comes back, always with the cautious and inherently condescending tone of a man who thinks he knows what's best for me.

Because that's what this is all about, isn't it? Like, let's be honest—Wyatt isn't holding himself back because he thinks his professorial pride would be injured by fucking me again. He is on some martyr shit. He thinks if he was with me again, really with me, he'd be doing some kind of irreversible harm to my studently innocence. And while I appreciate that he is considerate of the potential power imbalance, said power imbalance hardly even exists. *Doesn't* exist. Not really.

So it's just Wyatt wallowing in the swamp of his own indulgent self-sacrifice.

But he still wants it. All this time that's passed since we had sex . . . it's changed nothing. Wyatt *wants this*. He wants *me*. And maybe that's egotistical to admit, but he literally just told me to stop being modest.

Why are we still pretending? Why am I still letting him decide how *I* feel or set the standards for what I should find to be exploitative?

If that phone hadn't gone off, we'd be kissing right now. His hands in my hair, on my body, slipping beneath the hem of my shirt. And I'd have my tongue in his mouth and my fingers latching around his belt loops as he shoved me back against the table behind us, developer fluid sloshing in the trays and spilling onto the vinyl floor.

My skin still feels too alive where he touched me, that place on my hip burning with the memory of his hand.

If we were together, he'd murmur sweet things in my ear about how much he misses me every time I'm away.

When he comes back . . . if he comes back . . . this ends. I'll cup his face between both my hands, and I'll kiss him so hard he forgets he's ever kissed anyone else.

I exhale and slide another print into the developer. I get through just one more of them before the door opens again, and I listen to the sound of Wyatt's footsteps as he moves through the small maze of the light lock. I turn around, summoning up the courage to take those last steps forward, and immediately stop in my tracks.

Wyatt stands in the entryway, his phone hanging from one hand with the screen still lit up in red scale thanks to some screen-filtering app.

His face is streaked with tears.

27

WYATT

“What happened?” Ely says immediately, closing the distance between us in three quick strides. “Wyatt.”

I’m not really capable of speaking. I’m strangely aware of my face, the way my skin stretches over bone. I feel like I’m wearing a mask. Ely reaches for both my hands and squeezes tight, like she’s trying to anchor me down in this reality—she doesn’t realize, of course, that it’s impossible. I’m already untethering.

“What happened?” Ely says again.

I look at her, finally, really *look* at her. Her eyes are big and worried, but right now, in a way, it’s as if I’m watching her on TV instead of in real life. My fingers twitch against the backs of her hands. I taste metal in my mouth, sour and sickening.

“That was my mom,” I manage at last. The words come out dry, cracked. My tongue feels like a slug that’s been doused in salt: shriveled up and dehydrated. Barely functional.

“Your mom,” Ely says, and I can guess what she’s thinking. My mom—the one I haven’t spoken to since shortly after I came out. The one who let my dad kick me out of my childhood home, then may or may not have sent me a Hannah Wilke book in secret—half an apology.

I'm distantly aware that my face is wet. This is all happening to someone else, some other Wyatt. A Wyatt who is crying. Which makes no sense, because the Wyatt that lives in my chest is tight and smooth and unscarred, like a river-weathered stone. Unfeeling.

"Yeah. She. She, uh . . ." I shake my head, a dog trying to clear water out of its ears. "Sorry."

"Don't apologize."

"It's my dad," I manage at last. "He's . . . dead."

28

We end up in my office, which is a much safer place to have this conversation, considering anyone could walk into the darkroom at any time to find their professor having a breakdown by the developer trays.

I maintain the presence of mind to lock the door behind us, and we both end up sitting on the floor behind my desk, legs stretched out on the carpet. Our clasped hands rest between our hips, a part of me continually surprised that she hasn't yet pulled away.

"You know," I say after we've been silent for a good three minutes. My gaze is fixed on our hands, her thumb rubbing a warm pattern against the backs of my knuckles. "I don't even care that he's gone. He was . . . he was a terrible person. A terrible father. Not just because he didn't accept me but in general. He was mean and violent and made everyone around him feel like they had to walk on eggshells all the time. The world's better off without him in it." I'm sure Ely is horrified by this confession. Who wouldn't be? Doesn't matter what my father did or said. I shouldn't actively be pleased that the man is dead.

But fuck, didn't I spend most of my childhood wishing he'd swim out too deep into the sound, deep enough that no one would find him before he sank down past the barnacles and algae, all the way down to bedrock?

The sight of my father's face, red with that unique cocktail of anger and alcohol, is a permanent resident in my memory. And it surges up again today, flashing against the backs of my eyelids every time I blink.

But right now he's cold in a coffin somewhere, that red skin gone waxy and pale.

"Fuck him, then." I lift my head. Ely has her mouth set in a thin, hard line, her brows knotted together like she's bracing for a blow. "Fuck him. I'm sorry you had to put up with that. I'm glad he's dead too."

I puff out a heavy breath that almost but doesn't quite reach the threshold of being a laugh. I'm dizzy all of a sudden, almost giddy with it all. "Yeah. Pretty much."

I finally draw my hand away from hers and drag those fingers back through my hair. I wish she wasn't seeing me like this. I'm supposed to be the rational one, the steady presence, ten years sober with all my shit together. But here I am, the truth of me: anxious, chronically irritable, still clawing my way through life day by day. I want to find the key to my own brain and fix it, but I've tried that enough times to know wishing myself better isn't how this works.

"So what are you going to do?" Ely asks at last. "Are you gonna go?"

I told her, on the brief trip from the darkroom to my office, how my mother had asked me to come to the funeral. At the time I'd had to bite my tongue to keep from saying, *I think the hell not.* Even the sound of her voice took me back to that place: to the smell of salt water, the crunchy feel of ocean grass underfoot, the roar of my father's voice.

I shudder, tension drawing my shoulders up toward my ears before I can force them back down. "I don't know. I don't— I'm not sure I can face him again. Even dead, I don't . . ."

My father's face used to go so damn red when he was angry. Maybe it was the Irish in us. It was like his rage went liquid and pooled beneath his cheeks.

Against my will, one of my hands drifts up to rub at the knob on my collarbone, the only remaining scar from the time my father shattered the bone.

Ely clutches both her knees, gripping so tight her knuckles have become pale mountains straining against her skin. "You don't have to. You don't owe them anything."

I nod, and I'm pretty sure—like 65 percent sure—that I believe her. My dad used to love to say how he gave me life and a roof over my head, so I owed him obedience and whatever else. Being an adult, looking back, I can see that for what it is. But the scars still run deep. I thought I'd healed—thought I'd left that pain in the past—but it's still there, hidden but *there* all this time, like a piece of broken glass still sharp enough to cut.

"Come with me," I say before I can think better of it. "To North Carolina. I can't do this alone. Come with me."

"What?"

My face is wet—I'm crying, right in front of her. I hadn't even realized. I look at her properly, right in the eyes, so I can't be tempted to take it back. "I mean it. Come to the funeral with me. Please, Ely."

A pathetic request, pitiful. I'm like a child who needs his hand held to cross the street.

"Okay," she says.

"Really? You mean it?"

Ely reaches over and takes my hand again, clasping it between both of her own and gripping tight. "Really. I'll come with you. I mean it."

29

ELY

Flying over North Carolina, all I can see outside the airplane window is green.

I have my brow pressed against the glass as I watch the trees grow from moss to little clumps of broccoli, until at last the plane is low enough that I can pick out individual cars on the highway and count the number of people with pools in their backyards—which is not many, at least compared to California.

The wheels hit the runway, and I turn to look at Wyatt, who has been ignoring the view in favor of staring down at his own fists clenched atop his knees.

"Hey," I say. "You good?"

He presses his lips together and nods. "Yeah. I think so. Just . . . been a long time since I've been back here, you know?"

I do know. I haven't forgotten the way my hands shook when I landed in New York at the start of the summer. Just being back there, even miles away from anyone I'd known in my old life, felt like a risk.

"We can leave anytime you want," I tell him. "If it ever gets too much. We can fly home. Or we can rent an Airbnb on the beach and do whatever we want for the rest of the weekend. Okay?"

He finally looks at me, a weak smile curving at his lips. "Yeah. I'm gonna hold you to that."

It's a long drive from the airport to the coast, where Wyatt's family lives. The land outside goes from lush and verdant to sandy and arid. Hanging one arm out of the window of our rental car in the heavy, humid heat, I feel like I can smell the ocean long before we're even close. I've never felt anything like the air here. It droops over you like a damp blanket. Even when we close the windows to put the air-conditioning on blast, I can't forget how hot it is. Every breath feels weighted.

Wyatt puts on music, and we spend most of the ride talking about concerts we've seen, stupid things we did in high school and somehow got away with, places we want to travel—good conversation but avoidant. We keep skirting carefully around the real thing neither of us can stop thinking about: what waits at the end of this drive.

"I still can't believe you were in the Marines," I say as we drive past what the signs tell me is a Marine Corps air base. I have no idea if Wyatt was stationed there or if anyone in his family was. "You don't really strike me as the type."

I'm not sure if the comment strays too close to sore subjects. Wyatt's grip shifts on the steering wheel, but there's no telltale clench of his jaw or tightening of his brow.

"The military would pay for college, if I wanted to go," he says eventually. "And I did."

My brows go up before I can stop them. This is the first I'm hearing of Wyatt being interested in college. After all, he never went—his artistry is almost completely self-taught.

"So why didn't you?" I ask, and this earns me a huff of a laugh from Wyatt.

"Lots of reasons. I lost the chance when I got dishonorably discharged, for one. The Marines weren't gonna pay for college anymore. And anyway, I got hooked on drugs shortly after that, so even if I could have afforded it, there wasn't much of a future for me in school anyway. At least not as far as I could see at the time."

It's the same story I've heard a million times before. It's my own story, in some ways, minus the military enlistment. I wish I could crawl back in time and find that fragile young version of Wyatt and show him an image of his own future. Maybe if he'd known that everything would turn out okay, that one day he'd be a famous artist, grown and happy . . . maybe it would have changed things.

But that's probably just a flight of fancy. It wouldn't have changed anything for me. Baby Ely was hell-bent on self-destruction, and finding out I eventually got clean would have only made me want to self-destruct faster to avoid the risk of my own future happiness.

It's late afternoon by the time we arrive in Wyatt's hometown. It's one of those small beach villages with clapboard houses and a historical landmark sign posted at every corner, the waves lapping at the pylons of every aging dock. Charming, kitschy, but ever so slightly gone to seed, its best tourist days somewhere fifteen years in the past. We drive past rows of seaside cottages raised up on stilts with clover lawns and ornamental piles of seashells decorating their whitewashed porches. But we don't stop at any of those. Instead we turn inland, following winding roads past an ancient cemetery, an abandoned gas station, a shell-shocked but still open video store, into a different neighborhood.

Here the houses are smaller, one story with peeling paint and pockmarked driveways. Overgrown grass creeps up through the cracks in the sidewalk, ancient oak trees curling gnarled branches toward the sky, window units dripping water down the sides of walls and staining the wood.

Wyatt's house is at the end of the lane, huddled up against a brackish marsh. It's two stories, unlike the rest on this street, but somehow still gives the impression of squatness. We pull in to the driveway right behind a rickety, half-rusted pickup. The house itself looks like it might have been painted robin's-egg blue once upon a time. But despite the faded paint, the shrubs in the front garden are meticulously trimmed, and the mailbox is planted amid a bed of flowering pink begonias.

"This is it," Wyatt says as he shuts off the engine. But he doesn't get out of the car—just sits there with both hands still gripping the wheel.

I reach over on impulse and grasp his knee, giving it a brief squeeze. "Hey," I say. "It's not too late. We can still turn back. We can go find a shitty motel somewhere and pretend none of this ever happened."

He lets out a brittle laugh. "Yeah. I suppose we could."

But that seems to be enough to jolt him out of that frozen moment. He gets out of the car, and I follow a moment after.

30

WYATT

We don't even make it all the way to the house before the front door opens and an ancient dog comes hobbling out on matchstick legs. It's been almost fifteen years, so it takes me a second to recognize my childhood dog. Roscoe's gone white around the nose, but when I kneel down to let him lick my face, his tongue is as wet and warm as I remember. And just for a second the fist around my heart unclenches a tiny bit, and I laugh as Roscoe snuffles at every inch of exposed skin. He even smells how I remember, like salt water and wet fur.

"Hey, buddy," I say, scratching at his neck and resisting the urge to bury my face against his shoulder. If I did that, I might never be able to let him go again. "Did you miss me?"

"Roscoe!" a familiar voice shouts from the front doorway. I've been in the Northeast long enough now that her southern accent sounds foreign to my ears, like warm honey. "Roscoe, get off him!"

Roscoe limps obediently toward the house, only to change his mind halfway there and attempt a wobble back toward me. His tail is wagging so hard I have to hurry forward and grip his collar so he doesn't fall over.

"Good boy," I murmur, and twist my fingers in his fur as I gather the courage to look up.

My mother stands on the front porch, wearing one of her church dresses with the white collars. I'm too far away to see her face properly, but there's no mistaking the way she grips the support beam on the porch, her body listing to one side like she can't quite stand upright. She didn't say anything about being ill—but then again, when Roscoe calms down enough to let me stand and move closer to the house, I realize her weakness isn't due to illness.

My mother's face goes through a complicated series of expressions, all equally uninterpretable—but then the spell breaks, and she staggers forward, half tripping down the front steps. She closes the distance between us, and before I can open my mouth to speak, to apologize or I don't know what, she flings both arms around my shoulders and yanks me into the tightest hug.

I suck in a sharp, startled breath and freeze.

"My baby," she says, the words muffled against my chest, where I'm sure she can feel my heart slamming against my rib cage. "My boy—you've gotten so big."

Her graying hair tickles my chin, her fingertips pressing hard against my shoulders. She smells like floral perfume, even though I never knew my mother to wear perfume. I never knew her to be much of a hugger either.

I find Ely's gaze over my mother's shoulder, feeling somewhat frantic. I'm not sure whether I desperately want Ely to save me or just to explain what the hell is happening here, because this, whatever it is, is the last thing I expected.

The moment stretches on long enough, my arms hanging useless and indecisive at my sides, that my mother finally pulls back and looks at me properly. Her cheeks are wet with tears.

"Hi, Mom."

"My sweet baby," she says. Her voice is trembling. "I'm so

sorry. There aren't enough words to tell you how sorry I am. I've missed you so much, honey. But your father . . ."

But my father what? I want to say. I'm sure my father *was* the driving force behind me getting kicked out of this house. But it's not as if my mom stood up for me. She could have fought on my behalf. She could've argued. Instead she was just a helpless wisp standing by, like part of the backdrop. An extra in the scenes of her own life.

I look down at my shoes in the sparse grass. My therapist used to tell me to try to find the word to describe what I felt—to learn the difference between anger and frustration, anxiety and anticipation. But if there's a word for this feeling, I don't know what it is.

"Let me bring the luggage inside the house," I say, and take a step back, out of her arms' reach.

Ely tugs the duffels out of the back seat of our rental. When she passes mine over, our eyes meet. I've never been the greatest at reading facial expressions, but right now, the question in her eyes is louder than spoken word.

"I'm good," I murmur, low enough that only she can hear.

"You must be Ely," my mother says as we head up the cracked pavement back toward the house. "Wyatt told me you were coming. I'm so glad to meet you. I'm Mary."

"Nice to meet you," Ely says from behind me. I'm already ahead of them both, taking the steps up the front porch two at a time. I don't know what I'm in such a hurry for. Getting inside that house isn't gonna get me out of this situation. I can't run away anymore.

"Your brother's in the kitchen," Mary says once we've taken off our shoes in the foyer, suitcases clustered around the foot of the stairs. "He'll be wanting to see you, I'm sure."

Of course Liam's home. I don't know why I assumed he wouldn't be. It's our dad's funeral.

"I didn't remember you had a brother," Ely said.

"Yeah. He's my twin, actually." I probably should have told her that sooner, but it's hard to talk about your family when you don't exist in their world.

My mother leads us down the hall and into the kitchen, which looks just like it always did: snipped right out of a 1970s Polaroid, complete with yellow tile floors and Formica countertops. Liam's at the table. He's bigger than I remember—tall and bulky, far too big for the plastic chair he's in. He's let his beard grow out. I push down a pang of envy; the most I've ever been able to manage is a weak stubble.

He's out of that chair before Mom or I can say a word, clapping one beefy hand on my shoulder before I can even consider stopping him. "Bro," he says. "You don't even have fuckin' *Facebook*."

A laugh escapes me, high-pitched and frantic. I don't even know how to respond to that. Liam looked me up on social media? All this time, my brother was trying to get in touch with me, and I had no idea. At least, that's what he's telling me.

But what reason does Liam have to lie?

For a moment we're both silent, staring at each other, Liam's gray eyes anxious beneath knit brows. He's not gonna break. He's waiting for me to make the first move.

And I do. I pull my brother into a rough embrace, breathing in the dizzy scent of Old Spice as he pats me on the back the way guys do in football movies.

"I couldn't get ahold of you anywhere," Liam says when we finally separate. "I tried. You never picked up when I called. And when I googled you, all I could find was bougie articles about you being some fancy-pants art snob."

The situation is still awkward but maybe less so. Something about how nervous Liam seems, maybe. Like he's the one who wants my attention and affection for once instead of the other way around.

I snort. "I guess they're not wrong. This is Ely, by the way. Ely, meet my brother, Liam."

Ely steps forward, smiling, to shake Liam's hand. God freaking bless her for being chill about this. I'm not sure I would be so mellow in her place.

"Nice to meet you," she says.

"Likewise. Now that my twin brother has a girlfriend, I'm looking forward to living out my life dream of telling you all the embarrassing shit Wyatt got up to as a child."

Ely's pretty cheeks turn pink. "I'm not—"

"Don't you dare," I cut in, shoving Liam a half step toward the table. "You gotta *earn* embarrassing story privileges, and you're running fourteen years behind."

All four of us laugh. I don't look to check, but my mother's chuckle is somewhat wet sounding. The knot in my stomach twists a little tighter.

I feel like I'm living in upside-down land.

"I'll take the luggage upstairs," Ely says. "Let you all have some time to reconnect."

Oh god.

"No, let me," I jump in before anyone else can agree. "They're heavy."

I can't help glancing at Mom when I turn around, though. Her face is slick with tears. And I can't decide if that makes me want to cry myself or punch a wall.

"Your bedroom's ready for you, Wyatt," my mom says. She doesn't use my deadname. My real one seems tremulous on her lips, like she's still testing it out. "We . . . I—I kept it, after you left. In case you ever came back."

"Dad wanted to turn it into a poolroom," Liam offers.

"And why didn't he?"

The words come out harsher than they should. Or maybe exactly as harsh as they ought to be.

I know what it must have cost her to fight my dad on this. But it just feels so . . . Like, Jesus, okay, stand up to him when it's about a bedroom but not when it's about your son? Cool. Priorities, I guess.

"Sorry," I say. Liam looks shocked. My mom, stricken. I feel guilty, even if I shouldn't. "Long trip. Uh. So . . . yeah, let me get that luggage."

And I get the fuck out of there before this can blow up any worse.

At the top of the stairs, though, I'm faced with a fresh problem: With Liam staying in the house, there's just the one bedroom left for me and Ely to share. One bedroom, one bed.

Shit. Maybe I should have explained the whole *not-my-girlfriend* thing to my family after all.

I'm still hovering in the doorway, staring at my childhood double bed, neatly made with faded dove sheets, when Ely comes up. My mom must have changed this. The room used to be all pink and glitter and bows. Now the coral throw pillows are a muted green, and the curlicue white furniture has been replaced by solid wood pieces. Cheap ones, probably from the thrift store, but it puts a lump in my throat.

I cough and move into the room properly, giving Ely room to come in after me and pull the door gently shut.

"You okay?" she asks. She's noticed the bed—I saw her gaze linger on it for a second as she looked the room over—but she hasn't said anything. Even though she surely realizes there's not a fourth bedroom hiding in this tiny clapboard house. "That seemed . . . tense."

Understating it, frankly. "Do you think I was an asshole?"

Both of Ely's brows go up. "What? No. No, of course not. You could've laid into them harder, honestly. They would have deserved it."

"But they changed their minds. It was all my dad in the end. He scared them."

"Was it?" She shrugs. "I mean . . . maybe. I wasn't there. I don't know what it was like living around him."

I do. I remember the fear. It still got me even years after I'd left the state. I remember hearing a familiar-sounding voice on the subway and feeling the floor vanish from underneath me, reeling through space and memory until I realized I was nowhere near him. I wasn't a little kid hiding scared in his childhood home. I was just another dope fiend scaring tourists off public transit.

So, yeah. Maybe I can see it. Maybe I know exactly why my mother never even tried to call me, all those years. If she really did send that book, it would have taken all the courage she could save up. She probably sweated the whole rest of the week, waiting for someone to mention seeing her in the post office around him. *Say, Mrs. Cole, what were you mailin' off the other day, anyhow?*

But understanding doesn't seem to make me feel better. Resentment still curls its vine tight around my insides. Those thorns stick in deep.

The funeral isn't until tomorrow, which means we've got a long night ahead of us. I should have thought of that when I bought the plane tickets. We could have landed later, spent less time here. Could have flown out tomorrow night instead of the next morning. Shortsighted.

"Sorry for dragging you down here," I manage eventually.

Ely shakes her head. "No. Don't start with that. I'm glad you did. You shouldn't have to do this alone."

You're such a good friend, Ely said the other week. I replay that in my head very intentionally, over and over again. Good *friend.*

"I can sleep on the couch," I say.

"Don't be stupid, Wyatt. It's *your* room."

"Honestly, that's part of why I don't want to sleep in it." Memories are painted all over the walls in eggshell white. Even a fresh coat hasn't covered up that depression in the wall where Dad shoved me so hard I dented the drywall. The dresser is still positioned discreetly in front of that spot.

I suppose it's not like I only have evil memories here. Liam and I would hang out sometimes and play "murder zombies" with his action figures. I'd stolen our mom's lipstick and would smear it all over their bodies to look like blood.

I kick my duffel where I've dumped it on the floor by the dresser. All that's in there is my funeral suit, pajamas, a change of clothes, and my toiletry kit. I didn't even bring my camera, which I usually take everywhere. There's nothing I want to memorialize here.

"Want to go out?" she suggests. "Walk around?"

"Sure. We can if you want."

Downstairs, my mother is making a racket in the kitchen. I can't hear him speaking, but I'm sure Liam's in there with her. Ely and I make it out the front door without being intercepted, which feels like its own special ops mission.

The street heading into town is sand dusted; the wild grasses that grow out on the dunes aren't quite enough to hold erosion at bay. The sun bakes down on the tops of our heads; I'm glad I brought a hat. Walking around this place with a baseball cap shoved on my head and my hands stuffed in my pockets, I feel like I'm fourteen again. Always playing at being a man. Playing at being Liam, really. Up in New York, I might pass; here, I feel like you could take one look at me and tell. I feel like I'm wearing a cheap and badly sized costume, one that might come apart at the seams any second.

It's been a long damn time since I've felt this insecure. And I hate this place for it, all over again.

"What are you thinking about?" Ely asks eventually, once we've turned a few corners and are in sight of downtown. Or what passes for downtown, anyway. Really it's just a few bars, a couple

B and Bs, and a tourist shop masquerading as a "general store." Every single restaurant on this street serves seafood.

"Oh, you know. The usual emo teenage nonsense. *I gotta get out of this one-horse town,* et cetera, et cetera. I guess there are some things you never grow out of."

"Where did you hang out when you were younger? I'm guessing not here and not at home."

I snort. "Yeah, hard no on both of those options. You remember that bridge we drove over to get here? The one off the mainland?"

She nods.

"There's a little access road that cuts beneath it. On one side you've got some dinghies tied up, although who knows who they belong to, because I've never seen them get used? On the other side there's this patch of flat grass where me and Liam used to go smoke blunts and listen to the car radio. It was a shitty spot, trashed with all the garbage people threw off the bridge overhead. But it had the best view of the sunset on the whole East Coast."

Ely gives me a look. "Maybe we should have gone there instead."

"Maybe. I have no idea if it still exists. If it does, it's probably even more trashed than it used to be." And I'm worried that if I go back now, as an adult, it won't be how I remember. I don't want to dull one of the few good memories I have from growing up.

We wander along the boardwalk until the road ends—abruptly, as if the town used to exist past here but one night the sound rose up and swallowed the rest of the street in a mouthful of salt water. It's almost dinnertime, the sunlight taking on that amber quality of late afternoon; we have no choice but to head home.

And like the middle school kid I once was, I'm already dragging my heels.

31

When we get back the house is thick with the spice-syrup aroma of candied yams roasting in the oven, my mother flitting back and forth between stove and kitchen counter. As always, she's juggling a circus performer's worth of tricks: the yams but also collard greens, chicken, a pitcher of sweet tea with the sugar still dissolving, a pan of rolls cooling on the island. I have no idea how she got this all done in the time we were out, unless she started before we left.

"Hope it's not awful," says Liam, and that's when I realize—he's not just in the kitchen watching Mom work. He's got juice splattered on his apron from stirring the greens; more to the point, he's *wearing a dang apron,* which means he's actually helping our mother cook. I wonder if he does that at home with his wife and kids, too, or if it's just a special occasion since he's taking care of Mom this weekend.

"It smells amazing," Ely says, saving me from having to come up with a reaction that isn't just standing around like a fish gulping air.

Liam salts the greens, and for some reason that's enough to

make me open my mouth and say, “I didn’t know you knew how to use salt.”

The actual words might pass as a joke, but my tone pushes it over the edge into cruelty. Liam flinches and a split second later the guilt sets in, feeling like a swallowed rock.

“I’m not completely useless,” Liam says.

“I’m surprised to see you cooking, that’s all,” I say.

“Liam’s been very helpful,” my mother says, wringing a dishcloth in her hands. “Ever since your father got sick . . .”

“Took cancer for my dad to let a man help out in the kitchen, huh?” I say.

Liam just shrugs, which is honestly the best anyone could expect in response to something like that. *Yeah. Our dad was a piece of shit. What about it?*

I should probably lay off Liam. He never did anything to me—he was always a good brother. Always there to stand between me and Dad, every chance he got.

He doesn’t deserve this.

My mother says to me, “You were just so good at it, sweet pea. Remember that chocolate chess pie you used to make? People begged me for that recipe!”

“Well, joke’s on Dad, then, since I turned out to be a guy after all,” I say.

Her flush reaches her graying hairline. “Wyatt . . .”

“Come on, Mom. Don’t defend him. He was an asshole. He terrified Liam out of the house two years early, remember? Liam was literally living on Manuel’s mom’s pull-out sofa until he graduated high school. I’m glad Dad’s dead. I only wish he’d died sooner.”

And of course, my mother bursts into tears.

Liam and I both stand awkwardly by, Liam probably caught in the same conundrum as I am: Comfort Mom or stand by the obvious truth? In the end it's Ely who wraps an arm around my mother's round shoulders and pulls her in close, murmuring some soothing words under her breath that I can't hear.

A part of me wants to get angry about that too. Because how dare Ely suggest, even implicitly, that I should have kept my mouth shut? How dare she prioritize my mom's bullshit grief over what Liam and I had to live through?

Only I can't pretend not to know where Ely's coming from. She'd probably kill to be in this position in the first place, with her mother consenting to even be in the same room as her. Here I am, taking the opportunity Ely would die for, and I'm stomping it into the ground.

The worst part of it is, none of this is even my mom's fault. Not really. I spent my whole goddamn childhood resenting her for not stopping Dad's abuse. But she was just as trapped as Liam and I were. She was his first victim. Aunt Cathy said when Mom was pregnant with us, our father pushed her down the stairs and hurt her bad enough that she had to go to the hospital and tell them she fell cleaning the dock.

But I can't just keep my mouth shut entirely. If I do, all the resentment will stay trapped behind my lips and rot there. It'll take over everything.

"You should have stood up for me," I tell her as Ely strokes my mother's steel-wire hair. "If not before, then when Dad kicked me out. You should have said something then."

I don't know what I expect her to say. She's always had some excuse, even if it's just some misguided need to maintain harmony and keep everybody happy no matter what. Really: to keep *him* happy, because my happiness never seemed to factor into it.

But what she actually says is "You're right."

"I— What?"

"You're right," my mother says again. "I'm so sorry, Wyatt. I was—I was scared, but it's no excuse. I should have been there for you. For both of you. I should have done . . . something. I don't know."

"Why didn't you?" Liam says. He's still in his stupid fucking apron. "I'm not gonna ask why you didn't leave him—I know it's not as easy as that. And obviously I don't think either of us . . . We aren't asking why you didn't stop him."

He glances at me, looking for backup, and I nod. Jesus. I hope Mom isn't getting the impression that I expected her to put herself between me and him. The only thing worse than how things ended would have been watching him hit her because of me.

God. I'm the stupidest person alive. I should never have opened my damn mouth.

"Of course not," I say. "Never. We know . . ." I'm just digging my hole deeper. "I just wish . . ."

I can't. I can't even figure out how to say what I want to say without making everything worse. I drag one hand back through my hair, twisting my fingers around a fistful and pulling it taut enough to feel pain.

My mom slips out of Ely's arms and moves to where Liam and I are standing. She looks so small now, smaller than she ever did when I was growing up. Her arms hug her own stomach, fingertips digging in at her sides.

"I did," she says. "I wish I'd said more, but I *did* say something. I told him . . . I said how much we loved you. We both loved you. Him, too, whether you believe it or not. But . . . he just . . . He wouldn't hear it. And maybe I could have pushed harder. I should have. But it was already late at night, and we were in bed, and I could just hear what he'd say, if I kept talking—I knew exactly where we'd end up, and I couldn't. It was easier to just stop."

The tears that had welled up in her eyes slip free now, cutting long tracks down her faded cheeks.

"It was easier to stop," she echoes. "So I stopped. And I . . . I lost my baby. I lost . . ."

My heart can't take more of this. I feel shredded inside, bloody, a mess of a person who never should have opened his mouth in the first place.

"You didn't lose anything, Mom." I close the distance of the last two steps between us and wrap my arms around her shaking body, pulling her in tight. My mother buries her face against my chest, and I breathe in the stale scent of her shampoo and here we are, the both of us crying in the middle of the kitchen right in front of my brother and my . . . my Ely, as the pot of collards boils over on the stove.

32

ELY

I don't get time to talk to Wyatt before the funeral the next day. He insists on sleeping on the sofa, of course, even if it means he looks a little bit raggedy from poor sleep come morning. It doesn't help that we wake up so late we barely have time to eat breakfast, shower, and change into appropriate clothes before heading to the church.

Saint Francis's is an old whitewashed building, home to the town's small but tight-knit Irish-American community. Having never been to a Catholic Mass before, I find myself completely out of sync with all the other mourners: I'm constantly standing when I'm supposed to kneel, and I don't know a single one of the hymns. I have to force myself to be still during prayer, rather than rock back and forth to my own private rhythm as I murmur the words under my breath.

But I'm not here to pass as Catholic. I'm here to support Wyatt. Although I'm not sure how much he really needs my support anymore—it seems like his family is more than happy to welcome him back with open arms now that his father's tyranny is taxidermied in that coffin.

Don't be bitter, I chide myself. Being anything less than thrilled for Wyatt would be asshole territory. And I *am* happy for him.

I'm just sad for *me*.

It's not until the evening, after most of the mourners have left the house, leaving behind their casseroles and lily bouquets, that Wyatt pulls me aside and murmurs, "Let's get out of here."

A narrow sandy road leads away from the house, past the marsh toward a swell of sandy dunes. We clamber over the low hills, scratchy beach grass whipping against our calves. The beach on the other side is dark and empty, the black ocean crashing against the shore and washing tiny sea-worn shells onto the sand.

"You hanging in there so far?" I ask him as we kick off our shoes. The sand is cool between my toes, almost damp feeling even this far back from the water.

"It's not so bad," he says, offering me a little smile. "I still can't believe I'm back here. Or that they even *want* me here. I guess a part of me is still waiting for my dad to come crashing through the front door calling me all kinds of names and telling me I'm no kid of his."

We make our way across the beach to where the waves tumble against land. The ocean water is frigid, the air tasting like salt and grass.

"So it was just your dad, then," I say.

I wonder what it must be like to see your entire life totally recalibrated like that. All the assumptions Wyatt had built up in his head about what his mom and brother might think overturned, just like that.

He shrugs and leans over to pick up a shell, turning it in his palm before giving it up to the water again. "I guess so. He was kind of like that. He was . . . Everyone was afraid of him. You never knew which version of him you were gonna get. Sometimes he was all hugs and throwing balls around in the backyard and making pancakes shaped like Mickey Mouse. Then other nights he came home, and we'd spend the next morning patching up the holes he'd punched in the walls. I swear I don't know how Liam turned out so well adjusted. Whatever genes he got clearly didn't pass down to me, 'cause all I did was slowly try to kill myself for four years straight."

"I'm sorry," I say. I don't know what else there is *to* say. I hesitate to take his hand, even though all I want to do is lace our fingers together and hold on tight. Instead I touch my fingertips very lightly to his elbow, just long enough—I hope—to remind him that he's not alone.

Wyatt shakes his head. "That was a long time ago. And now he's dead. No point spitting on his name anymore."

Maybe that's why Wyatt is a better person than me, because I'm not sure I could hold myself back. I still harbor enough resentment toward my own family to power a small city.

"Thank you for coming," Wyatt says after a moment. He's stopped walking, standing there with the tide lapping against his ankles and his hands stuffed in his pockets like a nervous schoolkid. "Seriously. I didn't have any idea what to expect on this trip. And having you here . . . it's made it easier. I know we haven't had a lot of time to talk or anything, but it makes me feel better just knowing you're around. Maybe that's inappropriate for me to say—"

"Don't you start," I warn him. But I'm smiling all the same. "I'm glad. And don't feel like you need to entertain me or anything. I just want to . . . to be here for you. The way you've been there for me."

This time I don't have to overthink it, because he's the one who reaches over and catches my hand in his. His palm is warm and dry against mine, a little gritty from the sand on the shell he picked up earlier, his thumb rubbing at the back of my hand.

I try to find something to say, something to fill the silence that stretches out between us, but my head is full of nothing but white noise. Wyatt's eyes are dark in the half moonlight, the crash of waves against the sand a dull roar.

When he kisses me, I suck in a sharp breath through my nose, and he cups a palm against my cheek, fingertips skimming my ear. I can taste salt on his lips and, when I press my body against his, feel his heart racing just as fast as mine.

"I'm sorry," he says half a second later, although he still hasn't really pulled back—his lips graze mine, his breath hot against my skin.

I slide both my hands into his hair and keep him close. "Don't be."

This time neither of us holds back. He kisses me like he means it, his tongue in my mouth and his hands sliding over my body, keeping me close. The ocean breaks against our legs, and the breeze picks up, tangling my hair around both our faces.

This feels like something inevitable, a conclusion we've been racing toward for weeks now. I wish I could pour myself inside his body, merge us into one being. I want to see the world as he sees it. I want to feel the air on *his* skin, the cold water and sand against *his* feet.

"Let's go back to the house," Wyatt murmurs against my lips, and there is no part of me that has the strength to resist.

The house is quiet when we make it back, Wyatt's mother and brother apparently off to bed already, exhausted from the long day. We creep up the steps like teenagers sneaking back in after a night out partying, muffling giggles, Wyatt's hand still laced with mine.

His childhood bedroom is, thank fuck, about as far away from his mother's as it could get.

"Did you really live here?" I ask in half a whisper, taking in the plain gray sheets and white walls, the books stacked neatly on the desk. The whole place is so devoid of personality that I find it impossible to square with the man standing next to me. The room reminds me of a photo from a Pottery Barn catalog, like it was designed around the idea of a child but never inhabited by a flesh-and-blood one.

"Yep," Wyatt says, hardly sparing a glance behind him. His gaze is too fixed on me. "Mom changed a lot, though. Degendered it. It's . . . a good feeling. Like maybe she really was just waiting for me to come back."

He slides his hands up my thighs, hiking up the hem of my dress. And I forget all about the weird museum room in favor of kissing him again.

The kiss breaks only long enough for Wyatt to strip my dress off over my head—and then his lips are on my neck instead, drawing a low sound from my throat. He cups my breast in one hand, thumb rubbing over the peaked nipple through the thin fabric of one of the flimsy bralettes I wear since my tits have never been big enough to justify actual bras.

"I hope your walls are thick," I mumble, face pressed against the side of his head, where I can breathe in the piney scent of his shampoo.

"Oh yeah. Liam got up to plenty when we were younger, and I never heard a thing." Wyatt unclips the back of my bralette. "That, or he was making it all up. Which might be the more likely explanation."

I've finally managed to get his tie undone without looking. "Please stop talking."

He laughs but obeys, and by the time he pushes me back onto the bed we're both naked. His skin is warm everywhere I touch. And I've been wanting this for far too long; I want to engrave every second of this night into my memory permanently. Underneath his weight I feel heavy, protected. I want to keep him held close forever.

It's nothing like our first time. He isn't that suave stranger I met in a club. He touches me now like I'm something gentle, something worth protecting.

Like he . . . *feels* something for me. Perhaps the same thing that I feel for him in return.

He trails kisses down my sternum, going far too slowly. I want more—I want him to dig his fingers into my hips so hard they bruise. I want him to shred me apart with his teeth.

But he's perilously, torturously gentle. He handles me like I'm something valuable and easily broken. He touches me like he never wants to stop.

"Did you bring . . . ?"

He shakes his head. "This wasn't exactly on my to-do list for the weekend."

Heat floods my cheeks. "Oh. Right."

"Don't worry, though." He nips at the corner of my jaw. "There are plenty of other ways to have fun."

His fingers slip between my legs and I gasp. The smirk on his face is more than enough reward for waiting so long—and the longer his hand is down there, the more incapable I become of actual coherent thought. And when he shifts down the length of my body to let his tongue take over, I give up on staying silent. I keep one hand tangled up in his hair while the other clasps tight over my mouth, holding back the moans.

His tongue is fucking magical, for one thing. He teases it around my clit too well, always not quite close enough. I arch my hips toward him, searching, yearning for more, but he won't give it. He just slides his tongue between my lips, licking at my entrance, then goes back to his torturous task at my clit. The heat that wells between my legs is unbearable; my thighs tremble on either side of his head, the hand in his hair pulling so hard I'm surprised he doesn't cry out.

"*God,*" I groan. "Please—Wyatt—oh god, keep going. I—"

The first climax that crashes over me feels like getting caught under an ocean wave before I've had time to take a breath. I'm trapped in the undertow, lungs straining for air, hips straining toward his mouth as I reach desperately for his hand, holding on tight.

He doesn't stop. He keeps going, slower this time, spending more focus on my inner thighs and dragging his tongue carefully, carefully up my taint and back toward my cunt. I hum and sink back into the sheets, languid and satisfied even as my body keeps rocking up against him. Even as he draws me closer and closer to the edge again.

The second climax is softer, like being rocked in a gentle tide. I'm still shivering slightly as Wyatt makes his way back up the length of my body and kisses me, letting me taste myself on his tongue. My hands feel useless as I rest them on his narrow hips, wishing there was something I could do to return the favor but remembering too well how firm he was in his boundaries last time—no touching him in return.

"I've missed you," I say softly.

He tips his brow against mine. This close, his brown eyes are dark and easy to lose myself in. "I've missed you too," he says, and catches my wrist in one hand, guiding it down below his navel.

My breath hitches. "Are you sure?"

A faint smile crosses his lips and he nods. "I trust you."

I lift up to kiss him hard as he rocks his hips down against my hand, chasing friction. I want to be the best he's ever had, the way he was the best I'd ever had. I want tonight to pop up in his memories every time he looks at me. I want him to fall asleep thinking about it. To remember it in the shower. I want to invade him the way he has invaded me.

It's only fair, right?

I finish him not once but twice; the third time we come together, and then the exhaustion chases us down and tethers us in a deep and sweat-slicked, satisfied sleep.

33

The next morning I can't stop looking at Wyatt. Something has changed between us now—I can feel it. It's as if last night wove a tether between us. Even when we're in separate rooms I'm hyper-aware of his presence, a weight tugging at the other end of that invisible rope.

He can feel it too, I think. I catch him looking at me when he thinks no one is watching. Our elbows bump over breakfast, and my skin burns up every time we touch. His cheeks pinken when I smile at him. It's like we're kids again, giddy with the secret of a first kiss.

We came down on a Friday—Wyatt had to teach until late Thursday afternoon—so we leave in as little time after the funeral as we came before it. The goodbye is full of tears, just as the hello was. But at least this time there's no questioning motives: Wyatt's mother can't stop smiling as she hugs him, holding on tight as if she never wants to let go. Liam makes Wyatt promise to text him as soon as he gets back to New York and even snaps a photo of the pair of them together for Instagram—although Wyatt, of course, insists Liam doesn't name him in the picture.

"Am I ever allowed to put you on Instagram?" I tease him once we're back in the car and well on the road. "You know candid photography is kind of my thing."

Wyatt shudders dramatically. "Please don't. I'd rather not have to look at my own face on film."

"But it's such a nice face."

"Says you. I'm the one who has to stare at it in the mirror every morning."

I wish he could see himself the way I do. The way everyone else does. I have to actively order myself not to start psychoanalyzing all the reasons why Wyatt might not like to have his photo taken. It's his choice, and that should be all I need to know.

"It seemed like a good trip," I venture at last. "Your family seemed happy to see you."

A small smile curves at his mouth. "Yeah. They did, didn't they? You know my mom already said she wants me to come back down for Christmas? I keep waiting for the other shoe to drop."

"I don't think there is another shoe. I think she really means it."

He laughs softly, incredulously. At least the envy is quiet today, nothing but a faint buzz in the pit of my stomach. It's getting easier to be happy for him. To stop running through scenarios in my mind of what my parents would do if I showed up on their doorstep.

Maybe this is enough. Maybe I don't need them—I have Wyatt now. I have Ophelia, and Diego, and Michal. I have my sobriety. I have a whole life that they aren't a part of.

And it's a pretty good life.

We don't make it back to New York until after midnight. I'm tired enough to consider calling an Uber just to make it from LaGuardia back to my apartment, but I'm also cheap, and it's a twenty-minute bus ride. I find myself dozing off as the M60 rattles its way down Astoria Boulevard, my weekend bag on the floor clutched between my ankles. My head keeps tipping over onto Wyatt's shoulder, and he keeps pushing me back upright, even though I wish he'd leave it.

He's been kind of like this the whole last half of the trip home, really.

The car ride from Wyatt's hometown back to the airport was normal. We listened to a podcast and had an obnoxiously pretentious debate about the intersection between visual art and conservation during which Ansel Adams was quoted at *least* twice. Wyatt's hand rested tangled up with mine between the two front seats, easy and companionable.

Security at Raleigh-Durham was the usual clusterfuck, and by the time we were settled in our tiny economy seats, it was hard to get a conversation off the ground. At one point I offered Wyatt my airplane peanuts, and I swear he didn't even realize I was saying his name the first three times.

And now the bus. My fatigue. The shoulder pillow that refuses to be a proper shoulder pillow.

Wyatt shakes me all the way awake at my stop. "We're here."

I blink the blur out of my eyes and follow him out onto the sidewalk. I keep trailing behind him, but he slows down every time, chivalrous even at one-thirty in the morning. I consider making us stop at one of the late-night shawarma joints, but honestly, even white sauce isn't worth delaying bedtime.

Only one thing is worth that.

We sneak into my apartment as quietly as possible, Wyatt carrying my bag for me as I lead the way back to my bedroom.

He sets the bag down next to my dresser, then lurks awkwardly in the doorway, both hands stuffed deep in his pockets. "You good?" he whispers.

"Close the door," I tell him.

"What?"

"Close the door."

He obeys, although he still looks confused about it—the absolute idiot—so I do what I can to put his confusion to rest. I kiss him.

For a moment he kisses me back, pinned between me and the shut door with his hands on my hips. But too quickly he breaks away, turning his face away from mine and using that grasp of my hips to push me—gently—back.

"This isn't a good idea," he says, and something cold shoots into my gut.

"What do you mean?"

He scrubs a hand over his face, blowing out a heavy breath. "I mean this isn't a good idea. You and I, doing this again."

"What the fuck are you talking about?" I take a step back, both arms lifting to wrap reflexively around my middle. "It's not a *good idea*? That isn't what you thought last night."

"I know what I thought last night. And it's not—I don't—it's not that I *regret* it. I don't. I just—"

A brittle laugh finds its way up out of my chest. "You don't regret it. Right. And that's why you're suddenly changing your mind on all this again—because you regret sleeping with me exactly zero percent."

I can't believe we're having this conversation again. After all this time—after *everything*. He still sees me as someone who needs protecting. Someone who can't make her own decisions. Or maybe he doesn't feel like I do, that we're inevitable.

Maybe last night, when I thought we felt the same way, I was wrong. Maybe it was all in my head.

And he's still squinting at the wall like it might be hiding an escape route from this conversation.

"Can you at least *look at me*?" I say, and he finally does. His eyes are huge and doleful, like a kicked puppy's. I really wish he wasn't so good at making facial expressions that make me feel like an asshole.

"Nothing has changed since the last time we talked about this—"

"Everything has changed. What do you even mean?"

"You're a student *under my care,*" he presses on doggedly. "Not to mention, you just relapsed. And we're both obviously going through stuff."

This has gotta be a fucking joke.

"I never should have brought you home with me," he continues.

"And why is that?" I ask, even though I know the answer. I can't help the tears in my eyes. I cry when I get angry. And right now—right now, I'm fucking furious.

But I don't think I ever could have predicted the actual words that come out of his mouth next.

"It was a bad idea. You told me about what happened with your own family. Bringing you home to mine was . . . You still haven't really faced your family, have you?"

"Excuse me?" *That came out of left fucking field.*

"That's why you are struggling so much with your project. You're avoiding them."

It feels like he's shoved me and I've toppled all too easily. I'm left choking on my own rage. He's coming up with every goddamn reason we shouldn't give in, because god forbid he let himself want me. God *forbid* he relinquish one ounce of control.

And I hate him even more because I fucking *fall for it.*

"Wow," I say. "Low blow, thanks. Easy for you to say considering *your* family welcomed you back with open arms. At least you get to have a family. I went with you to North Carolina to face them, for your father's funeral, and back *then* it was okay to sleep with me. So what does that make me? Your security blanket?"

I pace the brief distance to my bed and back, wishing I could stop myself from crying. But unfortunately, the old angry cry is back again. It's a curse.

"Fuck you," I mutter. "Fuck you, fuck *you*. Fuck all of this." The tears are coming too fast to stop now. I wish Wyatt would be decent enough to turn his goddamn back.

So convenient, Wyatt's *boundaries*. All firm and self-righteous, right up until he's all fragile and needs some warm human comfort.

Wyatt has the decency to look hurt by what I said, and for a second I regret it. He's given me no reason to think he isn't full of shit, but that's . . . It's so inconsistent with the man I know. The man I *thought* I knew, at least.

Maybe I'm the problem—maybe it's the same story playing out over and over again. It's not even about me being his student at all. It's just *me*. Maybe it's the same thing Chaya said: that I'm too intense. I'm too much for anyone—no one can stand to be too close.

And I'm too cowardly to face the consequences of my own mess.

I swipe both hands across my wet cheeks, furious with myself for not seeing it sooner. I've been humiliating myself this entire time, throwing myself at him repeatedly. He doesn't want me. He pities me.

"I'm not trying to hurt you." Wyatt's voice is gentle, as if he's trying to calm a wounded animal. "I know it doesn't seem like it right now, but I promise this is the best thing for both of us."

I snort. "And you would know all about that, right? Just go. Just . . . leave. Get out."

But he stays where he is, shifting his weight from side to side. "Ely . . ."

"I said *get out*!"

Wyatt shakes his head. "I don't think that's a good idea right now, do you? You're upset. You're angry. . . . You *just* had a relapse. Someone should be here to make sure you're okay."

It takes every ounce of self-control I've got not to literally scream at that. "And you think that person ought to be you, huh? Can't be Ophelia, or Diego, or my own goddamn sense of self-preservation. Nope. It's gotta be you, Wyatt Cole, white knight and Most Responsible Man in the World. How long is it you've been sober for again? Ten years? Don't know how I could forget considering you bring it up *all the fucking time*."

He flinches as if I've physically struck him, recoiling back toward the shut bedroom door. And every part of me wants to dig in deeper, peel back layers of skin and fascia until I know he really, truly hurts. Until he hurts like *I* hurt.

"Get the *hell* out," I say, and this time he listens.

34

I do my best not to speak to him for the rest of the summer.

It's easier than it sounds. Turns out, most of the time random professors have no reason to speak to random students that aren't in their classes. Which I could have told Wyatt, of course, if he hadn't been so keen on keeping his head shoved in the sand.

I still see him. Hard not to, in a program this small. We pass each other in the halls, and I avoid his gaze even when I can feel him trying so hard to catch mine. If I enter the darkroom and he's in it, I leave. I time my coffee breaks to avoid his. I don't linger late after class finishes anymore; I go home, where sometimes I find Diego popping open a fresh bottle of wine that I never drink or Ophelia scribbling furiously at her tablet—or, some days, I hear the muffled sounds of her crying from behind her shut bedroom door. Diego insists that she's fine, that it's some dramatic, overemotional artist thing, and I'm enough of a dramatic, overemotional artist myself to know he might be right. But still, I worry. I know better than anyone that "tortured artist" isn't always a joke.

I throw myself into working on my capstone project. Partly to prove Wyatt wrong but mostly because I have to: The end of the program is coming up fast, and the last thing I need is to miss my deadline on top of everything else. The photos for my capstone are turning out even better than I'd hoped, with or without Wyatt's help. I find myself looking at them even when I'm not working—or maybe it's just that work-life balance has ceased to mean anything because all I want to do *is* work. I have pictures from so many different streams of Jewish life now—secular, Chassidic, Reform, Open Orthodox—both Ashkenazic and Sephardic, from every borough in New York.

I don't really fit in at any of them.

With one exception.

Michal's invitation, as it happens, is open-ended. And she replies to my text in approximately half a second when I ask, saying that I'm welcome at their place anytime, and my camera is just as welcome as I am.

It feels odd, to be there again without Wyatt. Which doesn't really make sense, because I've only gone to a service with Michal's friends the one time. Maybe it's just that Wyatt feels integral to the memory, as if the place and the people and the feelings wouldn't exist without him.

But they do, it turns out.

I start off on the sidelines, trying to get the shots without interfering too much with the service itself. But between the verses of one of the Psalms, Michal appears at my side and loops her arm through my elbow, tugging me in to stand between her and Kinneret where I don't have to zoom in at all to catch the joy on people's faces.

It's so much like and unlike what I experienced growing up. It's the same songs, the same prayers, the same delight at welcoming the holiday that comes every week. But if growing up I used to count down the minutes until services would end—no matter how much I loved Shabbos, no teenager wants to sit through hours of listening to men pray from a balcony behind tinted glass—tonight I never want to leave. Even after my job is done, my camera packed away so I can focus on actually experiencing the holiness of Shabbos, I linger over the oneg table picking at what's left of my challah so I don't have to go.

"You should keep coming back," Michal tells me as we walk back to her place. "I can tell how much you like it there."

"I should," I say, surprising myself. "But I live in Queens. If I decide. . . . That is, if I ever want to be shomer Shabbos . . . I mean, to be observant again. . . . Well. I can't exactly avoid violating all the rules against using money or carrying things on Shabbos to come all the way to Brooklyn. I have to get back home somehow."

She shakes her head. "Taking the bus here is better than not coming at all. And you are always welcome to stay here for Shabbat. Shoshana and I would love to have you. Anytime."

It's so nice, and it punches me right in the gut.

The old me, the shadow self, peers up at me and whispers, *Too far. Don't expose them to you. You'll only hurt them.*

But I know better now. I've had Ophelia and Diego. I've had Michal herself, this whole summer.

So I smile and throw both arms around Michal's shoulders, hugging her tight. "Thank you," I say. "I will."

When I get back to my own apartment, I shut myself in my bedroom and dig out a candle. It's not a classic Shabbos taper, just a grapefruit-scented votive I bought in Long Island City last weekend. But it counts. As I light it, I murmur the blessing under my breath: "Baruch atah Adonai, Eloheinu melech ha'olam . . ."

It's not much—it barely qualifies as observing Shabbos—but it's something.

And it counts.

35

WYATT

"That's a big story," Ava says once I've finished explaining the whole Ely thing to her. It reminds me of what Marcus said when I texted him after we got back from North Carolina: **that's a lot, Wyatt. What are you gonna do about it?**

Is everyone on planet Earth reading from the same script or something? "How to respond when you find out your friend/colleague/sponsee has fallen in love with someone totally inappropriate."

Maybe Ava is running through the faculty-staff handbook in her mind as we speak, trying to remember if she needs to report me.

No. That's mean. She's my friend. I should trust her more than that.

But these past two weeks since coming back to the city, my brain's been an anxious minefield. I keep trying to shut it up with offerings of cheese, long photo editing sessions, and Haze cuddles, but no good. That little ticking time bomb has started up in the back of my brain again, whispering, *Drink, drink, drink. Oblivion is the only answer.*

I've been trying to catch Ely alone and find a moment to

apologize. To grovel if I have to. But the worst part is I don't even have the luxury of angsting over how you can ruin a good thing with a simple, childish mistake. I've been ruining Ely and me over and over, repeatedly, for two months straight.

"Pretty much," I say in answer to Ava's comment. What else do you say, anyway? *Punch me in the face and throw me in the Hudson so I can worry about not drowning instead of all the relationships I ruin?*

"So how long until you realize you're being an idiot and get back together with her?" Ava asks, in the same tone of voice she uses to ask if I'm done with the developer in the darkroom.

I stare at her. "Wait," I say.

"I'm serious!" She shrugs, spreading both hands out. "The program is almost over anyway. And you're clearly deeply invested in this girl. I hate to watch you ruin a good thing out of a misguided need to play white knight. It sounds much deeper than all that."

Well, when you put it that way.

"Rude," I say.

"Yeah, okay, Mr. Man. She was right and you know it."

So, I'm a moron. I built this whole conversation with Ava up in my head, and that's it. I should have known better. Ava's my friend, after all.

I seem to be full of assumptions these days. About Ava, my mother, my brother.

And maybe I made some assumptions about Ely too.

I mull over what Ava said for the rest of the day. Her voice gets louder every time I see Ely in the halls. She won't even look at me, just clutches her bag closer to her chest and scurries by with her gaze fixed furiously on the ground. She's still angry with me. Or upset. Both, probably. One afternoon I find my Hannah Wilke book on my desk in my office, and the weight in the pit of my stomach is like a bullet never extracted.

She should be angry. She's *right* to be. I could have told her from the start, *Let's talk about this in the fall,* and it would have been fine.

Instead I pushed her away, then pulled her in, only to push her away again, and I hurt both of us.

That thing she said about me using her for emotional comfort, then shoving her away—it's the worst thing anyone has ever said about me. Even with every awful thing I've done, all my past crimes, her words hurt the most. They feel the most intrinsically true—like Ely has identified my worst fault: That I'm selfish. That I only care about other people as long as they can make me feel safe and wanted, two things I never was growing up.

And then I never bother filling their cups in return.

But knowing I should talk to Ely—that Ava agrees with Marcus on this point—isn't quite enough to overcome the awful heat that seethes in my gut every time I think about the prospect of actually doing it.

Piece-of-shit wannabe man, my father's voice sneers, and I down the rest of my seltzer in one gulp. The carbonation makes me gag badly enough that I almost run to the sink, just in case.

So instead of being a decent person about it all, I just steep in my own misery and try to get work done . . . even if my work seems particularly shitty as of late.

"This is worse than a total beginner's," I say, showing Haze the best of my latest projects. I was doing better art when I was high. Which is saying something, considering one pleasant surprise about getting clean was that my creative eye improved dramatically.

Haze stares back at me with his big round judgmental cat eyes.

"You're right," I tell him. "This can just be a first draft. Starting over."

I work until even the bar across the street shuts down for the night, the music and the laughter fading until the only sounds are light traffic, the hum of my window air conditioner unit, and Haze's soft snores.

Liam has started texting me. That's a highlight, at least. He seems to be a night owl as well, so I get messages from him half the night and usually wake up to one (or more) in the morning. He's working as a lineman, which you would think would be a physical enough job to make him sleep like Haze during a dead nap, but apparently not.

It's weird to be in contact with him again. I still feel like I have to put on a front of sorts, like I've got to impress him or he'll decide I'm not worth his time after all. One night I confessed this to him, and he replied: **dude I'm your brother, brothers are forever.**

Embarrassingly, I screenshotted that text and added it to my photo Favorites album on my phone.

A sick part of me is still jealous of my brother. He grew up to be happy, and I had to fight to find my happiness.

Then again, I guess I don't know his whole story. Maybe he had to fight too. Maybe the happy I see in him came hard won.

But even Liam isn't immune to asking about Ely. **How're things going with the girl,** he says, and my dumb ass lies to him and says, **great,** because I can't bring myself to tell him the truth. Or maybe just because he's the only person who doesn't know any better and can't prove me wrong. In his world, Ely and I are an item. We still have coffee in the park and talk about photography. She still borrows my books and insists I don't need to sleep on the couch, beckons me to join her on the bed. She still wants anything to do with me.

The fantasy world I construct for Liam is a much better world to live in, I think.

36

ELY

I wait until Sunday, and I don't call her. I text. Not that it makes much difference at this point; if I can't bear to hear her voice over the phone, I'm not sure how I'll stand seeing her in the flesh. But by the time I'm sitting in this cramped coffee shop in Crown Heights, hyperaware of how exposed my legs are in shorts compared to those of all the women around me in skirts and stockings, it's too late to cancel. Every time the bell rings above the door, I inch a little closer to the edge of my seat.

I could always ghost her. It's not too late.

The door swings open again, and I do the same immediate forward lean and neck crane. Only this time I'm right. There's no mistaking her.

Dvora's once-wild hair has been neatly tucked beneath the cap of a modest sheitel, its straight black locks obscuring the tangled waves I know hide underneath. She's gained weight since the last time I saw her, no longer the gangly kid I shared a bedroom with but a grown woman. But I still recognize the structure of her long limbs and the irregular angle of her Cupid's bow, which makes it look like G-d put her mouth on crooked. She's still my sister, despite the stroller she lugs through the door behind her—and the other children she's probably had by now.

I expected all this, of course. But I didn't expect how much it would feel like getting the wind knocked out of me. I don't know why, but some part of me thought maybe it was all a big joke. If you'd ever asked me, as a child, what Dvora and I would be like all grown up, I never would have said this. I would have imagined us rolling into adulthood like slightly larger carbon copies of our previous selves. I thought we'd always spend our nights together, whispering secrets across the telephone wire if we couldn't murmur them into each other's ears.

But Dvora is an adult now, a real one. And I guess that means I am too.

Her gaze scans the restaurant, and when it lands on me, I lift one hand. Watching her maneuver the hulking stroller through the narrow aisles between the café chairs would be a form of schadenfreude if I didn't actually feel kind of bad for her.

Dvora always wanted kids. But that doesn't make it seem any less miserable to me.

"I like the wig," I tell her when she sits down, even though I don't.

"Thank you. So do I."

I wonder if she's lying.

The creature in the stroller makes a soft, disgruntled noise, and Dvora leans over to adjust something in the bassinet—from this angle I can't see her baby's face. For all I know it's an octopus in there.

"Thank you for agreeing to meet with me," I say after a moment, once the baby is satisfied with its new pacifier (or whatever it is). "You didn't have to. I know . . . I know I caused a lot of pain, before I left."

"And since," Dvora says, blunt as she ever was.

It might be fair, but her words still sting. I grip the seat of my chair to keep from recoiling too obviously. "I'm sorry. For everything. I know I . . . If I could go back, I would. I'll never forgive myself for expecting you to keep my secrets. Or for all the horrible . . . horrible things I made you watch."

Like Chaya's dead body, gone cold next to mine.

We just stare at each other for a moment, Dvora's gaze hot and narrowed. I don't have any right to wish she'd look at me any different. Not after what I did. So I look away first, dropping my focus to the scone I crumbled onto my plate waiting for her arrival. But a beat later Dvora softens and sits back in her chair, hands falling lax in her lap—and when I look up, that awful heat has cooled.

"I'm glad you're doing well," she says. "I mean . . . you look good, that's all. Are you really clean now?"

"Yeah," I say, and venture the tiniest of smiles. It feels so fragile on my lips. "A little over four years now." Not counting a few weeks back, anyway. But Wyatt's right—one slip doesn't erase all the work I've done. That still counts for something.

"That's great, Ely. Seriously. Congratulations."

"Thanks. Took a lot to get here, but I'm never going back." I reach for my scone before remembering I've already reduced it to a pile of crumbs. I awkwardly fiddle with the sleeve on my coffee cup instead. "How have you been? You . . . you got married, I see."

She smiles, even if the expression doesn't quite reach her eyes. "Eventually. Yes."

I can't help myself. "Eventually?"

She nods. "To Zalman Horowitz. Do you remember him?"

I do, vaguely. I'm pretty sure he was our brother Sholom's friend—one of the ones always running around shooting fake lasers out of their fingers at each other. Presumably he's stopped doing that now. "Congratulations."

Dvora shrugs one shoulder. "I was lucky he would take me, after everything. Our yichus wasn't worth as much after what happened with you and Chaya."

I knew that must have been the case, that my expulsion from our community would have left a black mark on my family's reputation, that even our established, respectable lineage—descended from some of the most revered rabbis and scholars from Lubavitch itself—wouldn't make up for what I did.

Dvora probably counts herself lucky she ended up married to someone close to our own age, even if he did have laser fingers.

"What about Malka?" I ask. "And our brothers? Did they . . . ?"

"Gedaliah and Sholom Ber have just started shidduchim, so we'll see. But Malka is married. She didn't fare quite as well as me. She started the matchmaking process right after you left, so she was still. . . . It was too soon, I guess. It took her four years to find her bashert. But they're happy together. She just had another son."

"Baruch Hashem," I murmur. *Praise G-d.* I don't know what else to say.

I wish I could have danced with Malka at her wedding. With Dvora at hers. I wish I could have seen Dvora's beautiful face emerge from beneath her veil, beaming with happiness.

Is she happy? Is her husband a good man? Did she learn to love Zalman and his laser fingers? Does he love her in return?

I can't ask her any of that. Maybe one day, a dozen years from now, if she ever forgives me. Maybe then.

But I doubt it.

I think about Malka and her last-chance husband, her four years of waiting, alone and wondering more and more if anyone would ever consent to marry her. I wonder if she hates me every day for making that her life or if she just smiles and turns her face toward heaven and recites the same prayers as always, her faith perennially unshaken.

She was always a good girl. So much better than me and Dvora.

"I'm sorry," I find myself saying again. Apparently the first time wasn't sufficient. "Seriously. I didn't think about how this would affect you. I was so selfish, and stupid, and—"

I can't finish. My voice has gone thick, and I'm suddenly hyperaware of everyone else in this coffee shop. The girl at the table next to us is reading a book with no headphones in. She's probably listening. Probably thinks I'm such a piece of shit.

"Yeah," Dvora says. "Yeah, you kind of are."

Are. Not "were."

Can't really blame her for not making the distinction, though.

"Forget shidduchim. Didn't you ever think about what it would be like for me without you? You're my sister. You were my best friend, Ely. I was twelve years old the first time I saw you get high." Now she is the one with tears swelling in her eyes. She looks away, fumbling with something in the baby carriage again.

The urge to reach out and embrace her is unbearable. But that part of our relationship died eight years ago. I can't resurrect it. Not with wishful thinking and not alone.

Whatever Dvora is doing in that stroller only seems to make things worse. A small wail emits from behind the bassinet's rounded cover, and Dvora's mouth twists into an upset moue as she clicks the brake off and rocks the stroller back and forth in short, quick movements.

"I used to idolize you so much," she says. "I wanted to be just like you. You were always so cool with your art stuff and your secret parties and your friendship with Chaya—"

We both flinch at the same time. The red in Dvora's face deepens, and she clenches the stroller just a little tighter.

"I'm sorry," she says. "I shouldn't . . ."

My heartbeat feels like a stampede of hooves in my chest. "It's okay. It's been a long time. I . . . Don't apologize. Not for that. Not for anything."

She nods, a brief, jerky movement that yanks at my heartstrings. A large part of me regrets coming here. It hurts too fucking bad.

But it's the right thing to do. I owe Dvora this.

And . . .

"I'm glad you let me come," I say after a long moment. "I know I don't deserve this. You have every right to tell me to fuck off and never darken your doorway again. But . . . I'm glad."

She nods again, but her expression seems softer somehow. And she isn't rocking that stroller quite so furiously anymore.

When Dvora and I say our goodbyes and head off in opposite directions, it feels like the final closing of a door. I stop at the end of the block and turn to watch her disappear into the crowd. This might be the last time I ever see her—I want to etch her figure into my brain, short and curvy with that pristine wig, her hands gripping that huge black stroller. I want to meld this image somehow with my memories of her when we were young, as impossible as that seems.

I won't get Wyatt's happy ending here. And that's my own fault; I know it. Wyatt never did anything to his family to deserve being pushed out. But me . . . I did. And maybe it's time I came to terms with that.

But I don't know what the future holds. Dvora did come here, didn't she? She met with me. And maybe that's all she can do right now. But in a few months or years, she might heal. She might reach out.

I'd love it if she did.

But if she doesn't, I'll understand.

On my way to the bus stop I call Michal and take her up on her invitation. Starting now, I'm not spending another Shabbos alone.

37

I finish my capstone project with just a week to spare before Parker's final gallery show.

It feels like the end of an era—only a summer, but my time at Parker seems like it's lasted years. California is a fever dream in a lot of ways, fuzzy as a distant mirage. I never thought I'd come back to New York and certainly not for good. But now that I'm here, I can't imagine uprooting myself again.

"You're staying for another semester, right?" Michal says halfway through the show. We've abandoned our posts by our own exhibits to wander around, wine or sparkling water in hand, pretending to look at the other displays. "You're not leaving us after one summer."

"I'm not staying another semester. *But,*" I say before Michal can interject, "I've signed on to the lease for my apartment. So. I'll be around at least a little while longer. I got a job at Sotheby's as a cataloger in their photography department."

"Congrats! That's a big step."

"It's a start, anyway." It's still not where I want to end up. It's not doing photography full-time. But I need something to pay the bills, and from what I've read, freelancing in New York City isn't gonna cut it. "What about you? Another semester?"

She nods. "They can't get rid of me that easily. Besides, Ava said she'd work with me on an independent study next semester. How can I turn that down?"

"I mean, you can't."

"Exactly."

Dr. Zhu appears at my shoulder at that moment, squeezing my elbow lightly. "Elisheva? There is someone looking for you at your exhibit."

I wave my apologies to Michal and head back, weaving through the crowd to the corner of the room that has been appropriated for my own little mini-gallery. There's a man in a clean, fitted suit there, a glass of champagne in his hand, and he smiles at me when I approach. It's not until I'm only five feet away that I place where I've seen him before.

"Elisheva Cohen?" Henrik Andersson says, and when I nod, he goes on: "This is your work? I'm very impressed."

He doesn't seem to recognize me as the student he tried to pick up earlier this summer, but I'm counting that as a good thing. I follow his gaze to one of the sample pieces from my project, featuring a carefully cut out photograph of myself in secular clothing pasted into a blurry crowd of frum scholars and mothers crowding a Brooklyn sidewalk on Shabbos morning. I've stitched threads through the work, tying people together—everyone tied to someone else, except for me.

"Thank you," I say. "It was a really fun project to put together."

He extends a hand to shake mine. "I'm Henrik. I curate a gallery at—"

"I know who you are," I interject before I can stop myself. And I honestly don't care that I sound like a simpering fangirl, because that's exactly what I am. Henrik's gallery at PS1 is one of the *best* art galleries in the city, known for discovering some of the top rising talents in the visual arts world.

He laughs, so at least he's not offended by my rudeness. "Well, it's a pleasure to meet you. I've been following your portfolio"—*What does that mean, what does that* mean?—"and I'm really impressed with how you've evolved. I'd love to talk more about this project, if you're interested." He produces a business card from a slim steel wallet and passes it over. "Please give me a call."

"Yes," I say. "I mean . . . I will. Thank you. Wow."

He grins again, showing white teeth. "Great. Well, I'll let you get back to all your adoring fans. Looking forward to hearing from you, Elisheva."

I watch him go with my heart still beating a thousand times a minute. It takes all my concentration not to just stand here grinning in front of my exhibit like a complete weirdo. But also like . . . *holy shit.*

I'm sweating a little bit still, so I sneak off to the washroom to splash some cold water on the back of my neck—this mascara isn't waterproof—and give myself a little calm-the-hell-down speech.

When I return to my exhibit, Wyatt is there. He's facing away from me, looking at the photos with his hands clasped behind his back. My gait falters for a moment. I could just . . . walk away. He hasn't seen me. I could avoid him and hide over at Michal's spot until he goes away.

But it's not like I've done anything wrong. I refuse to feel embarrassed about this forever.

So I press my shoulders back, inhale, and make myself go up to him.

"Turned out pretty good, right?" I say.

He nods, still gazing at one of the photos—one I took in Crown Heights after I met Dvora, the street busy with post-Shabbos shopping, the men walking in pairs with their hatted heads tilted toward each other in deep conversation, plastic bodega bags slung over their elbows. The women with their strollers and shopping, children skipping along in their wake.

"It's fantastic," Wyatt says at last. "This is really good work, Ely. It's evocative."

Henrik Andersson thinks so too. I bite my tongue over that. The last thing I want is to seem like I'm bragging. "Thank you."

"I saw Henrik Andersson over here earlier. He looked impressed."

Well, so much for playing coy. A smile finds its way onto my face despite my best efforts. "He gave me his card. Looks like your cockblocking at Carolina's show failed after all."

The grin that splits Wyatt's face is immediate and hopelessly earnest. "That's great. You deserve it. So much. I'm so happy for you."

He says it with the kind of gusto that is contagious. And if I weren't already half-giddy from Andersson's offer, I'm sure I would be now. "I know. I can't believe it. I keep thinking there's no way this is really happening. Like I'll call him and he'll change his mind."

"He won't change his mind. He has a good eye, and he knows talent when he sees it."

Coming from Wyatt, that means a lot. And I might be a creep, but I know from reading Wyatt's Wikipedia page that he's been exhibited in Andersson's gallery himself. It was one of his very first major breaks, in fact.

I'm still smiling like a freaking moron, no matter how bad I try to get myself under control.

"Don't do that," Wyatt says.

"Do what?"

He gestures toward my face. "You always cover your mouth when you smile."

I'm pretty sure the observation just made me flush bright red, and I have to resist the urge to cover my mouth yet again as I force an awkward laugh. "Sorry. I guess I'm just self-conscious. I have big teeth."

"You have *what*?"

"You know. Big teeth. The dentist said they were two standard deviations above normal size."

Wyatt shakes his head very slowly. "That's the stupidest thing I've ever heard."

"No it isn't."

"Um, I think I would know, not you." His lips quirk up at one corner. "Besides, I like your big teeth."

God. Okay, now I really *am* turning into a tomato. Maybe instead of covering just my teeth I should cover my entire face next time.

The silence that punctuates his words is unbearable. If we were alone, I might— I don't know what I'd do. But we aren't alone, we're surrounded by total strangers, and I'm still so high off getting Henrik friggin' Andersson's card that I'm not sure I'm even thinking straight.

"Did you put in a good word for me?" I can't help asking. Because maybe that's all that offer even was: the nepotism of the art industry, Wyatt's good fortune trickling down to me, his protégé.

"Nope. I don't do referrals, as a general rule. This was all you."

All of a sudden there's a wet heat prickling at my eyes. I turn away from Wyatt and pretend to be staring at my work again, although I'm sure I don't do a very good job hiding my emotions from him. He knows me too well at this point.

His hand finds my shoulder and gives it a gentle squeeze. "Like I said, you deserve it. You've earned this, Ely."

"I tried," I say. "I tried really hard."

"I know." He hesitates for a moment. Then says: "Are you coming back to Parker next semester?"

I shake my head. "I got a job. So I'll be around but not . . . here."

He's silent for long enough that I have to actually look at him again. Wyatt's expression, for once, is unreadable. I can't dissect a single interpretable emotion from that face.

"What?"

"Are you leaving because of me?" he asks. He keeps his voice low, as if—despite the bustle and loud murmur of the gallery crowd—he's still worried about being overheard. "I know you were invited. Am I the reason you aren't staying?"

I make a face. "Don't be a narcissist. Not everything's about you."

"Why, then?"

Trust Wyatt to be completely undeterred by my name-calling. I blow out a heavy sigh. "I don't know. I want to focus on my original ideas, not assignments. My scholarship money ran out, and I don't want to pay tuition. The Sotheby's job pays great. I just got the card of a curator at a major museum. Pick your favorite reason; there are a million of them."

"Well," he says, "I'm happy for you. And I think you'll do just fine, with or without Parker. Although I'll miss you."

I raise my eyebrows. "You'll miss me? I'll still just be an L train transfer to the G, transfer to the 7, transfer to the N/W, and then a nine-minute walk away."

Am I mistaken, or is it Wyatt's turn to look a little pink in the cheeks? "So you're staying in New York long term, then."

"At least for the medium term, yeah. That's the plan. Why? Are you entertaining some seriously inappropriate daydreams about following me back to my apartment once we're done with this thing?"

Fuck. Shit, I need to learn to keep my mouth shut; *I keep freaking* catapulting *myself into these awkward-ass situations—*

"Pretty much," he says.

I blink. "Oh."

"Is that okay?"

I can't believe that's an actual question he's asking. "Yes. I mean . . . yeah. It's okay. But if I'm honest, I'm a little fucking surprised."

His mouth twists into a grimace. "Yeah. That's fair. I've . . . I've been an egotistical, scared-out-of-my-mind douche."

"Yep. Go on."

"I should have been clear with you from the beginning. I should have put you ahead of my reputation and my own . . . feelings about what any of this said about me. Yeah, sleeping with a student is fucked up—"

"Because you can't *un*sleep with me," I say, and he nods, then goes on:

"But it wasn't just that. It's more. I—I love you, Ely. Goddamn it, but I do." He laughs, a desperate, broken sound. "I love you, and that scares the shit out of me."

And now—now here we are, standing in this gallery, me staring at him as if I've never really seen him before in my life. This man, this perfect, *beautiful* man, and he said—

Did he really say that? Am I imagining things?

I love you.

"If I'm honest with myself"—he drags a hand back through his hair, messing it up horribly, which doesn't at all fit with the cool-guy perfectly coiffed look he's affected for this show—"I've always tried to control everything. After I got clean, especially. I didn't want to ruin anything. I worked so fucking hard to be here, and . . . And you too, *you* worked so hard to be here. I was terrified of messing it up. For either one of us."

I shouldn't trust him.

But I do, as it turns out. Possibly because he's standing there fumbling around like a dumb sloth, and right now, I love that look for him. He should try groveling more often.

I can't figure out what to say, although Wyatt is looking more and more distressed. I mean, he should. But enough is enough, and I'm starting to feel kind of bad for the man.

Should I say, *I love you too*? My mouth feels dry, like my tongue won't work properly. Have I waited too long now? Is it too late?

"Listen," he says after it's clear that my fumbling for a response is going nowhere. "I . . . I've got something for you. I hope it's not weird. I was planning to give it to you anyway, but I didn't get around to it, and . . . and regardless of how you feel about me—about us—I still hope you'll keep it."

He pulls his backpack off his shoulder and digs around inside for a sec, then emerges with a small cardboard box tied with a somewhat-wilted ribbon.

I don't know what to do besides take the box. I tug at one end of the ribbon until the bow unravels. And when I open it—

"Oh my god. Is this—"

"It's a Leica range finder. Thirty-five millimeter. Hannah Wilke shot in thirty-five millimeter a lot. But you can't find thirty-five millimeter anymore, and this, I thought you might—"

"Wyatt, this thing costs almost *six thousand dollars*!"

He looks a little bit like he wants to die on the spot. "I didn't pay for it," he says quickly. "I mean, I did. But it was a while ago. This was the first expensive camera I ever got myself. I thought maybe you could use it better than I can now. Or at least, I'd love to see what you do with it."

I'm staring at him with my mouth hanging open. A friggin' Leica. A *friggin', frick-frick Leica. His* Leica. The one he shot *Cloudburst* on. And he wants to see what I make with it. He wants me to make art with his Leica.

"Wyatt—"

"There's more," he says. At this point he's clearly just rushing to get it all out before I can tell him to fuck off again. "Look."

I lift the camera up and there it is—a roll of thirty-five-millimeter film. Still good.

"I only had the one roll left," he says apologetically, "but . . ."

"You didn't need to do this," I breathe at last.

He messes up his hair even worse this time. I really, really want to reach up and fix it for him. To slide my fingers into those chestnut waves and—

"I'm sorry; I know. I'm not trying to, like— This isn't a bribe. I really did plan to give it to you anyway."

This man. This *man*. This *incredible,* fantastic, gorgeous man.

I can't help smiling now, the expression creeping across my face despite my best efforts. Wyatt's clutching his backpack in both hands now, holding on for dear life.

"Okay," I say. "That's fine. I'll accept your apology, pending future discussions."

Wyatt still looks so pitifully remorseful, all cow eyes again—what is it with this man and the bovine woe? I stop him before he can utter another heartbreaking apology.

"And," I say, "I meant to say it. I *want* to say it, and I want—I want you to know how much this means to me. I love you too, Wyatt. More than anything."

Wyatt's shock is so artistically satisfying, it could be a gallery show on its own. Maybe my next collection will be called *Meditations on a Fish Mouth*.

"Really?" he says at last. His cheeks are flushed. I wonder if his heart is pounding as fast as mine is. I'm clutching the Leica like someone might swoop down and steal it, but I wish I were clutching him instead. I wish I could bury my face against his strong chest and breathe in the scent of him as his arms curl around me and hold me tight.

"Really. So much." I take a breath and then another one, a steadying one. "But it's kind of weird having this conversation right now, with the whole . . ." I gesture, indicating the entire gallery, the students and critics milling about.

He laughs, his shoulders finally settling down to their usual position. "Yeah. Sorry. I probably could have chosen a better location for my grand declaration of love."

"Just a tiny, tiny bit. But since we already fucked that part up," I say, "we should go back to your apartment. And then we should have sex. Lots of sex. As soon as possible. In fact, can we get out of here right now?"

And there—that's the suave fucker I met at Revel. He quirks up a corner of his lips. "I think we have a solid fifteen minutes before the crowd starts to dwindle. But at that point . . . absolutely, we can make our daring escape."

He hesitates a second, that vulnerability creeping back in. "Ely, I really do . . . I care about you. More than you can imagine. You mean the world to me, and I almost lost you. I never want to make that mistake again. I promise you I won't."

He takes a half step closer to me, then another. And then he slides his hand along my cheek and he kisses me—right there, in front of everyone.

I almost drop the Leica, but Wyatt—thank god—is quick enough to slide his hand between us and cup it beneath mine, holding the precious camera bracketed between our bodies as his other hand slips around the small of my back and pulls my hips in toward him.

When the kiss breaks, I'm off-balance, giddy and effervescent, like my whole body is filled with Wyatt's damn LaCroix.

"I can't believe you," I say. "You just did that. In public. At a fancy art show."

"I did," he says.

"Hello to you *too,* Professor."

He lets out a laugh, low and husky. The thrill that slithers down from my stomach to my thighs at that is nearly enough to make me slip with the camera all over again.

Those next fifteen minutes crawl by, of course. I manage to fumble my way through small talk with the occasional guest or professor, every conversation made about fifty times more interminable by the way I can't stop sensing Wyatt's presence. It's as if some primal part of me knows exactly where he is in the room at any given point in time.

Terrible move, Ely, I want to tell myself.

But terrible move or not, I trust him. And I wouldn't exactly say I'm a trusting-easily kind of person, so I feel like that has to say something. Right?

Either way, things have changed now. We're just two people with too much in common, two people who really want to have sex with each other.

Who—god help me—*love* each other.

Your move, Wyatt Cole.

38

ONE MONTH LATER

I honestly don't remember any details about my first New York gallery opening.

I guess I can confidently say there were a lot of people there with fancy credentials, and if I think too hard about the specifics, I get a shaky feeling in my gut that could be excitement, anxiety, or an impending stomach flu.

The whole time I kept muttering, "What the fuck? What the fuck? What the fuck?" to Wyatt until he finally detached himself from my parasitic side to make me—his words—"face my admirers."

I've only really resurfaced into coherence now that we're already back in Brooklyn at Wyatt's place, in that quiet moment before everyone else arrives, as Wyatt curls his hand around the back of my neck and pulls me in close to bury his face against my hair and whisper, "I'm so proud of you. You were amazing. You're amazing."

I take in a deep breath of his smell, pine-fresh men's deodorant and crisp detergent. My hands fall to his hips: warm, steady, an anchor holding me down.

Every moment with Wyatt is one that I wish I could bottle up and keep forever. I wish I could pull those bottles out when I'm away and release the memories to relive them.

This past month has felt like a dream. The best kind of dream, of course. My portfolio is littered with photos I've taken on my new Leica—including several of Wyatt himself, hunched over his negatives or lying in bed with the sheets bundled around his hips and the dawn light silvery on his skin.

Even the boring moments feel effervescent—scrambled eggs in the morning, fighting off Haze as he tries to steal our food, curling up on Wyatt's tiny couch to watch Nicolas Cage movies. Ophelia and Diego adore him, which is good because if they didn't, I'd probably have to fight them. Diego even adopted Wyatt as an unofficial test subject for his more adventurous food creations.

I wouldn't change a thing.

"I love you," he says, and the words are so soft, so warm in the dim interior of his apartment, words I could curl myself into forever.

I tighten my fingers at his sides. I almost don't want to breathe too heavy, like existing in awareness of my body might make the moment tremble and break.

Every moment we share now feels so precious and hard-won.

"I love you too." I tilt my head to kiss his neck, right over his pulse point. "So much."

He pulls back and looks me in the eye, traces his thumb along my cheekbone. When his lips meet mine, I forget we're expecting company, at least until the infuriatingly loud buzzer screeches to herald Michal and Shoshana's arrival.

"You killed it," Michal says, clinking her glass of seltzer against mine. "I feel like I know a celebrity."

I can't help rolling my eyes. "Oh, please. Says the girl who just had her work featured in a *Vogue* editorial. Sharing an MFA program with you is gonna be intimidating as fuck next year. I'm glad I don't have to do it."

"It's not too late to come back to Parker! I need someone to suffer through deadlines with me."

"Well, I personally welcome you to the grown-up world," Shoshana says. "Before you know it, you'll be buying blazers and debating which washing machine to buy with the rest of us."

"I'm a grown-up!" Michal pokes her wife in the side with her elbow. "I have very serious opinions about washing machines."

The buzzer blares again, and I nearly trip over Haze on my way to let the next round of people in. I rescue the black cat from getting trapped underfoot by carrying him around for the next twenty minutes, at least until he decides he's sick of me and launches out of my arms to go hide on top of his cat tree. Shannon texts me at some point to make sure I'm still sober. I finally made myself message her again after the summer program ended, resurrecting our friendship from the graveyard of all the ones I'd abandoned or trashed. I'll never stop being proud to text back **100% well and with it.**

There are enough people here that I don't even hear the bell ring for Ophelia and Diego's arrival. Someone else must let them in, because out of nowhere Diego barrels into me and flings both arms around my neck.

"My dear," he says, "you were phenomenal."

"Sorry we're late," adds Ophelia.

"Fashionably!" Diego says, rolling his eyes. "Anyway, it was mostly Ophelia's fault. This is what happens when you go cheap on glitter eyeliner, dear; you have to redo your makeup about fifteen hundred times to make it look right."

"It was not *fifteen hundred—*"

"But who knows? Maybe you can afford nicer stuff now that you actually got paid. Or you can, like, cover all three of our rents. I dunno, just an idea!"

"I saw your ad on the way here," I say, and dig out my phone to flip through the photos until I find the one I snapped of the gin ad on the subway, Ophelia's illustration so gorgeous and perfect that I honestly can't believe I know the actual human who created it.

"A banger," Diego says approvingly. "Ophelia Desmond, corporate artist. Now do more and hire me as a personal assistant. I hate my job anyway."

"Didn't you just get a new job?" asks Wyatt, who doesn't know Diego well enough yet to know any better. "Aren't you literally working for the mayor?"

"Like I said. I hate my job."

"You spent all of last night going on about how fulfilling it is to be in a position to make an actual difference, and the mayor is chill and secretly socialist, there's a flavored seltzer machine in the break room, and the girl at the desk next to you looks like a young Barbra Streisand," I remind him. "You drank three martinis and monologued about it for like ten straight minutes."

"And?"

The party goes on pretty late considering it's a dry event and everyone is living it up on seltzer and nonalcoholic beer alone. Once it's over, Wyatt and I lie on the living room rug, fingers laced together atop Wyatt's thigh, as Haze walks across our bellies.

"I hope it's like this forever," I say, eyes half-lidded.

Wyatt squeezes my hand, and I exhale long and slow. A damp cat nose nudges my cheek.

"It won't be," says Wyatt. "Bad days always come. But we can try." His thumb rubs the back of my hand. "We can fight for it."

I turn my face toward him and open my eyes. He's already looking at me, the amber lights from the street outside glowing gold on his skin. I lean over and kiss him, his stubble scratching against my jaw. I don't know what time it is, except that it's past three, and as exhausted as my body feels, my mind still tilts helplessly toward his.

"I love you," I say again because it deserves to be said again. It deserves to be said a million times.

His mouth smiles against mine, and I draw my phone out of my back pocket and take a photo of us. I'll keep tonight for a lifetime.

ACKNOWLEDGMENTS

No book is ever written alone. I'd like to thank the community that made this possible: my partner, my newborn child for saving screaming episodes until after I finished a chapter, my parents, my friends (in particular Ryan, Shelly, Emily, Tracy, Casey, Colin, Sara, Rishi, Joel, Jen, Arjun, Mac, and Ruthanne)—as well as my Narcotics Anonymous family across the globe.

Editorially, I'm so lucky to have worked with the best team on this project. Thank you to my editor, Shauna Summers, as well as Mae Martinez, Cara DuBois, Sara Bereta, Erin Korenko, Pam Alders, Cassie Gonzales, Kim Hovey, Melissa Folds, Taylor Noel, and Saige Francis.

This book literally wouldn't exist without my agents, Holly Root and Taylor Haggerty, who sent me the TikTok that inspired this whole thing. Seriously, who knew late-night TikToks could go so hard?

So much appreciation as well to Maggie Enterrios, who gave me amazing advice on illustration as a career and told me everything about how visual artists make their big breaks. The Hannah

Wilke Collection & Archive kindly helped me perfect the portrayal of Hannah Wilke, Wyatt and Ely's photography idol.

Thank you to my coven/cult friends too. Y'all have been there to support me through some of my darkest times, and I am so much stronger for having known you all. Finally, I can't say enough how much I love every reader who has found themselves in any of my books. You're the reason I write. Thank you.

PHOTO: © EMILY MARTIN

Victoria Lee grew up in Durham, North Carolina, where she attended an arts school and played piano competitively. She has a PhD in psychology, which she uses to overanalyze fictional characters and also herself. Lee is the author of *A Lesson in Vengeance* as well as *The Fever King* and its sequel, *The Electric Heir*. She lives in New York City with her partner, child, and two overzealous but adorable pets.

victorialeewrites.com
Instagram: @sosaidvictoria